I0706328

TAKE ANY CHANCE

A GAMING THE SYSTEM NOVEL

Brenna Aubrey

SILVER GRIFFON ASSOCIATES
ORANGE, CA, USA

Book Layout ©2024 BookDesignTemplates.com
Cover Art ©2024 Cover Design & Typography: Vanilla Lily Designs

Take Any Chance / Brenna Aubrey. – 1st ed.
ISBN 979-8-88908-028-2

www.BrennaAubrey.com

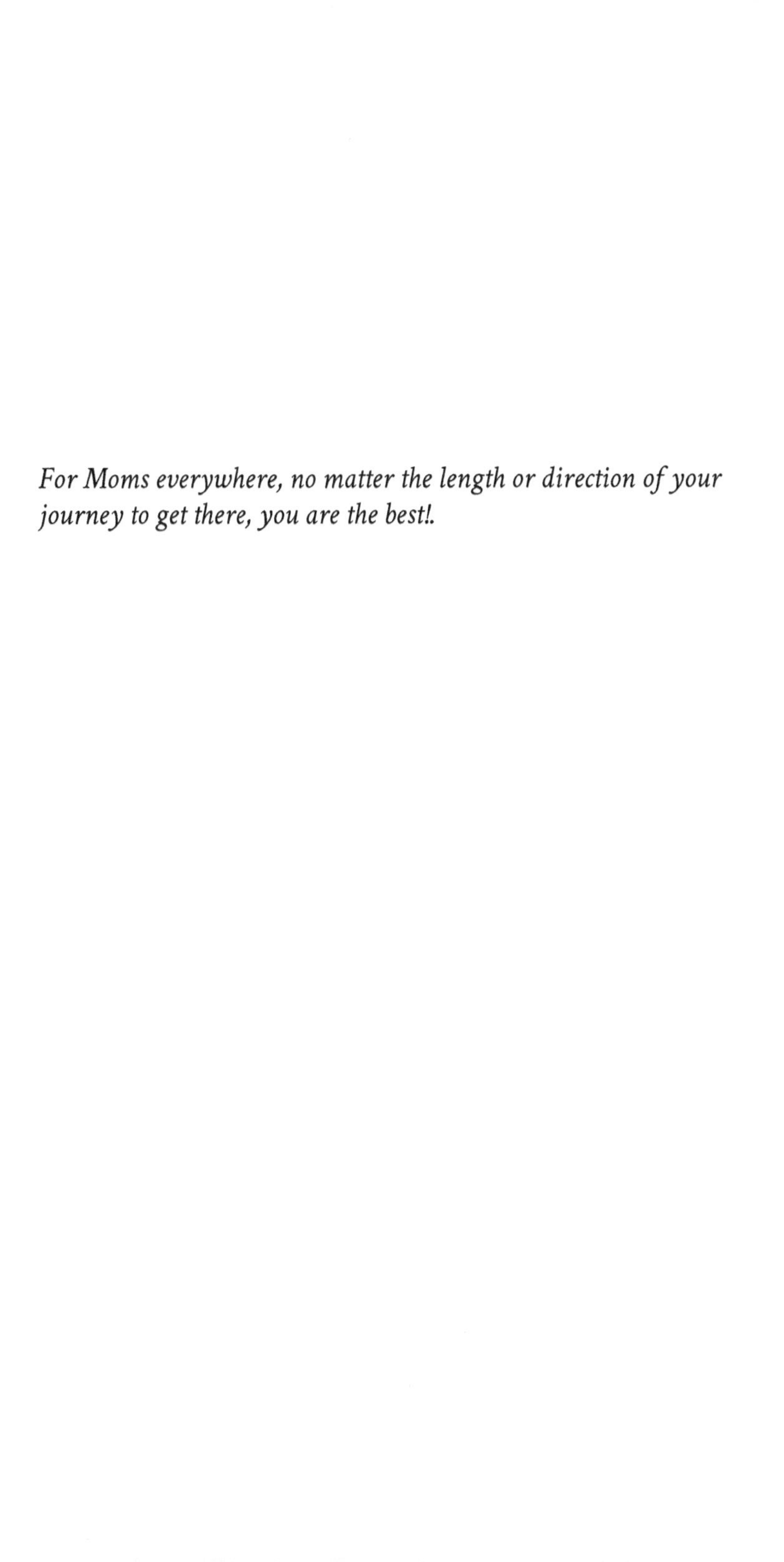

For Moms everywhere, no matter the length or direction of your journey to get there, you are the best!.

ACKNOWLEDGEMENTS

To the wonderful readers and fans of the Gaming the System series. Thank you, thank you for being on this wild ride with me. Your enthusiastic support and love of these characters has bolstered me throughout years both amazing and difficult. Sometimes I have to pinch myself and ask if this is my real life and is this my real job? So much love and appreciation to you. I can't express enough what you mean to me. I hope you opt to stick around for more stories in my connected worlds.

This book would not be possible without the many who have helped and contributed to its inception. My warmest thanks go out to you, Kate Mckinley (aka the "Smut Doctor") and Sabrina Darby, brainstorming partners and beta-readers extraordinaire who aren't afraid to ask the hard questions (even if they make me cry). To Kelly Allenby for her gems of wisdom and for being a wonderfully supportive fangirl. To Dayna Hart for her editing prowess--her scalpel is razor-sharp and she's not afraid to use it.

Many thanks to the talented visual artists who also contributed to this project. To Lindee Robinson for the excellent photography of real-couple models Elena and Marcus Filip (and their son, Leonidas) for the teaser and promo images and for the alternate print cover. Many thanks to Kristie of Vanilla Lily designs for the gorgeous neon cover (and the entire cover redesign of the series). Much love to my brilliant friend, Penny Reid, for her generous contribution to the rebrand concepts. Also thanks to go out to Sarah Hansen of Okay Creations for the alternate print cover design.

Last but never least, to my family who, by now, respects what it takes to go into making a book and knows that as the deadline approaches, the urgency ratchets up by a few degrees, or a hundred. Thanks to my husband for putting up with my short replies, my "why are you coming in here?" glares and for the generous amounts of coffee you supply. I love you. For my kiddos...well this one was done mostly while you 2 were off being young adults and taking on the world. I've missed you and not a day goes by where I don't wish you were still living here and freely interrupting my writing time. Just like Mia's dream, you are both my miracles and my dream come true. I'm so grateful to be your mom. Xoxo

I have to admit my eyes aren't completely dry writing this. However, please remember, this isn't "goodbye," to your favorite characters in the Gaming The System series. It's "see you soon." They'll be back and in some really surprising ways. <3

CHAPTER

ONE

MIA

I STOOD SHOULDER TO SHOULDER WITH FRIENDS AND colleagues, facing the brilliant light of a setting sun, staring toward my future as if it was a physical monolith situated on the horizon. Sure, we were all dressed like we'd just stepped off the set of a Harry Potter movie. All I needed was my maroon and gold Gryffindor scarf to complete the look. Our caps and gowns were black, decorated with the dark green stripes of the School of Medicine. From our caps dangled green tassels. Excitement crackled in the air around every one of us. Without a doubt, we had worked our asses—and possibly other body parts—off to be here.

Here I was, in line to mount the steps to the stage. *Me*, Emilia Kimberly Strong Drake, soon-to-be MD.

Hard to believe, and yet, here I was. After an arduous academic—and personal—journey, to get here.

Here I was, finally, facing my future.

"This is so surreal," my friend Louisa said at my shoulder. "Can you even believe it?"

I quirked a smile at her. "My body feels like I'm eighty years old and I've been through the wringer. I can absolutely believe it. Because if this is just another one of those fake-out dreams I've been having, I'll fall on the ground and throw a tantrum right now."

She smiled wide, showing off her beautiful, even white teeth. Louisa had big, brown eyes, deep brown skin and shoulder-length, tightly curled dark hair. And she looked as exhaustedly relieved and content as I felt.

"We're here, we've made it. I can pinch you if you want, but definitely don't be throwing tantrums. Think about your family out there watching us. And I'm pretty sure I spotted your ridiculously sexy hubby."

I laughed. I'd spotted him, too. He was in the center of one of the loudest cheering sections out there, led overly enthusiastically by my mother and assisted by Jenna, my hopefully-soon-to-be-someday stepsister-in-law.

"Have you found your husband in the crowd?" I asked her.

"Not yet. Midwesterners only get rowdy at football games. But I have a feeling that's going to change this evening."

"What's this evening?"

"Well...I have a secret I haven't told anyone yet."

I frowned. "Do I get to know the secret?" I whispered loudly.

"I can't tell you yet," Louisa said.

I arched a brow. "Are you sure? Don't tell me that you're backing out of the St. Joseph's residency, or I'll never forgive you."

"Oh no. No way. We're going to be interns together, for sure. But after that..." She shrugged dramatically. "Who knows?"

I turned to her. "Lou, please tell me you aren't ditching me. You and I are the only ones from UCI who matched with that program."

"I'm not planning to ditch you. However..." She bit her lip, gave me an enigmatic smile, and shrugged dramatically. Then she very deliberately patted her belly.

I raised my brow at her. "Indigestion? All that questionable fast food we ate while studying for exams?"

She shook her head. "You can't tell *anyone*. I haven't even told Josh yet."

"You're pregnant?"

She grinned, eyes sparkling. "How'd you guess?"

"I have stunning and non-scientifically verifiable powers of extrasensory perception."

She snickered.

"Or maybe it's all that incredible glowing you're doing," I added.

She waved a hand in dismissal. "Please, I'm not in the glowing stage yet. I just found out, and you are the first human soul I've told. I peed on the stick this morning. The second line appeared right away."

"We should get a blood draw and send it to the lab so you can verify."

She smirked. "Already did that on the way here. Should have the results anytime now. I marked it stat—in red, and double-underlined. Those dudes at the lab are always blowing off the stat orders. I get tired of it."

I laughed and turned my attention back to the stage for a moment, stepping forward before reaching out to grab her hand and squeeze it. "Congratulations, Lou. I'm so happy for you."

And I was. She'd been trying for a while, though I'd sometimes wondered about her timing. Doing a medical residency, especially during intern year, while pregnant was no joke—or so I imagined. But this marked a victory of over a year's struggle.

And so great was my joy for her that I only felt the tiniest pangs of self-pity. It happened sometimes. And it had been over a year since I'd opened the discussion with my own husband that I'd like for us to start trying again. So far, radio silence on his end.

I hadn't pushed. As hard as our previous struggle had been, I wasn't the only one affected by our loss. Nevertheless, I always swallowed a little lump when reminded about it, even on a day where I was finally achieving a lifelong dream.

I was now six people away from mounting that stage, receiving my degree and stole, shaking a few hands, and being declared a doctor.

So many years and so many experiences had led to this one point and time. I was grateful for them all—even the painful ones, because I'd learned so much from them.

"Are you okay?" Louisa asked, taking in my pensive features with a decided frown.

I immediately plastered a smile on my face to cover whatever resting-bitch-face had settled there. "I'm absolutely over the moon for you. *And* especially honored to be the first human being that you—*didn't*—tell." I punctuated that last with an exaggerated wink that made her burst out laughing. The guy in front of us, Del, turned and gave us both a stern look. But hey, who cared? He was going off to do a residency in New Jersey, then on to specialize in orthopedic surgery. I'd likely never see him again.

I squeezed Louisa's hand, but we didn't talk again as we were now very close to the stage. Butterflies stirred in my belly and, to be honest, something else did, too.

Longing. I could be happy when thinking about Louisa's news while also realizing that we'd be medical residents together at the same hospital. I'd be watching with a front-row seat as her pregnancy progressed. There were other feelings, too—a little tinge of something deep in my heart. It wasn't sadness but more a feeling of something missing. I was envious that Josh, her husband, had been all-in with this every step of the way. He'd be absolutely over the moon about it.

My partner? He was still in the "needed to be dragged kicking and screaming into it" phase. And given his near-legendary stubbornness, that wasn't going to change anytime soon.

But even with that baggage, I wouldn't trade him for anything.

It was my time to climb the steps to the stage as my name was announced. I felt no regrets or even the slightest sliver of sadness. Only gratitude for everything I currently had.

A little while later, as the ceremony was about to close, we were asked to stand, shoulder-to-shoulder, to recite the Hippocratic Oath.

"I swear to fulfill, to the best of my ability and judgment, this covenant...I will respect the hard-won scientific gains of those physicians in whose steps I walk, and gladly share such knowledge as is mine with those who are to follow....I will remember that there is art to medicine as well as science...If it is given me to save a life, all thanks....May I always act so as to preserve the finest traditions of my calling and may I long experience the joy of healing those who seek my help." And with one big collective sigh of relief and excitement,

we all gave out three cheers instead of the traditional cap throwing. Apparently, newly minted medical doctors were too dignified for that.

Just a short while later, Adam found me in the crowd, my mom and Peter in tow, Jenna and William straggling behind and book-ended by my best-friend-forever, Heath. My mind-blowingly handsome husband drew admiring looks he didn't notice as he waded through the crowd toward me, and my grin widened as he came closer. His smile lit up his face, dark eyes gleaming with pride. Our gazes met, and I felt as ooey-gooey inside as I did the first day I'd met him. My stomach did a little flip, and I moved toward him.

I sighed happily when he wrapped me in his arms tight, kissed my cheek and whispered his congratulations in my ear. "You did it. Now I can brag that I play 'doctor' with a real doc every night."

I laughed. Yes indeed, that gratitude and joy in the moment were pushing out everything else, and those feelings of longing and envy were soon forgotten.

Chapter Two
MIA

LESS THAN A WEEK LATER, I WAS IN ITALY WITH ADAM. We'd gone to the airport with the pretense of him taking me along on a business trip to San Francisco. It was completely in line with my husband's style of being the surpriser while hating being the one surprised. One of the many strange dichotomies that seemed to exist in my husband's psyche.

So far it had been a glorious ten days. We'd toured some of the major cities, stayed a few days in Tuscany and done some wine tasting while visiting the cutest little Italian hamlets. Then we'd finally ended up in glorious Venice for nearly an entire week.

Who'd've thunk it? That my workaholic husband, who was so very non-impulsive, would drop everything to whisk me away during the break between graduation and the start of my medical residency?

Truth be told, I hadn't been harping on his work addiction lately. Because it seemed that I'd developed one of my own. So, to continue doing it seemed hypocritical. Instead, I'd been sure to stress how important work-life balance should be for both of us. And while the concept of work-life balance on the road to becoming a medical doctor was almost laughable, we somehow found a way, even if it was just in tiny doses for now.

And he was objectively improving. He put his phone away when I reminded him to, instead of just pretending to do it. And we both took steps to appreciate the present moment instead of worrying about the future or mulling over the past.

And presence was exactly what we were practicing in this deliriously romantic city as we, hand in hand, strolled the tiny alleyways, watched passersby, caught a water taxi to neighboring islands, casually window-shopped and stopped for gelato whenever we felt like it.

We'd already seen the major sites in the city during our first few days here, joining the madcap tourist crowds that would rival some major rock concerts in St. Marks' square. We'd enjoyed a full tour of the lavish Doge's palace and the glittering St. Mark's Basilica standing right beside it. We'd walked the famous covered bridge that was the Ponte Rialto hand in hand, overlooking a canal teeming with motorboats and old-style traditional gondolas pushed along by gondoliers in black-and-white striped shirts.

But after that, instead of pushing for more touristic site-seeing, I'd asked him if we could slow down to just enjoy being in the city and soak up the ambiance. After the lion's share of the tourists left in late afternoon, the city transformed into something otherworldly and quietly enchanting. We'd watch a gorgeous sunset—each one different—and stroll the twilight-cloaked walkways looking out over a twinkling lagoon toward the neighboring islands. I was completely in love with this place, the delicious food, the kind, if tourist-weary locals, and Veneto wine. I was also completely in love with the man walking beside me, who often wrapped an arm around my shoulders or waist.

This afternoon, we'd crossed our fourth consecutive bridge when Adam started complaining. "Jeez, these bridges are going to be the end of my knees. I have an old war injury, here."

He rubbed his right knee. Last November, at the annual paintball war between Draco Multimedia and Blizzard Entertainment—or, as I liked to secretly deem it "Dick-Measuring 101: Battle of the Nerd Programmers"—Adam had sprained his knee when he'd missed his footing and tumbled most of the way down a steep hill.

When I'd first been notified that my husband was in the ER of the hospital, it had nearly taken a year off my life until I'd realized it hadn't been serious. He'd been ordered to stay off of his knee as much as possible for the next three weeks. Guess which driven, workaholic CEO had ignored those doctor's orders? Even when I had tried to enforce them, he'd found ways around it.

Now I observed his slight limp with a near-heartless eye. "Well, you're in your dotage now, so I'll be sure to slow down. Gotta make sure gramps can keep up with me."

I liked milking the fact that Adam was now into his thirties.

"Very funny," he said with a glare. "I guess that makes you my sugar baby. If you keep making me go over these damn bridges in this condition, I'm going to require some serious medical attention to help me through the rest of my day. And also, a very pleasurable way to get my mind off the pain."

I grimaced. "Have I mentioned that you're a *dirty* old man?"

He peered at me out of the corner of his eyes. "Only every damn day since I turned thirty. If I'm going to be an old man, then *dirty* is the only way to go."

I laughed. And dirty was the way I liked him, too. It was weird how, at the end of each day of this trip, I found that my cheeks ached from smiling too much. I loved this man...not only was he devastatingly handsome and insanely smart, but he was also hilarious, kind and so into me he didn't care about anyone else around us.

Our vacation became a string of moments where we enjoyed the sights, the tastes, the experiences, but no more than the mere opportunity to spend days, nights and long silent hours in each other's presence, without the need to talk. Our vacation transformed into a dream, a snippet of time where he wasn't being pulled in one direction and me in the other and barely having time to meet in the middle.

This was time for us. To rediscover who we were to each other. To breathe before we had to hit the rat race once more.

On this day, the late afternoon sun made our shadows stretch across the empty town piazzas as we emerged from the third small church we'd visited that day. We crossed the stretch of ancient stonework hand in hand.

Adam let out a long sigh. "I've seen more saints' bones to fill the Ossuary of Time." He wore a good-natured grin, running his free hand through his hair and rendering himself even more handsome than usual in the process.

I arched a brow and affected an instructional tone I knew would amuse him. "The Ossuary of Time only exists in Yondareth."

"My dear, sweet wife, if you haven't realized by now that Yondareth *is* my real life, then there is no help for you."

I laughed. "I wish you were just joking, but I believe you. It's your world—we players all just live in it, right?"

We walked on for a moment, turning a sharp corner as we wandered aimlessly into some residential district and passed some shops filled with Murano glass, Burano lace and other local items.

As he hadn't replied to me, I glanced over at Adam. He had a wistful look on his face, as if deep in thought. A breeze rose up, stirring my skirt and the stray strands of his dark hair. I frowned. "What's wrong? Your knee hurting still?"

He shook his head. "Nah, I'm fine. I'm just thinking a lot."

"That happens when you don't stare at your phone all the time. You're forced to think."

"Not sure I'm a fan," he said with a grimace.

I stopped walking and turned to look directly into his face. "Adam...?"

He shrugged. A cluster of small children in the nearby square were playing some game with a ball that looked like a cross between soccer and dodgeball, shouting to each other in Italian and laughing, teasing. Seagulls called overhead.

He hesitated, then shoved his hands into the pockets of his jeans. "I dunno. I guess that sometimes I feel like real life is a dream. A fantasy. We're so blessed that sometimes it feels like..." He shook his head, clearly not wanting to continue with the line of thought.

I shook my hand, that was still tightly entwined with his to urge him on. "Feels like *what?*"

He raised his solid shoulders in an exaggerated shrug. "Sometimes I get this dread in the pit of my stomach, like I'm waiting for the other shoe to drop."

I blinked. Wow. I mean, my husband tended toward the dark and morose sometimes. It was just part of his nature. The events in his past and in his childhood hadn't helped with what might have been a natural tendency to begin with. Something he clearly had found difficult to shake, even in the good times.

I moved up to him and pushed the errant dark lock of hair off his forehead, then caressed his cheek, his chiseled jaw while gazing into those dark, dark eyes. "Adam, don't forget that we've been there, done that, got the fucking t-shirt. We've *endured*. We deserve this happiness. Let's enjoy it. There's a lot to be said about living in the now. We are here in this beautiful, ancient place. We are each other's person. I love you more than I did the day I married you. Can you not sit back, soak up that happiness and enjoy it? Don't mess up your head with dreading some mythical time when it might evaporate."

He visibly swallowed, the bump in his throat bobbing. The expression on his face was deadly serious.

"Shit, you're scaring me." I searched his gaze.

"No, there's nothing to be scared about. It's just this vague feeling that I should be moving on to the next step of something, and I don't know what that is. Like we've now achieved these goals we'd worked so hard for in our twenties and now that we're—"

"Hey! Speak for yourself. I'm still in my twenties for two and a half more years. You're the only senior citizen here."

He grimaced at me. "Gee, thanks."

I raised my brows and gave him a cheeky smile. "It's your fault for robbing the cradle."

He smirked and then leered at me openly, reaching out to grab my butt. I let out a little yelp, and we both laughed. "I'm just a dirty old man, and it's been a long time since you've been in the cradle, baby."

After a delicious dinner at a small, out-of-the way restaurant that we'd wandered into, where we'd dined on the patio out under the stars and drank a full liter of sparkling local Rabosello wine, we stumbled home, both of us well past tipsy.

Fortunately, Adam wasn't so far past tipsy as to be unable to perform once I'd ripped his clothes off. I think a few of the buttons on his shirt actually did go flying in my desperation to get him naked. It hadn't been all that long since the last time—just two days ago—but we were on each other like it was a yearly conjugal visit and he was a prisoner serving a life sentence.

"Wow, my sugar baby is—"

"Don't finish that sentence unless you want to immediately kill the mood, dude," I muttered between frantic kisses and even more frantic unbuttoning—and unbelting. Without warning, he grabbed both my arms and fell backward onto the bed, pulling me down on top of him.

We both started laughing hysterically, like it was the funniest thing ever. Then he stopped with a long sigh. "That wine tasted like fizzy fruit juice, but I think a liter is way too much for the two of us."

I divested him of the last scraps of his clothing and had him joyfully naked underneath me. I began trailing kisses across his delicious, hard chest. "Speak for yourself."

"If I hadn't had any, I think I'd be getting drunk just from the wine on your breath. Like when someone reeks of pot and you get a contact high just by breathing near them."

I laughed. "You've been spending too much time in the Den with your game testers again."

"Oh, hell no, I never go in there. Those kids are animals. Even Kat can't keep them in line."

"Less talking about work and more touching my boobs, okay?" I growled at him, grabbing his hands and putting them where I wanted them.

He grinned, palming them obediently. "You don't have to tell me twice." As he often did, his finger traced the tattoo I'd gotten last year—the one just over my lumpectomy scar that showed the constellation of Draco.

And soon we were all over each other, mouths and hands and legs interlocking.

It was fast and furious. We did what we do best—we improvised. When he finally rolled off me, we were both out of breath and way too sweaty. He flopped onto his back beside me.

I took a deep breath, staring at the ceiling. "Wasn't I on top when we started?"

He sighed heavily. "There was a lot of rolling around. I lost track."

I blinked, bringing up the edge of the fitted sheet that had once been nicely fastened to the mattress. "We tore the sheets off the bed."

He laughed, running a hand through his thick, dark hair and leaving it standing straight up in the process. "That's my horny little sugar baby."

I rolled over onto my side and smoothed a hand over his disheveled hair. Then I leaned down and gave him a long kiss. "Hey," I said. "I want to talk to you about something."

His dark brows twitched up and his smile hesitated only a little. "Uh oh. Well, if it's about my wife, she doesn't know about us yet, and I—."

I put a finger over his mouth to stop him. "I'm being serious, even though we had all that wine. Maybe it's what's giving me the courage to finally bring it up."

His brows furrowed for a moment in concern, but he sobered and gave a slight nod, urging me to continue.

"I think it's time...."

At my hesitation, he tilted his head. "Time for what?" he prompted.

"For us to start trying for a family."

He licked his bottom lip and stared at me as if trying to focus his eyes. It was probably a mistake to bring this up when we were both most of the way to drunk.

"What is this *really* about?"

"You know, I've been thinking about this for a while. I brought it up on our first anniversary. We tabled the discussion while you told me you needed to do some research on all the risks. I got distracted by my last year of med school. How is your research project coming along?"

His jaw bulged where it tensed and he turned to stare at the far wall, probably to avoid meeting my gaze.

"Is this about *me*, Adam?"

He frowned and turned back to me. "What? No. But we are both really busy. I just don't see—"

"Or is it about *you*?"

He rolled his eyes exaggeratedly and suddenly sat bolt upright in bed, slipping into the bathroom.

I got up to follow him, and before I could needle him further, he turned to me. "We are way too drunk to be having this discussion right now."

"On the contrary, maybe we need to be a little drunk to be honest about how we feel."

He turned away from me, stepping into the large shower in our fancy accommodations, and turned on the faucet, holding out a hand to test the water.

"So, I'm not being honest?" he called over his shoulder.

"I didn't say that." After quickly using the toilet, I stepped into the shower behind him. He moved into the spray, clearly letting me know I wasn't welcome to shower with him if I was pressing him on a subject he didn't want to discuss.

Tough shit.

I held out my hand to test the water, and it was on the colder side of lukewarm. "What the fuck? Since when are you into taking cold showers? *After* sex? Isn't that defeating the purpose?"

Despite the undesirable temperature of the water, he shoved his dark head under the spray. I glared at his muscular back.

"So that's it?" I challenged. "You're in full avoidance mode?"

"What? Can't hear you," he replied.

My eyes narrowed. "You're shivering, and you look one step away from hypothermia."

He turned to face me, still dominating the space directly under the spray so that I couldn't get any. "It's invigorating. I feel invigorated."

"Your lips are turning blue. Be careful how much you expose yourself to that water. You'll start getting shrinkage."

We both glanced down at the body part in question at the same time and fortunately I had just enough wine in my system to be able to laugh at the situation. Because maybe the way he turned tail and ran like a coward the minute I said "start a family" might have made me cry instead—or at least shake my fist at the sky.

CHAPTER
Three
MIA

OUR DISCUSSION DIDN'T RESUME UNTIL WE WERE ON THE flight home. I was merely trying to pin Adam down on a time for when we could have a serious talk about it. He wouldn't even give me that.

I leaned forward, resting an elbow on the arm of my airplane seat in our adjoining first class pods. "Should I call your assistant and ask her to pencil me in? How about next Tuesday between three and three-twenty?"

Comfortably ensconced within his own pod, his arms were folded over his chest. "I really want to watch something but forgot to download a new movie. We get free Wi-Fi in first class, but I'm sure their streaming speed is for shit."

"Adam—"

"Are you using your tablet?" he cut me off.

"Oh, I downloaded a couple 80s movies. Right up your alley. John Hughes. You like his movies, right? That Kevin Bacon one? *She's Having a Baby.*"

Adam's side-eye game was perfected long ago, long before we met, and he shot me some of it right then. And you know what? I didn't give a shit.

I responded with my sternest stare, punctuated with true exasperation. "When are we going to talk about this seriously?"

His eyes narrowed. "We sure as fuck are not doing it right now on this plane surrounded by two hundred of our closest friends for the next twelve hours."

I raised my brows in hope. "So, Maggie will pencil me in for twenty minutes next week?"

He rolled his eyes. "Emilia, please."

I rummaged in my carryon and shoved my tablet at him. "Here, have a ball. Enjoy the tablet, since I don't plan on talking to you except for basic survival needs until you tell me when we're having this conversation."

He took the tablet from me and threw me an unreadable but careful look. "Basic survival needs, huh? Does that include—"

"*No*, it doesn't. You'll never become a member of the mile high club at this rate."

He blinked, threw still more side-eye my way, then unlocked my tablet without another word while slipping on his noise-canceling headphones.

He must have liked my John Hughes suggestion, at any rate, because a few minutes later, he had the opening sequence of *Ferris Bueller's Day Off* playing on the screen.

I blew out an exasperated breath that was lost on him due to the headphones. Hopefully, he got the message when I pressed the button to raise the divider between our two pods.

I rolled over to catch a nap, but my thoughts were racing too much to let me doze off. This man had to give in someday.

Someday. But Adam's stubbornness was legendary. And try as I could—and had in the past—I was, quite honestly, no match for it.

And as I had to be at the hospital all day tomorrow for my intern orientation, who knew when we'd have the time to talk again? Unless he made the overt effort to be home for dinner that night—and he only hit that mark about half the time, messaging me by early afternoon to tell me whether it was going to happen.

The next morning, fighting jetlag, I got up extra early, put on my hospital scrubs and a bit of makeup, and headed out the door. I allowed Adam to grab me up into a hug and land a peck on my cheek. "Have a good day at orientation. Try not to fall asleep in the middle of a presentation. Might be a bad look."

I arched a brow at him. As if I'd fall asleep on my very first day as an actual doctor. How many years had led up to this day? And now, it was finally here.

"Forgive me?" he asked, tilting his head in that way that made him fetchingly handsome while he implored me with those dark, compelling eyes. Must be nice to be so fucking irresistible. But I was Mia Strong, and I could resist even the sexiest man on the planet.

For a little while, at least.

"You're forgiven the second you put our chat on the calendar and follow through with it." I tugged against his grip, reaching out to grab my purse.

He didn't release his hold. "It's your first day as Dr. Mia. Don't go to work mad at your adoring hubby."

"I'm not mad. I'm...*exasperated.* I'm—"

"Aroused?" He arched a brow at me, and I almost laughed at him. Instead, I smacked his chest, right on his firm, hard pec.

"Stop it. I'm annoyed. I'm—I'm—*disappointed.*"

His dark brows twitched together. "Disappointed?" And at my nod he added, "Ouch."

I tilted my head as if to ask, *do you blame me?* And he slowly released his hold on my waist. Before stepping away, I landed a peck on his cheek. "Maybe I'll see you tonight depending on when you can break free."

"Have a great first day, doctor!" he called as I closed the front door and headed out.

It was nearly noon and after four straight hours of going over policies and procedures with our senior resident, several fellows, and attending physicians, we were more than ready for lunch. My brain felt fried. Funny that I could take hours and hours cramming medical terms, suggested dosages, and drug compatibilities, and feel refreshed after a short break, ready to dive in for more, but give me a bunch of legalese and my brain shut down after mere minutes. This reaffirmed that the medical track was the one for me and I should steer far clear of law, should I ever decide on a later in life career change.

"Dr. Strong, you have a delivery," came a voice over the mic as we were breaking up for lunch. "Check in the mailroom."

I turned to Louisa, whose brows raised as she asked me. "What's all that about?"

I shrugged. "No idea. I haven't ordered anything, though now I have this handy dandy list of suggested items." I gave a sarcastic wave to my notes listing equipment we were supposed to provide ourselves while undergoing our internship—such as a stethoscope, otoscope and the like.

Her eyes lit up. She'd had her hair done into cornrow braids since I'd last seen her at graduation, and they looked amazing on her. She claimed it was a move of sheer practicality. "Let's go see what it is, and then I'm dying for a bite to eat. I can't believe we only get thirty minutes."

"Medical school was only the beginning of the masochism, I'm afraid." I smirked at her as we made our way down to the mail room, per the summons.

I knew the minute I got to the mail desk which delivery was for me. A massive bunch of flowers—red roses prominent.

"I was told I had a delivery." I grimaced sheepishly. "Dr. Strong?"

"Yup," the woman pivoted, grabbed the massive floral arrangement by the heavy vase and pivoted, depositing it on the counter between us. Her nametag read Elaine, and she beamed at me, making a big show of peering around the flowers. "What a great way to start your first day as a doctor. Somebody loves you," she cooed.

I glanced at the card and rather than it being typed out or scrawled in some florist's hand, I saw, printed out in my husband's very distinctive handwriting: *Dr. Emilia Strong* and then in tiny writing just underneath and in parentheses: *(aka Mrs. Drake)*.

"Aw look at that. He even put both your last names on it," Louisa said, eyes lighting up. "I wish Josh was this thoughtful—and romantic. *Dayum*, woman. All this and hot as hell on top of it."

"Oh, he's hot?" Elaine asked, still invested in the conversation from where she crouched to see us around the massive arrangement. "Tell me more. Got a pic?"

Louisa actually pulled out her phone and fished up a picture of us at graduation standing with our husbands and pointed him out to her. She bent to look, eyes widening. "Wow!"

She gave me a look, maybe wondering how I ended up with someone with Adam's stunning looks. Currently, I wasn't exactly looking my best in my unglamorous hospital scrubs, hair pulled back in a ponytail, and with only light makeup.

"Oh, that's not all," Louisa leaned forward to dish. "On top of being super hot, he's also a bil—"

"Okay, time to go!" I snatched up the vase, wrapping my arms around the unwieldy base so I wouldn't drop it. "Thanks so much, Elaine," I said to the mailroom lady while sending a pointed glare Louisa's way. She responded with an apologetic shrug.

I had to carry that damn thing all through the cafeteria line while every eye in the room seemed fixated on it and me. "Aren't you going to read the card?" Louisa asked.

"Eventually," I answered. "Thanks for handling my food tray. I just want one of those Cobb salads with a little ranch dressing on the side."

When we finally made it to a small, two-person table, the damn arrangement took up so much room, we had hardly any place to fit our plates.

"Go on, read the card."

I pushed out a loud sigh. The card probably bore a profuse apology. And I'd rather not have to explain exactly what he was apologizing for which would eventually lead to her feeling bad and—worse—possibly apologizing for being pregnant or talking about her pregnancy, which I didn't want at all.

I could just make up what it said, couldn't I?

I snatched up the card from its little holder, but before I could open it to read, a presence made itself known, hovering near us at the table. Our senior resident, Dr. Craig Iverson, stood staring at the massive jungle-growth of flowers that seemed to be growing bigger by the second. *Jeez.* Adam never did things halfway and apparently that trickled all the way down to his taste in apology flowers, too. Goddamn it.

"Doctors Bluth and Strong? Good. I just wanted to let you know that I have you down for three twelve-hour shifts each this week. Dr. Strong, you're on..." He clicked an app on the tablet he was carrying and scrolled. "You're working the next three nights starting tomorrow and Dr. Bluth, you'll follow—" He interrupted himself, throwing another look at the massive arrangement. His eyes landed on the envelope in my hand and he tilted his head, reading it. For some reason, I wanted to reach out and snatch it away.

"Wait, what?" Louisa protested. "Can't Mia and I work together sometimes? Are you always going to schedule us opposite each other?" Louisa said, eyes wide with alarm.

Dr. Iverson blinked. "Well, this isn't a girls' club, Dr. Bluth, but I'll see what I can do next week."

I immediately felt myself prickle at the tone of his voice. "Dr. Iverson, 'Girls club' sounds a little...." I gestured with my hand to infer what I meant because the words were likely to inflame.

His eyes narrowed at me. "A little what?"

I blinked. He couldn't be this clueless, could he? "Well, as we are two of only five female interns this year, I think it sounds a little sexist to call it a girl's club just because we are requesting some rotations together."

His features froze. I'd said the s-word. That word was not liked by men in charge, clearly. I sighed inwardly.

"I apologize, Dr. Strong. I'll endeavor not to ever use the term again in any context—"

I held up a placating hand though it irked me to do so. "Please, I was just pointing out—"

"No, no. Fair enough. I have been called out. Now is there anything sexist in the sentence: You're working for the next three days, late 12-hour shift?"

I blinked, then swallowed. "Umm. No."

"Good. Thanks for keeping me on the straight and narrow." He spun and left, his bearing stiff. He was clearly offended. *Great, Mia.* I sure knew when to pick my battles, didn't I?

"Uh, maybe that wasn't such a great idea," Louisa said, watching him go.

I turned and peered after him, making a face. "Probably not, but hey, I bet today would be a great day to let him know you're pregnant and going to need maternity leave in about seven months. I doubt he'd have anything to say about it."

She grimaced at me. "Good point."

Before Louisa could pester me about it again, I pulled the card out of the envelope, opened it, read it, and tucked it into the front pocket of my new white coat.

"Well? What did it say?"

I made an exaggerated face. "Can't tell you. This cafeteria is rated PG, and let's just say the note was NC-17." I waggled my eyebrows for effect.

Louisa flushed, jaw dropping, eyes widening. "Oh my god, you are so damn lucky. What I wouldn't give—"

I held up my hand. "Josh is amazing. Stop saying that."

Later, during a particularly boring stretch of lecture, I fingered Adam's card in my coat. He promised that we'd have that talk as soon as he was back from the short business trip he was taking over the next few days.

Which suited nicely, since apparently, I would be working late 12-hour shifts for the next three days...

CHAPTER

FOUR

ADAM

I'D HAD TO SPEND A CHUNK OF MIA'S FIRST WEEK AS AN intern-year resident away from home. In addition, it was in one of my least favorite places—Northern California—at an exclusive CEO training program that my board of directors had slated for me. It was an honor, really, to be leading an important enough company to be considered for the program. But that didn't make me like it any more. And I'd have to return in a few months for a longer weekend retreat.

I was already dreading it, perhaps because this whole program was starting to outline for me how much I'd moved beyond the CEO thing.

Thankfully, I was able to return home on Friday night to my wife just waking up after her third night shift in a row. And we were able to spend a long Independence Day weekend alone, just the two of us rattling around that big house that felt so empty and yet so full at the same time. Chef had packed us a few meals and bought a few things for us to cook. Emilia was going to try a new recipe, which made me regret not having purchased one of those souvenir crucifixes near the Vatican. Just so I could send up special prayers that her cooking wouldn't kill us both. I stopped just short of saying that out loud. She'd just started talking to me again. No need to heedlessly rock the boat, even when just poking some innocent fun.

"You want to eat outside tonight?" She grabbed a crouton from the salad bowl and popped it into her mouth, crunching it. "I was thinking we could heat up the puttanesca and open one of those bottles of wine we bought in Tuscany."

Wine, hmm? I threw her some side-eye, wondering if the wine was some ruse to get me to loosen up. Was she always going to try to ply me with wine when she wanted to broach a difficult subject? And then the answer to that came just as quickly inside my own head—did I blame her? Wouldn't I do the same in her place?

I was being famously stubborn. And my wife knew me all too well. Point taken.

"Mmm," she said later as she bit into her pasta. "Chef never disappoints. This is amazing. Try it with a little bit of the chianti."

I eyed her while I took the smallest sip possible. She watched, frowned, and then went back to her meal. My eyes slid over the table setting. She'd put out a new tablecloth, set the table with a lone candle and turned the outdoor lighting down low. The lapping of the back bay water onto our own little private beach and the reflections of the passing boats and lighting from our neighbors provided the rest of the ambiance. She had some Italian-style concertina music playing low in the background on the Bluetooth speakers. It was romantic, thoughtful. Perfect thing for staying in. Since I'd soon be traveling again for business and she'd be pulling many more of these godawful long shifts, this was a brief respite where we could enjoy each other.

We'd learned a while ago to seize these opportunities when we had them, hence my whisking her away to Italy in the first place.

"So..." she said. "When's your next trip up north? I forgot to check your calendar."

I shrugged. "Couple weeks. I'd like to wiggle my way out of it. Maybe send Jordan."

Her brow twitched up. "Isn't it part of that elite CEO program you're in? Would they accept your CFO instead?"

I inhaled and then let it go. Why would this be so hard to bring up with her? I couldn't imagine.

"I'm, ah, thinking of putting Jordan in the hot seat for this and maybe..." I hesitated, then suddenly felt the need for more wine. I grabbed the glass and downed it in one fell swoop.

Emilia watched me closely. "Jordan is okay with that, I'm sure."

I nodded, refilling my glass. "Yeah, yeah. I mean, I haven't formally spoken to him about it yet, but I know him well enough to know he'll be good with it."

Her brow twitched up. "And you? What will you be doing instead?"

"Well, for one thing, I won't have to fly up to fucking Palo Alto every five minutes."

She grinned. "Everyone knows how much you love it up there." She plucked up her glass and took a dainty sip. I mirrored her. A slight frown creased the area between her brows. "Is everything okay? You seem...nervous."

I took a deep breath in and out. "I'm thinking about taking a step back."

Those beautiful golden-brown eyes widened. "From...?"

"From the company."

She blinked, clearly confused. "And do what? Retire on a beach in the South Pacific and sip Mai Tais all day?"

I shrugged. "I don't know. I just feel like I've come as far as I can in this job. And I know that sounds weird to you, but you're just barely starting out your dream job. I've been in this industry for well over a decade now. And I've worked long, long hours for most of it."

She frowned, setting down her glass and covering my hand with hers. "Are you sure you aren't just burned out? Maybe you need a leave of absence—or some breathing room—or a new project that excites you."

I heaved a long sigh. "The idea of creating a completely new game just exhausts me, to be honest."

She blinked. "Well, I know we have fun teasing you about your age, but I think thirty-one is a wee tad too young for retirement, don't you?"

I laughed. "I don't even think I'm capable of retiring. But it's tempting to be able to kick back and relax now that I have a doctor to support me."

She snorted. "A lifestyle supported on a resident's salary is not one I think you might find terribly fun."

There was another long pause. The wind kicked up, and the water rippled on the shore. Emilia's hand shifted, lacing our fingers together and she squeezed. I licked my lips, staring down at our linked hands. It felt so weird, this place we were in, so close that I'd never felt closer to her emotionally, and yet we were at such different stages in our lives, our careers. Every time she talked about going off to work, even when she was tired and had spent twenty hours there the day before, she got a dreamy smile on her face. She was clearly in her element. I envied that.

I hadn't felt that way about my own work for far too long.

Emilia's brow creased, and she looked like she was working through a puzzle. "You have choices. So many choices. Maybe that's part of the problem?"

I shrugged. "I've always known what I wanted and gone after it with intensity. I've always been driven, planning out my next moves surgically and strategically. I've always loved the thrill of the hunt and the acquisition. That heady feeling of success. Of winning and being at the top of not only my own game but of the industry at large. It's a high that no substance could ever replicate. I just..."

"Haven't felt it in a long time?" she completed the thought for me.

I hesitated a moment before nodding. "Yeah. That obvious, huh?"

She shook her head. "Actually, not at all. I can hear it in your voice, though, when you talk about it. And I wish you'd told me earlier. You know, since we're partners in this thing together."

I quirked a smile at her. "This game called Life? You're the pink peg riding in the passenger seat next to my blue peg?"

Her eyes widened at the reference and only belatedly, I realized that there were other pegs in those little Life cars, too. Pegs for children.

She bit her lip, thinking. "Sometimes *I'm* in the driver's seat. That damn game." She shook her head. "I always thought it was so bogus that you won by having the most money in the end. That's not the point of life—money. The point is to be *happy*."

I mentally wiped my brow that my reference hadn't reminded her about the little pink and blue baby pegs in the car.

"Maybe if they revamp it, they could add happiness points instead." I grinned.

She laughed. "The next genius project for the boy prodigy?" she arched her brows at me prettily. God, she was beautiful, and I never tired of appreciating it. I sat back, sipped my wine and soaked her up with my eyes. Tonight, she'd be in my bed, wrapped in my arms. I was a lucky fucking bastard.

And that's just where she was less than an hour later. We'd had just enough wine to get us enthusiastically in the mood but not so much as to make the process too awkward or clumsy, and with no actual danger of Whisky Dick—very important when you wanted to fuck your wife after four long days of hardly seeing her at all.

"You look so amazing naked. I wish you could be naked all the time." I leered at her when I had her spread out on the bed under me.

Between lusty kisses, with her arms looped around my neck, she laughed. "That would definitely cheer up some of my patients."

I dipped my head and captured her mouth again. "On second thought, I like that I'm the only person who gets to see you naked. The rest of the world doesn't deserve it."

"But you do?" she smirked.

"Fuck yeah, I do. I won a fucking auction for the right to see you naked."

She snickered. "You seem very fond of bringing up our sordid beginnings."

"Oh baby, I love getting *sordid* with you." My mouth sank to capture hers and there was no more talking. She was soon writhing, and I relished the feeling of that soft, supple body under mine.

She opened her legs readily and swept up in my own lust, I was ready to dive in—so much so, that I nearly started without a condom.

But I stopped myself just in time as the tiny thought flitted into the burning lust of my consciousness like a butterfly drifting into the center of a violent tornado. Of all the times for that to happen.

Because when I had to interrupt things to get up and go grab one out of the nightstand drawer, she said. "How about you just...skip it this time?"

I turned and gave her an acid look. "That's not going to happen. Either we're using a condom or we're not doing this."

"But..." she frowned.

"Please, Emilia." I wanted to fuck my wife, not have an argument with her. I plucked up the condom and turned to her with the question on my face.

She held my gaze, beautiful features clouding. I felt like shit for causing that, but what did she expect?

She rolled onto her side, propping her head up on her hand. "So, are we talking about this right now?"

I was about to snap at her. I was standing here half dressed, all systems go, with a gorgeous, naked woman on my bed. Did I want to stop things now and have this discussion?

Oh no. No, I fucking did *not*.

Didn't seem to matter. She was bound and determined to keep pressing the issue. My hopes that this was just a passing fancy, that it was a fluke brought on by her transition from medical student to physician intern were now being dashed.

"Emilia, you've been a doctor for ten minutes. You've done three shifts as a resident. How the fuck do you even know that such a thing would be feasible?"

"Because others have done it. Others are doing it right now."

"Right now?" I scowled at her. "Like who? Who's pregnant right now? And wives don't count—"

"Louisa Bluth. She's doing it. She just found out at graduation. She's almost at the end of her first trimester."

I sank heavily on the bed beside her.

This explained so many things. I ran a hand through my hair. *Fuck.* There went my leverage.

After long minutes where I just sat and stared at the wall, she reached out a hand toward me, then let it fall without touching me. "Well? Aren't you going to say anything? You said we were going to talk about this."

I let go a long sigh and miserably tossed the still-wrapped condom onto the nightstand. "Isn't that what we're doing?"

"I seem to be the one doing all the talking."

I rested my head in my hands, pressing the heels against my closed eyelids, fingers in my hairline. Was that the faint echo of a headache coming on? "Emilia, you're not going to like what I have to say, so I'm not saying anything."

"So that means no." Her voice was flat. I felt the bed jostle. She'd rolled onto her back, blowing out a long breath of obvious frustration. When I lifted my head to look at her, she was staring at the ceiling.

I half turned toward her. "*No.* The answer is: this entire subject scares the fucking shit out of me. I'm sorry. I can't control that. If I could, I would."

She turned her head to meet my gaze. "So, instead, you shut it down? What about research? I have piles of it, by the way. I can send you links to medical studies. I've been amassing information for months. But what good is sending it to you if you won't read it?"

"I'll read it," I replied quietly without looking at her.

"And then?"

I opened my hands and gestured in frustration. "Agreeing to read it doesn't mean I'll agree to all of it. I'm sorry. This will sound weird coming from me, but this is—and I readily admit to it—a purely emotional reaction. I feel it in the deepest part of my bones."

"What do you feel?"

"*Fear*, Emilia. Bone-crushing, paralyzing fear. Every time this subject comes up, it takes me right back to that time, right back to when I almost—" I stopped at a loss for words. I swallowed then added quietly. "It was my fault."

Her open hand hit the bed beside her. "It was *nobody's* fault. It was life, and shit happens."

"Yeah...*shit.* And you almost made a decision that would have ended me. I had no control over that—which, rightly so. It's your body. But at that point of time, I had no control and when I think back to it, I can't breathe properly. It's not logical, just...visceral."

Not another second passed before Emilia's hand wrapped around mine. Tight. I laced my fingers through hers and our palms fused together. I let out a long breath but still couldn't look at her.

"Adam," she said quietly.

"Yes," I replied in a flat voice.

"Come here." She tugged me toward her with our interlocked hands.

Slowly I uncurled myself and stretched out alongside her on the bed. She rolled onto her side and brought her free hand up to palm my cheek. I closed my eyes.

"Look at me."

I opened my eyes and locked my gaze on hers. She had the most earnest, honest expression on her face. One of understanding. I at once felt intense relief but also like an incredible failure. This woman, this woman who I loved more than my next breath...I couldn't give her the one thing she wanted more than anything. Because I was too much of a coward.

And there were tears in her eyes. *Fuck.*

"Thank you for telling me all that. I know it was really hard." Her voice was thick with unshed tears and her eyes glistened. I felt a scratchiness at the back of my own throat as if I might start in, too. Thankfully, I resisted. That would have just been icing on the fucking coward cake.

Instead, I reached out and dried her tears with my thumb.

"I'll wait, you know. I can wait," she whispered.

What if you end up waiting forever? Was it fair to do that to her? I reframed the thought because it was important not to hide that possibility from her.

"What if, a year from now I feel the same way? Or a year after that? Or..."

"Well, then we deal with it. We're still young. We have time for you to grow into the idea. You know how I feel, and I don't see that changing."

"There are so many what-ifs here. I'm not just reacting to the past. What if you do get pregnant and then we find out the cancer came back? Would you make the same decision again?"

Her eyes wandered off to stare at something only she could see, as if trying to envision the catastrophic scenario that my own dark mind had instantly gravitated to.

"I don't know. I'm going to be honest. I don't regret the decision I made before. It saved my life. But the likelihood of that ever happening again—"

"Don't say it's almost nil. It's only been a little over three years since you showed no evidence of disease. Five years is the benchmark. I know that much."

Her brow twitched. "Statistically, yes, but for my age—"

"Again, you were an anomaly to have developed that type of cancer at your age. You're already out of the standard mean statistically, so don't quote statistics at me."

Her grip tightened on my hand. "Adam, don't get worked up. I'm just saying...I'm just being honest and saying that I don't know. I. Don't. Know. And if we were to proceed, you'd have to become comfortable with that uncertainty. I don't think that's a comfort zone for you."

"That is a definite *dis*comfort zone."

Her brows knit. "I think there's a lot of uncertainty going on with you already, what with this deciding to step back at work without knowing what you want next. I think we should table this discussion until you've resolved some of the other uncertainty in your life."

I couldn't help but hear the disappointment in her voice even as she said it, but there was nothing but compassion in her eyes. It made me feel like shit. But I wasn't about to turn down her offer to table the discussion, even though a little voice at the back of my mind called me coward, yellow, wuss, gutless, ad infinitum—and wouldn't shut the fuck up.

I wrapped my free arm around her body and pulled her flush against me, landing a peck on her lips. "Thank you, my gorgeous, sexy wife. Every day, I wonder what the fuck I did to deserve you."

She grinned widely, eyes gleaming. "Not enough, clearly."

I pecked her again and pulled back to look at her once more. "Clearly."

She hooked an arm around my neck and pulled me in close. "I can think of a few things you could do right now to make up for the deficit."

"Mmm. I'm sure you can."

Her hand went to the fly of my jeans, but I gently pushed it away, reaching down to grab one of her soft thighs and pull it away from the other one. Without a word, I slid down her body, kissing a heated path down her bare skin until my head and shoulders were between her legs. The moment she realized my intentions, she sucked in a quick, sharp breath of excitement. It was that—and that alone—that I felt deep down in my bones, a straight shot of arousal that made me hard and ready for her in an instant. But her pleasure came before mine, so I kissed and licked and sucked her there until minutes later, she was arching her back and crying out with an orgasm.

Oh yeah. I loved doing that to her. I fucking craved it.

And in that moment, I wanted to give her everything. Give her the world. Give her whatever she wanted. Nevertheless, when the time came, I slipped on the condom.

She didn't say a word, and there was no judgement nor disappointment in her eyes.

And for that, I was very grateful.

CHAPTER

FIVE

MIA

OVER THE NEXT FEW DAYS, OUR CONVERSATION WAS never far from my thoughts. I mulled it over and replayed it in my mind, wondering what the hell the solution could be.

But I could not fault Adam for the raw honesty he'd showed me. For trusting me enough to bare his soul and his fears to me. But short of some miracle dropping from the sky, I couldn't see a way around this impasse.

I was willing to wait, for now. But could I wait forever?

That was a question that kept me up at night.

It only took a few weeks of being a resident physician to realize that I had to snatch a personal life whenever I could. As Adam was still working—though foisting off some of his workload onto Jordan—I took one of my days off to meet with Jordan's significant other.

"Oh em gee, thank you for getting here early and nailing down the table. I am flat out starving." April arrived, plopping down a designer bag the size of carryon luggage onto the bench beside her.

My eyes widened taking it in. "What's that for? Fending off muggers?"

"Haha. I have a lot of shit I need to carry around for the new job. Way too much shit."

I added sugar to the tea I'd been served before she got there. She flagged down the waiter and he headed her way with a menu in hand. "How's that going, by the way? Any better?"

"My boss is an asshole and doesn't think young people fresh out of school deserve to have a life outside their job. One night he had me at the office 'til ten p.m. I thought Jordan was going to go through the roof or get arrested for assault. Ironic, since he himself can be a boss from hell."

I blew out a breath. "And he's also an enabler—to my workaholic husband. The two of them egg each other on. If I wasn't a hundred percent certain of their sexual orientation, I'd swear those two were having an affair."

April's eyes widened and she stared off to the side for a minute, smiling lasciviously. "Oh. My. God. You just gave me the most amazing mental visual just now...*drool*."

I laughed. "You pictured it?"

"Two extremely hot guys getting it on? Of course I did. And if you didn't, you need to read more of my kind of books and fewer medical journals."

Our laughter was cut short by the arrival of the server. April glanced at the menu and quickly ordered. I took a little longer to decide but finally settled on a taco salad. As soon as the server left, I turned back to the conversation.

"So, Jordan's free to cheat on you as long as it's with Adam?" I laughed again.

"Well as long as I'm a spectator, then yeah."

"Just a spectator?"

"Well…" she tilted her head to the side, staring at that same spot as if the image were still projected there in her mind. Her cheeks grew pink. "I wouldn't protest if they decided to involve me."

Her grin widened further, and I couldn't stop laughing. "I should probably be pissed off about you imagining a threesome with my husband, but you're just cracking me up."

She joined in, a cute dimple forming beside her mouth. "It's just a fantasy. A perfectly safe one, I might add. The funny part is if there was ever even just the slightest hint of that scenario becoming reality, I'd be so terrified or self-conscious, I'd run away. But I talk a good talk when it's just fantasy."

I wiped a tear with my napkin once I stopped laughing. "Damn girl, you are just the medicine I needed, making me laugh like that within five minutes of sitting down."

"Oh, if you want a laugh, I could spend a minute or five hundred going off about my asshole boss. I am counting down the days 'til I can find a better job. I need to keep this one just long enough that it doesn't look like a red flag on my resume."

I stirred my tea for a moment and then looked up. "What if…you didn't have to look for another job after this one? Or worry about the blip on your resume?"

April blinked, then reached out to straighten her silverware. "What do you mean?"

"Well. You know that nonprofit organization project we keep talking about? I just feel like maybe it would be a good time to start doing something more than talking."

She straightened, blue eyes widening. "The nonprofit clinic? I absolutely love that idea, too. But I can't imagine that you're ready to take that on right now, are you?"

I shrugged. "Well...*ready* is a relative word. It seems a little crazy to do it now, yes. But you know me, I'm an overachiever, and for the next year at least it would mostly be planning and paperwork before we can even get anything going. Why *not* start working on it now?" After all, there were many other ways to feel fulfilled than dwelling on the thought and plan of starting a family.

April blinked. "Well...money, for one thing. NPOs may not be for profit but they do need money to get going."

I nodded. "I have that money from my inheritance just sitting there. I haven't wanted to touch it, considering the source."

"So, you're figuring using it for the NPO will clear out all the ick from your gross biological sperm donor? Not a bad plan."

I laced my fingers together over my place setting. "Exactly. I wanted to do something good with it but didn't know what. And I didn't even realize until our group ski trip to Canada, when you and I were throwing around ideas for it. Of course, it would be a big undertaking. Even with you at the helm, we'd need more help."

She bobbed her head, taking a sip of ice water. "We sure would. A lawyer, for one. Maybe Adam's uncle?"

I suppressed a grin. At least she didn't refer to Peter as my stepdad. Which he was. But none of us liked to acknowledge *that* bit of weirdness. It had been nearly four years, and all of it was perfectly normal and natural now. And yet, I never called Peter my stepdad unless I was trying to deliberately give Adam the ick. And for that purpose, it was highly successful.

"I think Lindsay Walker would give us a big discount on this. I ran the idea by her at a party last year and she said she'd love to work on something like that."

"Oh, okay," April said coolly, looking away. Clearly, she wasn't hip on the idea of Lindsay.

I frowned, wondering where that came from. It's not like Jordan had ever hooked up with Lindsay. I couldn't say the same for my husband, unfortunately.

April seemed to pick up on my unspoken question. "I don't know her very well, but she was close to Jordan at one time. It makes me a little..." she grimaced.

I held out a hand to placate her. "Oh yeah, don't be jealous. Nothing ever happened between those two."

April laughed. "I'm not jealous, though sometimes I get this weird feeling that she wished it had. Honestly, the fact that she and Adam were a thing for several years weirds me out more."

"Oh yeah," I took a sip of my tea. "It's weird but it's become more of a distant weird now."

April reached into her bag, pulled out a microscopic notebook smaller than my wallet, and unclipped a pen. "I take all my notes in analog now. Technology and I don't get along and I've lost too many files on my phone to get me into trouble. Like that asshole needs an excuse to yell, really. Anyway, let's see. We've got a lawyer. Do we have a timeline for this? Paperwork for articles of incorporation needs to be filed, but we also need to look at business requirements to do some projections."

She scribbled some more, and I sat back feeling overwhelmed. I supposed if someone asked her to write a prescription for amoxicillin, she might feel the same way.

Even after our food arrived, she was still scribbling notes into her little notebook. She'd barely glanced at her food—an Asian salad festooned with delicious looking mandarin orange slices and wonton strips.

"Aren't you going to eat?" I asked.

"Yeah, yeah, I will. I will. It's not like a salad is going to get cold, am I right? But if I don't write down all these ideas now, I'm going to lose the inspiration. This is so damn exciting, Mia. You don't even know. It's been my dream to start a nonprofit from soup to nuts."

"Well, people will definitely be calling us nuts, won't they? Especially me. I've got three years of medical residency to finish before moving on to my fellowship."

"You'll be our doctor of record eventually, but we can hire a physician to get things started. Maybe you could even do part of your residency under him or her?"

I blinked. Why hadn't I thought of that? "You're brilliant."

She gave me a preening smile. "Why, thank you. You're not so bad yourself, Dr. Mia. Put a bunch of smart women together in a room and we'll make magic—and possibly take over the world. For now, that's you, me, and Lindsay."

I almost snorted thinking of the look on Adam's face when I told him I was bringing Lindsay in to help me get my dream NPO started.

"You want to set it up in an underserved community, right? Do you have any ideas as to where?"

"Somewhere around here, obviously." I bit my lip, thinking.

April began eating her salad. "Immigrant communities would have the biggest need. Places like Santa Ana, Garden Grove, Fountain Valley. Isn't it wild how these cities in Orange County have such peaceful, glamorous names? Yet they don't much resemble those names. There's neither a lake nor a forest in Lake Forest, know what I mean?"

I laughed again. April was good for that.

She sighed about halfway through her salad without having come up for air. "Damn this is good. But I'm packing it away so fast, I might as well have shoved it in one of those horse feeding bags and attached it to my face. I'm sorry. Don't think I'm blowing you off in favor of my salad. I was just super hungry."

"It's not like I'm not doing the same thing."

After a few more forkfuls of salad and a long, thoughtful chew, April spoke again like she'd never stopped, "So the problem with putting your clinic in one of those communities is that you're going to need bilingual staff. In Santa Ana, that would be Spanish, in Garden Grove, Vietnamese, et cetera. And then there's the competition with other low-cost clinics. Since we talked about this last year and I started some initial canvassing, I couldn't help but notice that they are on practically every block in some of those communities. Which is wonderful for the community, really, but not so great for us trying to find an underserved niche."

"How bout we create our own niche? Make it a women's clinic?"

She brightened. "Oooh, that gives me so many ideas."

The girl was talking so fast, she hardly paused to take a breath. She was in her element, and I was here for it, asking her questions and her replying as we clarified my vision of the place and whom it would serve.

By the time we left, she had already started a bullet list with at least ten items we needed to tackle to get started. I promised her I'd send her my schedule for the next few weeks so we could meet again and possibly talk to Lindsay at that time, too.

I'd obviously made a good choice in future business partner, and I couldn't wait to get started.

Chapter Six

Mia

On my second day off in a row, since my husband was still working, I couldn't resist the opportunity to join my mom on a shopping expedition to help Heath redecorate his condo.

I'm not sure what was more fun, getting our trio back together again or mercilessly teasing Heath about some of the great possibilities he had open for redecoration.

"Why did I let you two drag me to IKEA of all places?" he said grumpily as we made it down yet another aisle full of ridiculous room suggestions.

"Because putting together the furniture based only on badly drawn pictures is so much fun," I quipped.

"It's to give us ideas, Heath. Color schemes, lighting, adding knickknacks," Mom said.

"Isn't that what Pinterest is for?" he asked, still unconvinced.

"I like looking at three-dimensional models. It's more inspiring." Mom stopped to snap a pic with her phone of a lamp she liked.

"Only if you like Danish modern, which I don't." His eyes narrowed.

I faux-punched him in the arm. "How are we going to get ideas for your hot pink steamy love den without looking around a little? I can see it now, big fuzzy pink couch—"

"Fuzzy? From what? Mold?" He arched a blond eyebrow at me.

"Faux fur," I scoffed.

He snorted. "That will go so well with the black and gray dungeon themed bedroom."

I made a whipcrack sound. "I think you should pick shades of gray...like maybe 40 or, dare I say, 50 Shades of Gray?"

We both dissolved into laughter while my mom scowled. "You two stop being so silly. You're interrupting my inspirational flow."

I raised a brow at her. "*Inspirational flow*, Mom? That sounds a bit...woo woo."

"So?" she arched a brow at me. "Artistic endeavors sometimes need a bit of woo woo."

I waggled my eyebrows. "Not to be confused with all the *woo hoo* that will be happening on Heath's fuzzy pink couch."

"*Woo hoo?* So, we're playing Sims now?" Heath said. "Do I need to put you in the swimming pool and take out the ladder?"

"Whatever, dude. You are so getting a furry pink *loooove* couch for your front room."

He scowled. "Very funny. Pink is *not* my color."

Later, after the grand tour of the display rooms, we went upstairs for lunch. Apparently as much as he liked to diss the furniture, Heath did love the IKEA Swedish meatballs.

"So, tell us about the residency. What's it like actually being a doctor?" Heath asked between enthusiastic bites of gravy-soaked mashed potatoes to go with his meatballs.

"Fun, exhausting. Fulfilling. It's pretty much all over the place. The schedule can get grueling at times. But working with patients is very rewarding."

"But the hours are long," Mom prompted.

"Yeah, well. Mostly you get used to it, though long call makes my eyeballs cross."

"Long call?" Heath asked.

"Thirty-hour shifts. It's purgatory." I rolled my eyes. "Though it would be a lot better if my senior resident wasn't such a jerkface."

"Isn't that *Doctor* Jerkface?" Heath smirked.

"Dr. Jerkface. I like the sound of that." I nodded. "Fitting."

Mom frowned, clearly concerned. "What's he doing?"

I recounted our rough first day where he got his back up because I pointed out his sexist choice of words. "And it all went downhill from there. He's super defensive and hyper critical. Makes comments about my chart notations, saying they're too precise and therefore I'm spending too long on them, which is a waste of valuable time. My attending physicians have said they like my charts, by the way. But this guy also calls me out a lot, pointing out mistakes in front of fellow residents, volun*telling* me for stuff on the floor. And the worst part is that since he's in charge of assigning rotations, he has me on the same one as him. So, I have to put up with him every day and I can't even tell myself that next month, I won't have to work with him. Over the next few months, I have three straight rotations in a row scheduled like this. Another intern said it's because he thinks I'm no competition for him so it's making him look better to our attendings. Nice, huh? It's really starting to piss me off."

"Huh." Heath blew out a breath, shook his head and shoved some more food in his mouth.

"What's so funny about that?" I glared at him, mildly irritated.

"To me, it doesn't sound like he's out to get you. Sounds like he's into you."

My glare sharpened. "Please."

Mom raised a brow and nodded her head slowly. "Sounds like it to me, too."

"What? No. I'm married." I gestured to my left hand. "Like you could miss this rock? It's not even a little bit subtle."

"Doesn't even matter, Mia," Heath countered, having come up for air from his pile of mashed potatoes. "He could be telling his little self that you're just waiting for something to tip the scales to bail out of your marriage and he might just be that someone to... tip *your* scales." He gave me a sly grin and a wink.

I made a gagging noise. "Are you saying all this to get back at me for the pink fuzzy couch comments? Because you're truly making me nauseous right now."

Mom shook her head. "Mia, you should at least be careful. This might develop into something you eventually have to take to human resources. If I were you, I'd document everything that happens that makes you uncomfortable. The date it happened, the time, the location, whether there were witnesses, and all that. It might amount to nothing, but if it ends up becoming something, then you have the incidents to back it up."

I bit my lip. She had a point. As for what had already occurred, it had only been a few weeks, and I could list out most of the stuff so far from memory. I made a mental note to sit down and do that tonight.

"I'll take that under advisement. For right now, I think I can handle it, but you never know, he could get intolerable. Whether he likes or hates me, the motivation behind his actions isn't my problem or concern. I'm not there to make him happy. I'm there for my patients and my attending physicians. Who cares what his reasons are?"

"The reason is he wants to get naked with you." Heath waggled his eyebrows.

I threw a French fry at him, and fortunately he took the hint and shut up.

Nevertheless, let's just say I wasn't overly excited for my next shift at work.

Ultimately, the senior resident wasn't my boss. My bosses were my attending physicians and those were the ones I was striving to learn from and impress.

In the ensuing days, things didn't get much better. Dr. Iverson became even more critical about my charts and scheduled me for extra time to review my peers' charts—under his supervision.

It was totally uncalled for, as my current attending had specifically complimented my chart notes. Iverson, however, required this one-on-one activity that lasted at least an hour after a shift. I was starting to wonder if Heath's suspicions didn't have a bit of truth to them.

I wrote everything down, and after that first week, made sure to dip out at the end of my shifts before he saw me. If he wanted to complain to my superiors about my refusal to meet with him, then I had ammo to throw at him in return.

After a week of ignoring his requests to meet, he dropped it.

In November, the holiday party gave me an opportunity I hadn't anticipated, since everyone brought their significant others as a plus one. I was willing to take the opportunity to find out once and for all if Heath might be right. Why not turn a boring social occasion into a fact-finding mission?

I wore my finest dress, black, strapless with a hem above the knee, and the most stunning arm candy. I wasn't one to turn down a chance to flaunt my ridiculously gorgeous husband to the world.

The party was a lovely affair at a hotel just over the city border, in the Anaheim Resort area. There was live music and great food and a humorous white elephant gift exchange which— I soon discovered—when combined with the average doctor's humor made it downright hilarious. Everything from duck-themed "quack" mugs to a t-shirt that read, "As a great doctor once wrote...." followed by lines of illegible squiggle.

I predicted that joke wasn't going to last many more generations before dying out, as most doctors nowadays documented their work and sent prescriptions electronically. I was no different.

"That explains so many things about why I can't read your love notes to me," Adam whispered into my ear.

I laughed and turned to him. "Aside from the fact that I never write them? The only way to your heart, mister, is through your phone."

He put a hand on his chest. "You wound me."

I leaned in, playfully touching the tip of my nose to his. "I'm sure it takes a lot more than dissing your phone to wound you."

He cracked a devastating smile. "The three of us have many happy memories together."

"From a certain point of view…" I arched my brow. "*Definitely not mine.*" He made a faux pouty face and I laughed, leaning in to kiss him. "You aren't dying of boredom, are you?"

He shook his head. "No. It's interesting. I'm seldom outside of my own geeky gamer bubble to socialize with normals."

"These are definitely not normals. These are geeks of a different persuasion. Instead of gaming, they read big fat boring medical journals and talk shop about weird diagnoses, bizarre symptoms, and hypochondriacs."

His gaze flicked past me and then returned to mine. "Tell me why that one dude over there keeps staring at us. Do you know him?"

So as not to be obvious, I turned to follow who he was indicating while reaching for something in my purse. When my gaze met Dr. Iverson's, my gut twisted. The minute our eyes met, he looked away, back at the emcee who was currently directing the white elephant exchange.

My eyes narrowed and I watched him for a moment, but his head didn't move again. I turned back to Adam. "He was staring at us?"

"Off and on, for a while. He attempted to disguise it a few times when I tried to pin him down."

"Hmm." I faked ignorance. "Maybe he's a hardcore gamer or something."

Adam rolled his eyes. "I have trouble believing that even the hardest core gamer would be able to recognize me on sight in a random nongamer setting like this."

"Well, it's either that or he finds you incredibly hot." I grin. "If that's the case, then I have to say he's got excellent taste."

He arched a dark brow at me, undeterred. "Are you sure *you* aren't the one he finds incredibly hot? And ditto the sentiment."

I swallowed but didn't say anything and endeavored to change the subject before Adam asked me if I knew him.

But my mind was on that for the rest of the night, unable to get what Heath had said out of my head. Why else would he be staring at us if it wasn't some sort of weird hope that he might have a shot with me? Once the idea was there, I couldn't get it out of my head.

The only thing that distracted me? When Louisa's husband pulled out his phone to show us their latest ultrasound. I examined it, expanding the image out to have a good hard look at it. I gave a little smile the second I saw it—the baby's gender. However, I had no idea if Louisa was avoiding looking at it so she wouldn't see.

We'd learned how to read these things during our OB/GYN rotation in medical school. "Uh, so are you keeping the gender secret or don't want to know yourself?"

Louisa smiled. "No, I was just testing you to see if you could tell what it's going to be. We're not having one of those crazy-ass gender reveal parties or anything, don't worry."

I laughed. "I'm thinking that the doctor equivalent of doing a gender reveal would be just passing around the high-res ultrasound for everyone to look at."

She grinned. Maybe that was her low-key plan.

Adam had pulled out his phone, only half paying attention to our conversation—or maybe hiding his own discomfort about the subject of the conversation.

"So," I asked quietly so as to not spoil their news for everyone else. "What's his name?"

"We have a shortlist. Will let you know when we decide."

I couldn't help noticing how she kept rubbing a hand over her rounded belly. "Is everything okay?"

"He's kicking a lot right now." Then she grabbed my wrist. "Here...feel this."

And almost as if on cue, the baby kicked right under my hand. That entire side of her belly twitched, and I gasped with surprise. How cool. I smiled.

"He's going to need a playmate, you know," she said to me with a sly grin and a pointed glance at Adam.

I could tell Adam was paying attention, though he wasn't looking at us, because the minute Louisa said that, he froze like a proverbial deer in the headlights.

I immediately leaned over toward him and nudged. "I'm parched. Can you grab us some more drinks?"

"Sure." He immediately popped out of the chair.

Louisa watched him go with a frown. "I hope I didn't say anything wrong. If I did, I'm so sorry."

I smiled and turned to watch Adam go, hoping he didn't think I'd staged that to push my agenda.

I laid a hand on her upper arm. "You're fine. But we're not in that place yet."

Louisa grimaced. "Sorry. I won't do that again."

"Tell you what, I'll forgive you if you let me feel him kick again."

Her mouth split in a wide grin. "Sounds like a deal." She grabbed my hand and put it on her belly, and I was rewarded in no time.

I had to admit, if only to myself, to the twinge of envy. Maybe, at times, more than a twinge. But I reminded myself that there would be a time for us, too. I just had to keep believing it.

CHAPTER

SEVEN

ADAM

I WATCHED OUR TABLE FROM THE CASH BAR WHILE I WAITED in line for the drinks. It was hard to tell what they were discussing but it seemed congenial. Louisa grabbed Emilia's hand again and put it on her pregnant belly. I turned my back to the scene, irrationally furious. I didn't need Louisa rubbing that shit in Emilia's face and though Emilia hadn't said anything, I knew this would cause some hurt.

A reminder that her husband was a coward.

I took a breath, stepped up to the bar, ordered our drinks and waited while they were made. Emilia was right. We had time. We were still young.

Which meant that I had time to get over this. Eventually.

When I returned to the table, Emilia was telling Louisa and her husband, Josh, about the new pet project that she had thrown herself into.

"I'm so excited about it," she was saying. "It's still early days and there's so much paperwork to do before anything else. Thanks, Adam." She flashed me a brilliant smile as I handed her a cosmopolitan. I set my drink down in my place and turned to Louisa and Josh. "What can I get the two of you?"

Josh was about to stand but I motioned for him to stay seated. "No, no. Please. I'm already up. Tell me what you're drinking?"

"Club soda with a lime twist for me," Louisa said with a sheepish—almost guilty—smile.

Josh piped up, "Your beer looks good. One of those, please?"

"Sure," I said.

Emilia grinned at me. "It's amazing how shockingly handsome the waiters are at this place, isn't it?"

"Maybe you'll get to go home with this one." Louisa laughed.

"That's a definite." I grinned, winked at my wife, and noped the fuck out of their conversation for a few more minutes. Thank God.

The one big advantage to having associated mostly with Emilia's friend Louisa and her husband was that they were not night owls, and we were able to leave this doctor shindig relatively early. Emilia seemed happy and we chatted like normal on the way home. I was mildly relieved that there were no lasting effects from all the baby bombs that had been dropped at our table.

In fact, the baby subject never came up again...until bedtime. Guess I shouldn't have called it a complete program before compiling the code.

She was sitting on the bed in her night shirt rubbing lotion into her legs and arms after a shower.

I plopped down on the bed beside her and she ran her eyes down my bare chest above my pajama bottoms. "Nice view."

I leaned over and kissed her. "It can be nicer, if you want."

"I'm too slippery at the moment. Give me a few, then you can do a striptease for me."

I cocked an eyebrow. "With music? You're quite demanding."

She leered at me, licking her lips. "I know how to keep the marriage alive and fizzling with excitement."

I snorted. "You're talking like you're the one who's going to be doing the striptease."

"Don't you wish." She smirked at me. "Nope, I'm the lucky spectator tonight. I want some wiggle in those hips, or I won't give you a tip."

"That's okay, I'll be the one giving *you* the tip—*and more.*" I ran my gaze down her luscious, if still slippery, legs. "You need any help rubbing that lotion into those gorgeous gams of yours?"

Without a word, she handed me the lotion bottle. Oh, hell yes. I was here for this. I lovingly spread a few dollops from the palm of my hand across her shapely legs, across her muscular calves. She let out a very quiet moan of pleasure, so I wasn't the only one who was turned on. By the time I got to her second leg, I was rock hard.

"Hey..." she said quietly as I was finishing up, rubbing my own slippery hands together and wondering how long it would take to get the gardenia smell off them. Oh well, if it meant I got to score with my wife, totally worth the residual flower scent for a few hours.

"Yes?" I raised a brow. "Did you want that strip tease now?"

She grabbed one of my hands and wrapped her fingers around mine. "I just want to make sure that you weren't too weirded out about all that with Louisa."

I knew exactly what she was talking about, but I shook my head regardless, as if I had no idea.

"I didn't know she was going to say something like that...about their baby needing a playmate. I know you heard her say it."

I shrugged.

"I'm okay and I don't want you to suspect—"

I shifted my hand inside hers, switching who was holding whose hand. My greasy fingers slipped over hers as I held them tight. "I don't suspect anything. It's good. It's all good."

She smiled and gave me a pointed look as she raised her other hand to smooth over my chest. "Oh, dude, it's about to get a whole lot better—for both of us."

Then she pulled me on top of her and I was helpless to resist her bewitching charms. The best part? I hadn't even had to do the striptease.

The next day at work was a whirlwind of meetings, briefings and piles of unanswered emails that had to be handled after careful cataloging and prioritization by my assistant. Without Maggie, I would have been sunk long ago.

Jordan and I shared a working lunch of cold subs at the table in my office while we went over the most important things that had to get done today and in the next week.

"So tell me all about that new CEO program the board has you in. Spare no detail."

I leaned back and, with a heavy sigh, stared at him. "I gotta go back up there soon for a full weekend retreat. Honestly, the next time the board wants me to participate in one of these bullshit things, I'm tempted to send you instead, starting with this program. Coming back to a pile of shit to deal with at the office doesn't make it worth it."

"Truth," he said right before taking his last bite of sandwich and washing it down with a bottled drink that resembled some sort of green-brown sludge.

"What the fuck are you drinking these days? Looks like a potion of lost hopes and dreams."

He shrugged. "It's healthy. April's on a kick."

I laughed. "I understand the incentive to comply now." I watched with unmitigated disgust as he took another sip of the sludge. "What the hell is she giving you in exchange for you drinking shit that looks like that?"

He sent me a sly grin. "Wouldn't you like to know?"

I held up a hand to stop any unwanted details. "Actually, I don't think I would."

"True. You'd probably be way too jealous."

I rolled my eyes. "On to more serious subjects."

"Like you sending me in as a pinch hitter on your next CEO retreat. I would like the record to show that I heartily approve of that plan."

I paused for a second, then laid the rest on him. "How'd you like to pinch hit for me as CEO, too?"

"Ha ha. Funny. I'm sure the Board of Directors would love it. I am, after all, ten times better looking than you are."

I smirked. "And infinitely more modest—"

"And charming. *Very* charming."

I chuckled. "*Prince* Charming, actually. With your very own Snow White on your arm."

He gave me a leering look. "We're so good, we could actually bring in the bucks making Snow White/Prince Charming internet porn."

"TMI."

"Rule 34 at work, after all. If it exists, then somewhere on the internet, there's porn for it."

I laughed. "While Walt Disney turns in his grave."

He shook his head. "We all know he's not in a grave. He's in a cryochamber at Disneyland under Sleeping Beauty's castle."

I arched a brow. "Is that anywhere near the movie studio where they faked the moon landings?"

"Right across the street, I've heard."

Sometimes I wondered if people outside in the atrium to the company officer's suites ever wondered what idiocy we were in here laughing about.

"So, wild conspiracy theories aside..." Jordan opened his pack of potato chips.

I gave him a disapproving look. "Would She-Who-Is-Making-You-Drink-the-Sludge approve of the potato chips?"

He made a face. "I'm not telling her, and neither are you. Now, about the CEO gig, what are you thinking?"

I slurped on the last of my unsweetened iced tea. Definitely much less healthy—but tastier—than the green-brown sludge. "Is this my performance review?" I arched a brow at him.

He gave a half shrug. "Straight up, I was just asking because you seem distracted lately. And also because you just asked if I'd pinch hit for you. You know I'd do it in a heartbeat if you were serious. So, I'm wondering what you really want."

I blinked. "Let me get back to you on it. Soon. If I don't, ask me about it in a month or two."

His brow arched. "You know I'm going to."

"That's why I asked you." With a smile, we finished up our bullshitting and I grabbed my stuff to rush off to the next meeting.

Never a dull moment around here, that was for sure.

CHAPTER

EIGHT

ADAM

I WAS BACK UP NORTH FOR THE RETREAT AND, AS EXPECTED, not terribly happy about it. And there was no place like Silicon Valley for inane, meaningless corporate meetings, networking, and over-budgeted galas full of bored businessmen who'd rather be at home gaming.

Or maybe that was just me.

I was now at the end of day one of our 3-day CEO weekend retreat. I already knew this program wasn't for me. But for the sake of sliding Jordan in to finish this, I intended to stay until I could set up that transition and discuss next steps.

Fortunately, I had a friend or two in the program along with me, so the weekend wasn't a complete loss. And now, in typical corporate conspicuous consumerism fashion, our group was being treated to one of the most exclusive Japanese restaurants in the Bay Area. It had been reserved just for us with a lavish display of food and décor to greet us, complete with vodka ice sculptures, sake fountains, and caviar spreads.

The day's meetings had left me bored and cranky. I really wanted to get outside.

Maybe after this, I'd go for a long run under the night sky.

Besides, I missed my wife. We barely saw each other as it was with our normal work schedules. We'd finally had the open, honest discussion about the baby question, and she generously accepted my viewpoint. But my constantly questing mind couldn't help but dwell on the implications of that discussion—and our differing viewpoints.

There was no small fear that this issue would grow and solidify and turn into an eventual wedge between us. Because, as if I didn't have eighty-thousand other things to worry about, I had to add this to the list as well. It was a constant, nagging judgment that sat at the back of my conscience and poked me with a jagged pitchfork every so often.

I tucked aside that thought and scanned the restaurant and the various businessmen milling about. At least I'd get some top-quality sushi out of this bullshit before I dipped out.

My friend, Dominic Fischer showed up shortly after I did, and we wandered around neon-lit colorful tropical fish tanks toward a table.

He had a whole entire life here—big house, electric car, full wardrobe so he could travel without bags—in a place he only resided during a fraction of the year.

Such was the bachelor life of an incredibly successful CEO. I should have gone into the automated car business, clearly, because his company, Tranxit, wasn't even public yet, and he'd been valued in the billions.

"Ready for some amazing sushi?" he asked.

I laughed. "I'm ready. But it better knock my socks off."

"Your socks haven't already been knocked off?" He shot me a look. I opened my mouth and closed it again awkwardly before he burst out laughing and slapped my arm. "C'mon, I know you, Adam. You've been bored off your ass all day. Let's enjoy our dinner, some sake. The night is still young, maybe we can get into trouble afterward."

I held up my left hand and pointed to my wedding ring. "The only trouble I like to get into these days is at home."

He laughed. "I didn't mean *that* kind of trouble. I was thinking of some head-to-head FPS action in the gaming room at my house."

Ah, you could take the genius out of the game room, but you couldn't take the gamer kid out of the genius.

All along the edge of the dining room, there were stations and an elaborate—and beautiful—buffet. One of the tables had a woman lying on top of the huge serving table while men filed past, chopsticks poised.

I tilted my head, taking in the display. "Is that woman...?"

"Naked? Yes." Dom laughed at my expression. "It's actually a form of art in Japan. *Nyotaimori*, it's called. Been around for hundreds of years."

I threw another acerbic eye at the line of men as they filed past. "Somehow, I don't think those guys are the art-lover type. And the last I checked, this group is far from a band of samurai warriors."

He laughed. "No, probably not. Are you hungry?"

Filing into line, I averted my eyes from the naked woman on display, knowing just how much my wife would be ranting in my ear if she were standing here. And honestly, there were some female CEOs present. Why hadn't the organizers thought to have a naked male sushi model as a counterpart? Did they think we dudes were too fragile to handle being near a naked guy? That presumed that we were all heterosexual, anyway.

I at least hoped they paid the model well. She lay perfectly still, staring straight in front of her. She was covered with strategically placed frond leaves and tiny flowers to cover her modesty and provide hygienic plating for the sushi, so at least there was that. And I wasn't above noticing that she was stunningly beautiful. Nevertheless, I chose the sushi set out on regular platters rather than on her body.

It was so distracting that it took me a minute to notice that Dom wasn't following me. When I turned to see what was holding him up, I caught him frozen and staring, pale-faced, at the sushi model. His bearing was stiff, and he looked visibly disturbed. Wasn't he the one just explaining to me that this *Nyo*-whatever was an acceptable art form?

"Dom? You okay?"

He blinked, tearing his eyes away from where they were fixed—on her face, and not the barely-covered rest of her. He turned to me like he'd just brought himself out of a daze. "Huh?" He looked like he'd just seen a ghost.

Back at our table, I arched a brow at him. "Is everything okay? You seemed kind of spooked back there."

He shrugged exaggeratedly as if to emphasize the point that he was totally nonchalant about whatever had just happened. "The model looks like someone I used to know." He shrugged again.

I glanced at his plate. He apparently had lost his appetite. And he was strangely quiet the rest of the meal, even after we were joined by a couple of chatty New Yorkers who started pumping him about his business model. I sat back and ate my sushi and watched him dodge their often pointed questions. He really seemed out of sorts and the guys detected it too, leaving soon afterward.

"Are you still up for that shoot-'em-up?" I asked him as I stood up and buttoned my jacket.

"Sure. Hold up a minute, will you? I'm just gonna give my compliments to the chef."

I frowned. He'd hardly eaten anything. The model had since been wheeled back into the kitchen and hopefully was now dressed in something warm, since it was cold as fuck in here. Dom pulled out several large bills from his wallet and moved to the cashier. Maybe he'd forgotten this was a corporate function, already paid for in the exorbitant price of the CEO retreat?

But instead of handing the cashier money, Dom took the envelope she provided. I stood some distance away, giving him the privacy he obviously desired as he pulled out a pen and quickly scrawled something on the envelope before stuffing several bills inside. He then walked over to hand the envelope to the chef.

I highly doubted that the model was just someone who looked like someone he once knew, but was, quite possibly, the someone herself. Especially since he'd just tipped her five hundred dollars cash.

There was definitely some hidden drama here. Something that left him deeply disturbed. It made me wonder what would go through my mind if it was someone I knew—or presumably, cared for—in the middle of that lurid display. A memory flashed in my mind. That time I'd first seen those photos Emilia had posted of herself for the online auction. They hadn't included her face but had showed off her partially clothed body. The moment I'd clicked to see them displayed on that computer screen like the menu for a meat-market, I'd felt physically sick.

I wondered if that's how Dom felt and if that large tip was his way of helping someone that he used to know, to make it feel better.

He'd gotten off a lot lighter than I had with my $750k auction bill.

Nowadays, I sometimes joked with Emilia about the auction. And so did she, but that wasn't with any true emotions or memories attached. But it was all too easy to spark the memories of that tumultuous time when she wasn't mine. When I wasn't in a position to protect her.

Now, I just wanted to give her the world. Making her happy made me happy. So why was I so stuck on this baby thing?

A few days later, I was able to sit down with Jordan and give him the highlights from the inane CEO retreat. He took notes and asked follow-up questions with intense interest. He was particularly persistent when asking about Dominic Fischer, grilling me for details. "Okay so, when do I meet him?"

I sighed. "I'll see what I can arrange. But since you'll be stepping in for me, it shouldn't be hard."

His brows twitched up. Yeah, it was time to have the formal talk with Jordan—and change his life forever.

"So, I think it's time, given that you'll be entering this CEO training program, that we fast track you for actually becoming CEO of Draco Multimedia."

He laughed and ran a hand through his hair. "A drastic move to keep from having to go back to Palo Alto again."

Unsurprisingly, Jordan already had a lot of knowledge on the process himself. Nobody could accuse him of not being enthusiastic. Just looking at the sheer amount of research he'd done told me that I'd be leaving the company in good hands.

And that was a relief. It was still my company after all, and I still cared.

And though I was still feeling the profound discomfort of the unknown ahead of me, I also felt some relief.

A chapter in my life was coming to an end which meant, naturally, somewhere, hopefully soon, a new beginning. Regardless, I promised myself I'd be ready for it when it found me.

CHAPTER NINE
ADAM

A WEEK LATER, I WAS OUT WITH HEATH, GOLFING, OF all things. We'd met up at a nearby fancy golf course in Anaheim Hills and spent some time enjoying the outdoors and catching up.

"Mia on call today?" Heath asked, placing his ball down on the second tee and setting up his shot.

"No. She's off work today."

His brow arched up behind his sunglasses. He didn't even have to ask the question.

"She's got a business meeting for this NPO project of hers," I explained.

Heath nodded, took some practice swings with his driver. "Sounds like you're not terribly happy about it."

I leaned on my club, watching him. "I actually think it's an awesome idea. I'm just not a fan of the timing."

Heath hesitated just a moment, straightening his grip, then took his swing. We watched the drive—halfway down the fairway and into the rough.

"Fuck this damn game," he muttered when the ball landed.

I laughed. "You're on the second hole and you're already cursing it out?"

He shrugged, stepped aside. "Mia has always been the quintessential overachiever, but I agree that this is a lot to take on during her intern year. I mean, her schedule has been grueling. Probably somewhere around what *you* would call a normal workweek, right?"

I snorted. "I haven't worked eighty-hour weeks for a while, or I'd be divorced."

"But now that the shoe's on the other foot?" He darted a worried glance in my direction behind his sunglasses.

I stepped up to set my ball on the tee. "Oh, not to fear. I've been prepared for this. I knew it was coming. She tolerated my schedule, my being away so much. I'd be a fucking asshole if I wasn't understanding of her schedule. She can't be a practicing doctor without her residency."

Heath snorted. "Well, I mean you're already an asshole."

"Yeah, but I don't want to be a *fucking* asshole."

He nodded. "Fair."

I took my shot. My ball, also, landed in the rough about fifteen yards past his.

"See?" he gestured. "I can already tell you're going to win this hole. So, I stand by my assessment of your asshole-ness."

Once we'd motored our golf cart up to the green, our conversation picked up again.

Heath volunteered his viewpoint. "I think she's anxious to get everything started because this NPO thing is a really long process, and she wants it all in place for when she can start her practice at their clinic. Plus, it's an empowerment thing, you know?"

I frowned. "Empowerment? How do you mean?"

Heath shrugged. "The biological sperm donor begrudgingly gave her all that money because his own wife and son insisted on it. Mia doesn't want to use it for herself because that would be acknowledging the bastard. Plus, thanks to you, she doesn't really need it, anyway. This gives her a chance to do something good with it. Gives her a chance to give him the big ol' fuck you. The man who essentially destroyed what little family she had, you know? She had half-siblings she never knew, a parent she never knew. It was just her and her mom 'til I straggled into their little family like a beaten dog."

He shook his head as he feinted a few putts, then, instead of swinging, set his putter to the side and leaned on it like a cane while he turned to me to finish his thought. "You know what she said to me the day I moved in after my dad threw me out? She said 'I always wanted a brother. I want a big family.' Hell, if she'd had the ability, she probably would have opened up a home for wayward kids right then and there." He shrugged. "She's always been like that. So I get why she feels so passionate about this clinic."

I took a deep breath and looked away. Heath had just given me a whole lot of context that I hadn't even considered. It explained so damn much, to be honest.

Heath turned and made his putt, setting his ball just inches from the hole. He moved up to it and lobbed it in easily. "And before you ask, no I still don't think you deserve her."

I laughed as I picked up my bag and took it back to our golf cart. Real men didn't use caddies, in my opinion. "I wasn't going to ask because I know you'll never change your mind about it. And to be honest, I agree with you."

But as we made small talk through the next sixteen holes, I couldn't get his words out of my head. *I always wanted a brother. I want a big family....she probably would have opened up a home for wayward kids.*

I knew this about her. It was not new information, but a reminder. She'd said those exact words to me with tears in her eyes the day I'd found out she had cancer. I knew this and yet now, I chose to conveniently ignore it. She'd always wanted a big family growing up but had never gotten her wish.

I could help her fulfill that dream now. We could start a family.

I loved Emilia more than anything. But did I love her enough to face my own dark fears and give her what she dreamed of? Did I love her enough to want that dream for myself, too?

Emilia and I spent the rest of the day together watching movies at home and ordering in, cuddling in the same lounger and making love. Just enjoying being in each other's presence alone.

But when I got a moment to myself, I found the link to all of the medical research she'd been begging me to read for months.

And I started reading.

I decided to make an appointment with an oncofertility specialist—a doctor who specialized in fertility in cancer and former cancer patients. Because I wasn't going to do this half-assed.

I was going to be me and be thorough. I wanted the whole truth, warts and all.

But there was no way I was going to chance losing her, even if it meant telling her I could never fulfill her dream.

Chapter Ten
Mia

"Hey there!" April plopped down, tossing her massive bag into the booth beside her.

"Want me to flag the waitress down so we can order something to drink?" I said, raising my hand.

April's brow furrowed as she dug a notebook and pen out of her luggage. "I just want a Sprite or ginger ale or something. My stomach's been bothering me."

I frowned. "Stress? Do you need an antacid? I think I've got something in my purse." I grabbed it up.

She shook her head and waved me off. "No, no. I think I'll be fine. It's just weird." She leaned in conspiratorially. "Just between you and me, I'm a week late on my period."

I blinked but didn't say anything, waiting for her to finish, noting how my breath froze in anticipation. Curiously, I was struck with an even stronger feeling of envy than when Louisa had told me her news at graduation.

April continued, "It scared the shit out of me because with the stomach issues and the late period...you know. And I'm such an idiot that it took me so long to realize."

I took a deep breath, fingernails digging into my palms before I ordered myself to relax. "Did you take a test?"

"I did this morning. Still no Aunt Flo, though. You, ah, don't think those things do false negatives, do you?"

I shook my head. "No. No, as long as you took the test properly, you're not likely to incur a false negative."

She put her hand on her belly. "Oh, thank God. Because when I realized what it might be, I practically had a freakin' meltdown. I actually asked Jordan to run out and get the test for me while I sat there in a state of panic for half an hour."

I frowned. "I'm sure Jordan must have been even more freaked out."

April shook her head. "That's the weirdest part. He was super calm the whole time, even before I got the negative result. And when I did, he seemed...I dunno, maybe a little disappointed? Or at the very least, not as relieved as I was, or as relieved as I figured he'd be."

I couldn't tear my eyes away from her, suddenly envious for an entirely different reason. "Huh. Go figure." *Jordan?* I never knew he had it in him.

"I know, right? Maybe aliens have abducted his brain or something."

I shrugged. "Have you two talked about having kids?"

She waved her hand. "I mean, in hypothetical terms, yeah, we have. He wants three. One of each and then a wildcard—that's what he says, anyway."

I bit my lip to suppress a grin. "Huh, if only you could choose like you're ordering off a menu."

April's brilliant blue eyes widened. "I have a lot I want to do before throwing myself into the mom thing because I want to take time off while they're little. At least for a little while. But of course, I don't really think I'd ever want to stop or pause my career, either. If I could get a work from home situation going with daily help at home, that would be perfect. First world problems, I know."

The waitress arrived on the heels of that statement, setting down her soda and my iced tea. April stuck a straw in her cup and took a sip. "Again, it's all hypothetical. I don't think I can get to that place for a few years, yet. I think I want my first before thirty, though, which gives me about three years."

"So, he wants three, how many do you want?" I arched my brow and sipped my tea.

"I dunno. One, probably. I was an only child—at least 'til my dad remarried and had my little sister and brother, but I was nearly in high school by that point. I definitely don't want a big age gap if I do have more than one. If I can help it, that is. My oma would be freaking out to hear me talking like this. She's so superstitious. Can't be planning on what you haven't already been given and all that."

I grinned at her. "Well, there's always the law of attraction and manifesting what you want."

She gave me a sly look. "I mean, we're pretty solid with that one, aren't we? Both of us manifested hot billionaires. Yours has even put a ring on it."

"About that...."

She held up a hand. "Please. I've already had one grown-up type scare today. We aren't talking about when or if Jordan will actually pop the question—again." We shared a knowing look. April had confided in me that during our group mountain ski vacation on our first anniversary, Jordan had been plotting to stage a flamboyant proposal, and April had been the one to kill the plans. What made that especially funny was that April liked to freak him out by overtly hinting that she wanted to get married. She apparently had been so convincing that Jordan had taken it seriously. She'd been able to talk him off the ledge, telling him that she wanted him to ask when he felt moved to do it and not because he feared losing her if he didn't.

Since then, there had been no further whispers of engagement from Jordan. And no more marriage jokes from April, either.

So far, Katya was my only married girlfriend and that had been a complete and total surprise; she'd eloped with her arch-nemesis, Lucas.

I had hopes that the year ahead would at least bring an engagement announcement, either from April and Jordan or William and Jenna.

Yeah, I was *that person*...the married woman who was so enamored of her state of wedded bliss, even after two years, that she wanted everyone she loved to partake. And sure, marriage wasn't easy, but I was still firmly in the school of thought that it was worth it.

"Well, who knows, maybe you'll both come to your senses soon." I grinned.

"Come to your senses about what?" Lindsay asked, having just approached from behind me. April smiled and scooted around in the booth toward me to make room for her to sit down.

"Hey Lindsay, how are you doing? Long time, no see," April said as Lindsay complimented her on her very large bag.

Lindsay slid into April's former spot, setting her leather legal pad cover aside. "Hey ladies. I'm doing great, April. Thank you. What are we discussing?"

April handwaved at me. "Oh, she's being a sappy married woman. We should definitely change the subject."

Lindsay laughed and flicked her blond curls back over her shoulder. Lindsay had been divorced for about four years now and had been a serial dater until recently. She was now living with a guy who was around her age, for once, and she seemed happy.

Lindsay laughed. "Oh yeah, I already got that from her. We should come up with some kind of signal to each other to change the subject when she gets like that."

My mouth dropped. "Wow. I'm sitting *right here*." Maybe I was starting to get annoying? I made a mental note to check myself.

"We get it," Lindsay replied smoothly. "You're deliriously happy and want all your friends to be. It's cute." She wrinkled her nose at me with a grin while I narrowed my eyes at her in response. "I'm serious. Don't always be so suspicious. Now, where's the waitress? I don't eat lunch this late and I'm starving. After that, we can get down to business. We have a world to conquer, after all."

And she was right. I did have a world to conquer—a man's world. And I was fortunate to be surrounded by smart women who could help me do it.

Chapter Eleven
Adam

After weeks of reading research and doing still more investigation on the downlow, I met with the oncofertility specialist and word-vomited my long list of questions to her. She patiently answered each one, mostly to my satisfaction.

And then I took some long walks and did a lot of thinking.

Then one day, weeks later, I chose to work from home in the morning and take the afternoon off, since it was her last day off for the next ten days. We'd successfully carved some time to be present and be together. No distractions. Just each other and the raw beauty of nature.

I even left my phone at home when we walked to the beach.

Yeah, a serious sign that Adam Drake meant business. Or rather not business, but a pivotal moment in my private life—and in our relationship.

It felt silly, staging things, but then I hadn't had a chance to plan the marriage proposal—at least the second time, the time that really counted.

But this, this I could make special.

We had a picnic on the sand and then took a long walk. As it was late fall, the air and the water were too chilly for swimming.

We stood overlooking the Newport Harbor Jetty right at the end of the Balboa Peninsula, less than a 2-mile walk from our house on Bay Island. Fishermen stood atop the rocks, casting their poles overhead into the sea below and the bell on the large buoy rang every so often, warning of rough seas coming in. Sea lions barked all around us from the rocks and from their perch atop the buoy. Sailboats and fishing boats were heading into the entrance channel to the back bay for the night.

I laced my fingers around hers and felt that same, satisfying twinge in my chest when she responded by tightening her hold on my hand. She leaned back, against my chest and rested her head against my shoulder.

I cleared my throat to speak after nearly a half hour of enjoying each other's company in silence as we'd walked along the beach to get here. "Looks like it's going to be a beautiful sunset. Just enough clouds in the sky to make some fireworks with the light but not too many to block it."

She glanced up at me, smiling cheekily. "Wow, my husband the sunset aficionado...and he's kept it hidden from me all these years. A secret romantic."

I shrugged self-consciously. "Romantic? I wouldn't go *that* far."

She laughed, bumping her shoulder against me. "I'm teasing, silly. Didn't mean to insult you. But you sounded almost poetic describing it."

I laughed. "Maybe I just spent too much time around my cousin."

She arched a brow. "Poetic? William? Well, I can see the artist angle. Any way you frame it, a southern California sunset rarely disappoints."

I pulled her closer against me, wrapping my arms tightly around her waist. Together, we took in the play of rapidly changing light across the sky. She shivered slightly as the breeze rose up, like it always did, the minute the sun sank below the horizon leaving a wake of dazzling, glowing colors in the sky behind it—gold and pale blue shot through with streaks of neon orange and magenta. Emilia's hair tickled my face, dancing on the breeze. I dipped my face and buried my nose in the perfumed cloud of glossy brown hair, inhaling deeply, savoring that vanilla scent. My eyes closed and my equilibrium drifted just slightly off center.

She nestled deeper against me with a sigh. "I love living so close the beach that we can just walk down the coast together to soak in the sunset."

I huffed a laugh. "Given our schedules that's, what, once in a blue moon?"

She sighed. "I wish that was just a joke, but I think the moon was a distinct shade of azure the last time we did this."

My arms tightened. Kids played across the bay in the Pirate's Cove on Little Corona beach, their laughter reaching us even as their parents' voices called after them saying it was time to go home. Her head lolled back against my shoulder. *Mmm...*I loved how this felt.

"This feels so good," she echoed my thoughts. "We should definitely do it more often. We're fortunate that we live on the side of the country where the sun goes down over the ocean, rather than rising over it."

"I guess we'd have to become early morning people if we were on the east coast. I do like living here, but I can't help but wonder..."

My voice trailed off and I swallowed, realizing that I was on the brink of ringing a bell that couldn't be unrung. Once the words were out of my mouth, I was committed. I couldn't back out.

Fuck. This felt so bizarre.

"What do you wonder?" she finally asked, tilting her head to look up into my face after I'd let that dangle for too long.

I shrugged, then swallowed, ignoring that dread at the pit of my stomach. *Here goes nothing.* "I just wonder if this is the ideal location...to raise a family."

Silence. The wind stirred her hair, tickling my cheeks. She went completely still in my arms. This time the long pause was on her side. I waited.

"You aren't...you aren't saying what I think you're saying."

I suppressed a smile. "And what's that?"

"That you're thinking about starting a family?"

I turned to look down into her face. Her eyes were wide, questioning, earnest. "And if I was?"

She let out a sharp breath—half anticipation, half frustration. "You already know I'm on board with that."

"So then...let's do it."

The wind kicked up, almost blinding me with her hair, but she turned in my arms, looking up at me with near disbelief on her features. "You aren't bullshitting me right now, are you?"

My hands clasped together right at the small of her back, hitching her against me. "If I was bullshitting, I'd be a worthless piece of shit, now wouldn't I?"

She frowned. "What—how—I'm just so confused. Last summer you were so determined to put this off. And I like to think I wasn't putting any pressure on you. Your decision feels abrupt. Have I been doing something to pressure you?"

I shook my head. "You haven't been pressuring me, Emilia."

"But—" she began in a voice thick with emotion. "You could always change your mind. That's an option, you know. It's not like I want to lock you into something."

I met her gaze, stared deeply into her eyes, then reached up and smoothed that soft, soft skin. Her eyes fluttered closed and my thumb traced the hollow of her cheek. "Yes, that's possible. But *you* know that I'm a stubborn fuck, and once I've made up my mind, it's hard to change it again."

She laughed, her eyes still closed. "Yes, that's true. You *are* stubborn as fuck."

"Hopefully not always in a bad way."

She gently shook her head, and, to my amazement, a thin tear slipped out from under her closed eyelids. I brushed it away, then kissed the cold, salty spot on her cheek where it had been.

Her eyes fluttered open, glistening with still more unshed tears. But it was the strange stew of emotions behind those beautiful eyes that held me captivated.

She cleared her throat despite the emotion. "But what about all your reservations and misgivings? You had solid reasons for—"

"I read the research. I read through the medical studies on that cloud folder you sent me. And just to make sure you weren't cherry picking the studies that corroborated what you wanted, I went out and read some more—what I could understand of them, anyway. Then I met with an oncofertility specialist at UCLA."

Her brows arched and she blinked. "Wow. You *did* do your homework."

I grinned at her and tilted my head like, would she have expected anything else? More tears spilled onto her cheeks even as she laughed.

"I trust they said something to make you feel okay with this."

I nodded. "According to the doctor, the risk is minimal enough that I can be comfortable with it. For a while, anyway."

"Like how long?"

I shrugged. "Depends. If this drags out a while, I might ask you to go get another scan. And if we have to start talking about fertility drugs, well, that's going to have to be a whole new conversation."

She slowly nodded. "We'll cross that bridge if we come to it. Or we'll explore some other way to have a family if we decide not to go that route."

I tucked a long strand of hair behind her ear. "I have research on all of that too."

She burst out laughing. "I have not a doubt in the world, Adam Drake. I know you well enough to know that."

More tears streamed down her face though she seemed calm and rational, as if the emotions and the logical halves of her were warring and neither knew which side was coming out on top.

She bit her lip and was quiet for a long moment. I nudged her, wordlessly urging her to voice the thought at the tip of her tongue.

"And you aren't scared anymore?" Her eyes widened, searching mine.

"I can't say that, no. I'm actually terrified. But I want you to be happy."

Her brows knit. "You can't agree to have a baby just to make me happy. You have to want it, too."

I smoothed the pad of my thumb over her lip. "I do want it. I can't promise that my controlling tendencies won't kick in sometimes. It's the way I handle fear of the unknown. And this is a huge motherfucking unknown for me. But I trust you. And I want it, too."

In the face of her obvious joy, my terror was muted, but not gone. It still sat there, like a bugaboo, in the back of my psyche. Watching. Always watching.

I ignored it, swallowed, and summoned my courage.

"Let's do this, Emilia. Let's make a baby."

CHAPTER TWELVE
ADAM

WE WALKED THE NEARLY 2 MILES HOME, HAND IN hand. And when we got home, as if cementing that momentous decision immediately, we made love. We didn't even make it to the house. In the darkness, she pulled me into a deck recliner.

As she pulled me down beside her, our lips locked in a kiss, I mumbled against her mouth, breathy and urgent. "Do you remember the first time we were in this chair together?"

Her mouth curved against mine. "Oh yes, I definitely do."

"I believe I destroyed your panties..." I muttered huskily against her soft, sweet-smelling neck.

"The first in a long line of panty massacres you've perpetrated over the years," she replied in a dreamy voice.

Under her fleece jacket, I cupped her breast with my hand, running a thumb across the nipple through her bra and the silky material of her blouse. She shifted against me and made a sound that set my blood boiling instantly.

How long had it been since we'd been able to just enjoy each other without a plan, without a schedule or agenda—without hunting down a fucking condom?

Mia reached into the cabinet right beside the lounge and pulled out two blankets, unfolding them quickly and pulling them over the top of me as I adjusted the back of the lounge to lie flat. The blankets covered me, and I covered her.

And for the first time in what seemed like forever, we took it long and slow. Once I had her out of her jeans, I ran my palm up her legs and kissed her and kissed her, savoring the silky feel of her skin, the scent of her. My beautiful, beautiful wife.

I tasted her skin and tore those panties right off her, taking care not to destroy them—only because she told me not to.

But as we kissed and whispered our truths to each other, I felt present in this moment. With her soft, giving body beneath mine and our long kisses and breathless gasps, I wasn't afraid. I was here for this. And that fact shocked me more than just about anything else.

When I paused to readjust the blanket after it slipped off me, Emilia snatched the opportunity to roll on top. She stuck her lip out exaggeratedly. "No fair, you're not naked yet."

"A condition that can be quickly remedied," I quipped back as I reached for my belt buckle.

"Oh no. It's time for me to return the favor of helping you disrobe."

Then she made me laugh as she waggled her eyebrows. Her palm smoothed over my crotch, fingers cupping my erection. I let out a gasp and flopped backward, flat on the lounge, ready to let her drive this bus for a little while. Ready to enjoy her touch, her direction. Ready to take this as slow as she wanted.

The slower it went, the easier it was to savor.

I helped her by lifting my hips and she slid my jeans off my legs, quickly doing the same with my underwear. She readjusted the blankets to cover us both because it was really starting to cool down.

Then, her head dipped.

When her mouth touched my cock, I was so wound up I almost jerked in surprise at the shock of pleasure. Oh fuck, that would not do to have our first go at baby sex be the time where I came prematurely in her mouth instead. But her tongue was undoing me all too quickly. With a gentle but reluctant nudge, I pushed her head away.

"Enough of that," I said in a hoarse voice. "Or substances won't be going where they're supposed to go."

She kissed her way back across my abdomen, my chest, until our faces were inches from each other once again. "Well, we don't want that to happen, or we might just have to do it again."

I hooked an arm around her waist and pulled her on top of me. "And again, and again. Such a shame that would be."

"Mmm yeah," her breath jolted the second I thrust into her, and then I just about blacked out at the sensation of being inside her without a barrier between us. She was wet, so ready and so warm, her heat almost suffocated me with bliss. Okay, so if I came now, at least things would happen the way they were supposed to, but where was the fun in that? I held her hips still for a long moment, savoring the feel of her and willing the initial excitement to pass.

Something felt different, and it wasn't just the lack of condom.

No, something had shifted in my head. As I finally loosened my hold on her hips and she slowly glided her hips over mine, I realized what it was. I, the ultimate overachiever, had just been given a mission and I was bound and determined to get it done and do it well. We were fucking with a purpose far beyond just enjoying ourselves and pleasuring each other.

No, now there was a third goal in mind. One that made my cock swell painfully every time I thought about it.

Fuck.

I had to stop thinking about it, or this would have the exact opposite effect of thinking about baseball during sex. But God if I didn't want to put my baby inside her right this fucking second.

Emilia sat up, her breasts and long neck bathed in moonlight as she tilted her head back, enjoying the ride. I swallowed, watching her. She was the most beautiful woman in the world to me.

And she was all mine.

And soon, she'd be the mother of my child. And fuck if that didn't excite me. I wanted it. I wanted her. Always.

Minutes later, when I couldn't hold back for another second, I grabbed her hips once more and held them still, thrusting upward as I came to climax, bathed in sheer, mindless pleasure. She let out a long moan and joined me, as we both topped that summit together. Her skin, soaked with sweat despite the chill, stuck to mine and we shared each other's hot breaths for long moments as we both surfed the afterglow.

I felt alive, clearheaded, and blissfully replete.

"Fuck," I said, still gasping for air. "Now I don't want to move. Just get me another blanket, maybe a pillow and I'll sleep out here."

"Mmm," she pressed her cheek to my chest. "That will not do. I refuse to sleep up in our bed alone."

I ran my fingers through her hair. "You do it all the time when I'm not here."

"Change of plans. I'll be keeping you chained to the bed until Project Baby has lifted off."

"Hmm. Does that mean I can start charging a stud fee?"

She stared at me, biting her lip. "I might have to start charging you for sex, then, so we can call it even. Otherwise, I think your high-value prodigy-genius sperm might be too out of my budget."

I frowned as if contemplating that transaction. "I'm afraid that the going rate for prodigy-genius sperm is twice the value of gold and therefore—"

"If you dare say that your 'baby batter' is more valuable than hot sex with your wife, then I'll be using teeth the next time I go down on you."

I laughed, making her head bounce on my chest. "Don't do that. You'll damage the baby-making equipment."

She grinned and kissed my chest. "You're going to milk this for all it's worth, aren't you?"

I cupped her breast, fondling it lovingly. "Oh yeah, I'll be milking in more ways than one."

That might have been a bridge too far. She elbowed me in the side—*hard.*

Well, this was fun. There were months and months of all the sex I wanted, whenever I wanted, to look forward to. Without a condom. That was a definite win-win in my book.

Until it wasn't....

Because oh my god, sex was also draining and damn fucking tedious when you weren't particularly in the mood.

"My god, woman, again?" I started one night over a month later. She'd just jumped me while I was in the middle of reading a book on my tablet. "You're a slave driver."

She arched a brow at me, smirking. "I'm an opportunist. And you're about to leave the country, so I need to take advantage of your vital body parts and genetic materials."

I blinked. "I feel exploited."

She leaned in to kiss across my bare chest, licking my nipple as she went and sending a zing right down to my nether regions. "Isn't that every man's dream?"

"Not when you're wearing it down to a nub multiple times per day," I shot back, setting the tablet aside with a long sigh.

She blinked. "You're right. I'm so sorry. I hadn't considered your advanced years. Fortunately, I'm qualified to write you a prescription for Viagra to handle that nasty case of erectile dysfunction."

I grabbed her, rolled on top of her and pressed my hard-on against her leg. "I got your erectile dysfunction right here, baby."

She laughed, throwing her head back. "Well hurry up. Whip it out and let's get this done."

I feigned irritation even as I maneuvered myself between her legs. "You sure know how to make a man hot."

Her brows arched as she hooked her arms around my neck. "I thought I just had to flash a boob."

I looked away, considering. "Yeah, that can work too, depending on how war-weary I am."

She licked her lips. "I might be ovulating."

"*Might* be...don't you know yet?"

"I haven't started charting my basal body temperature yet. Waiting for my cycle to reboot so I can."

I blinked. "Are you sure you don't want me to jack off into a cup, so you can keep it refrigerated for when I'm gone?"

She smacked my arm. "Don't be gross."

I leaned down and devoured her neck. "You started it with all that basal body temperature stuff."

She shifted under me, wrapping her legs around my hips. "Show me what you got, big boy."

"I've already showed you...hundreds of times before."

She bit her lip and tilted her head, giving me a coquettish look. "But this is baby-making sex. It's extra sexy. C'mon, let's do this." Her hands slid across my chest. "C'mon, old man."

Yeah, it was devolving into that...foreplay via taunting.

It worked. But again, not my finest moment.

Afterward, we cleaned up and finally settled down for the night. She flopped down onto the mattress beside me, splaying her arms above her head. "I'm *so* tired."

I kissed her forehead. "You aren't even doing all the work."

She rolled her eyes at me. "*All the work.* Are you losing your stamina now?"

I shook my head. "Taunting isn't going to work now. I'm tapped out. You aren't going to be able to egg me on into more sex tonight. No matter how hard you try."

"It's okay, I really wasn't trying. But you better be ready for me when you get back from your trip."

I reached over and smoothed her cheek. She smiled—I could feel it under my hand. "Oh, I will be, sugar baby, you can bet on it."

She kissed my neck, then rolled over. "Bring only your best swimmers."

I laughed, but damn, I did secretly hope this phase of the process didn't last very long. It was starting to suck all the fun out of sex, damn it.

Chapter

Thirteen

Mia

Our girlfriend group gathered to celebrate April's birthday three weeks after the fact because trying to wrangle five busy, professional women to meet at one time wasn't an easy feat. But on a Saturday afternoon in early winter, we got together at a local hole-in-the-wall bakery near the city of Orange in upscale Villa Park.

Here, we brought our cards and presents and greeted each other with warm hugs. I saw Jenna fairly often, as her man, William, was Adam's cousin and—ugh—I guess you'd have to call him my stepbrother, too, if you were categorizing. But again, despite that same weirdness factor with Peter, William's dad, being married to my mom, I never thought of William that way.

"Does anyone know if Heath is coming?" I asked.

"He is," Kat said. "But he's going to be pretty late and said that we should definitely start without him."

So, we did. Breakfast was served in short order: scrambled eggs, muffins, toast, fruit and every good thing.

And mimosas. Crap. I'd forgotten about mimosas. When the server stood next to me with a bottle of champagne poised over my glass, I held up my hand. "Just orange juice in mine."

That immediately drew attention.

Double crap. I glanced around at every single eyeball at the table that had turned and focused on me. Then I shrugged and gave a sheepish smile. "I'm on call. Can't drink."

It wasn't technically a lie. I was on second call, which meant I was back up for the doctor on first call, but they didn't need to know that. Nor did they need to know that I was currently trying to get pregnant.

But I had to throw these bloodhounds off the scent, or this hunt would be over before it had even started.

Jenna tilted her head, openly studying me. Maybe she was using her Reiki or woo woo powers to detect a lie.

I took the opportunity to change the subject. "How's your property out in the mountains coming along?" I asked. "When do I get to come up and see your garden?"

Jenna arched her brow and threw me a look that said she knew exactly what I was doing but went along with it, anyway. "Well, it's winter, so not much of a garden to see yet. Maybe we'll have a little gathering up there in early summer when the butterflies are out, and the bees are pollinating."

"Sounds dirty," Alex said, popping some scrambled eggs into her mouth and chewing before washing it down with the last of her mimosa. "Wish I could be here to see it."

Jenna's brows arched. "Are you off again?"

She nodded. "Yup. Spain this time. *El Camino de Santiago.*"

Jenna's eyes lit up. "Ooh, the pilgrimage trail? How amazing. Though I'm surprised you're waiting 'til May to go somewhere."

"Oh no, I'm actually leaving in March and will be gone until September. Six months in Europe. The perks of being a digital nomad."

Alex had scored herself a very nice job out of college, and since the pandemic, had been working 100 percent remotely. "How is your mom not constantly complaining about you being gone so much?" I asked, shaking my head.

Alex shrugged. "She complains but I'm not around to have to hear it. And I do call her every single week, rain or shine." She signaled to the server to top up her mimosa glass once more. "Light on the OJ," she murmured when the server went to pour.

I narrowed my eyes, wondering, then looked up to meet Jenna's light blue gaze. She'd no doubt noticed Alex's uncharacteristic behavior, too. Drinking more than usual, a flip attitude towards her mom—it just wasn't Alex. I arched my eyebrows at Jenna and she frowned, shaking her head.

Maybe she'd get to the bottom of it.

"Hey, we'll be in Europe the same time as you, I think," Kat said to Alex as she finished up her small bowl of mixed tropical fruit—fresh pineapple and banana topped with shredded coconut. "Lucas's family is hosting at their ancestral home in Netherlands."

"Ooh," April said, eyes widening. "The baron and baroness will be in residence, will they?"

Kat sent her a crooked smile. "Yeah, we were able to carve out three weeks from our work schedules, between deadlines and new projects starting up. I'd complain more about my slave-driver boss but, you know, his wife is sitting right over there so it might make it awkward." Kat shot me a mischievous grin and I laughed.

"I'm dying to see Amsterdam," Alex said. "I'd totally be down for checking out your digs there."

"Well, the home is in Utrecht but truly, I don't think Netherlands is that big, so we can definitely meet up."

While they discussed how they were going to meet up thousands of miles across the Atlantic, April nudged me and started a quiet conversation. "Have you heard from Adam when this whole shift in CEOs is going to happen? I can't get a straight answer from Jordan."

I broke off a chunk of fresh cranberry muffin and popped it into my mouth. "I think you can't get a straight answer because there isn't one. Once they get approval from the board of directors for the change, there will be a timeline in place. I think the meeting is happening sometime next month."

April nodded, frowning as she picked at her fruit cup.

"Is everything okay?" I asked.

She gave me a shrug. "Nothing scientifically verifiable. Just a vague sense of impending doom."

"How so?"

"It's a big change, going to CEO."

I gave her an ironic smile. "I mean, I've been married to the CEO for a while so I can assure you it's not that terrible."

"We don't see each other a lot as it is—and I work from home, so. I dunno. Maybe I'm just overwrought for nothing."

I put my hand on her arm to reassure her. "Adam's going to be around for the process of the transition, and they've worked together for a decade. If it's in anyone's best interest for a smooth transition, it's Adam's. But if you want, I can talk to him."

April blinked and looked at me with true appreciation in her eyes. "You are amazing for offering to do that. Let me sit with this for a little while, and if things start to really concern me, I'll get back to you, but in the meantime, don't say anything to Adam."

I nod. "Got it. I won't breathe a word. But maybe...if you just want a sounding board for your concerns, I might not be the best person to talk to, you know? As far as being unbiased."

April bit her lip and nodded. "Yeah, good point."

I took in a deep breath and let it go. "Besides, I don't want whatever happens between our two significant others to affect our own project together, you know?"

Her brows twitched up as if that had just crossed her mind. "You are very wise, Dr. Mia. Are you sure you shouldn't be pursuing a specialty in psychiatry?"

I grinned. "Did not love my psychiatry rotation in medical school. It's internal medicine for me, all the way."

At that moment, we returned to the table conversation where Jenna was telling us about how some kid nearly blew up the classroom in her Physics lab.

"Are you still enjoying teaching, generally, despite the mishaps?" Alex asked her.

Jenna turned to her bestie and former roommate. "Yeah, for the most part. I mean, teaching is the hardest job I've ever had, and I have to bring my work home with me practically every night—"

"Can't beat those summers off, though!" I winked at her.

"Yeah, that's a nice perk but it would be nicer if we got paid then. Gives me a nice chunk of months to spend with our gardening project up on our land and getting the house built up there."

"I heard a rumor that a certain someone might be popping the question soon," Alex blurted with her typical nonexistent filter.

Jenna blushed. "Who says he's the one who gets to pop the question? Maybe I'm the one who'll ask him."

A rush of joy hit me like a storm. "Oh my God, Jenna, are you going to?"

She turned to me and winked. "That's for me to know and you all to find out."

"I just want you to become my—whatever it would be? Cousin-in-law?" I replied.

"Sister-in-law, I'd think?" Alex nodded enthusiastically, practically glowing at the thought.

"They don't acknowledge that part of the relationship." Kat gestured between the two of them. "William and Mia are *not* stepsister and stepbrother, even though they totally are."

"I'd make an exception and call Jenna my sister-in-law."

"Yeah, just don't you go spilling the beans." Jenna pointed at me, then waved that finger around to the others. "That goes to all of you."

"I'll keep the secret in the vault, but you better put a ring on it soon, girl. I need a sister." I grinned.

"Well, you do have a stepsister—Britt," Jenna said.

I nodded, "True. My family's getting bigger and bigger by the minute." And I couldn't hide the beam of joy that shot through me, thinking that I might have another family member secretly on board, if not now, then very, very soon.

CHAPTER

FOURTEEN

ADAM

THE ONLY THING WORSE THAN HAVING TO LIVE UP TO sex-on-demand was seeing how disappointed Emilia got when it didn't get results.

She stood at the kitchen sink staring down into the basin as I made my morning coffee and reminded myself not to ask or comment about any recent tests. If it were positive, she'd have told me. And the frustrated—and even puzzled—expression on her face said enough, really.

"So which kind of shift are you on today? Late, early, or long call?" I said, taking a careful sip of the hot brew that had just percolated from the machine.

"I don't understand." She shook her head.

"What? I just wanted to know if I should make sure to be home early or—"

She waved her hand and that's when I saw the pregnancy test. She bent to shove it into the garbage can under the sink. "No, I mean *this*. My period's due tomorrow, and I don't have any PMS symptoms."

The first thing to hit me was the instant shower of relief knowing that we were well out of the fertile zone, which meant that she wouldn't be hitting on me tonight.

Not that it was a hardship that my beautiful wife would hit me up for sex, but I was starting to feel like the prized bull in the cow pasture. The pressure to perform was...intensifying. And now, it seemed, even my swimmers needed to step up their game.

I finished stirring a little sugar into my coffee then moved up beside her to put my spoon in the sink. She waited, then washed her hands. I pulled her against me as she was drying them and kissed her hair. "We've only been at this for a few months and we've been spending our entire adult lives trying to prevent what we're actively going after now. Maybe our systems are just a little...sluggish."

She blew out a breath and rolled her eyes. "That is not a medical diagnosis, and you're not—"

"The one here licensed to practice medicine. Yes, I'm aware." I arched a brow at her.

She blinked. "Huh, do I end up saying that a lot?"

I landed a peck on her nose. "Once in a while, yeah. I'm just saying that maybe we need to chill with all the pressure we're putting on this. It's not a race. We're young and—"

"I know for a fact that I'm ovulating based on the classic rise in temperature, the length of my luteal phase and—"

I turned her toward me, taking both of her damp hands in mine. "Emilia, breathe, please. I know this is important to you, but we have zero reason to believe that there's anything wrong."

Her brows knit, forming a deep ridge between them. "But it could have been the chemo. Something could have happened. I'm going to schedule an appointment to get checked out."

I drew back for a moment. "I thought you already did that? We met with the doctor. She said everything was fine."

She shook her head. "No, not the oncologist. A fertility specialist or that oncofertility doctor you saw at UCLA. They could run some tests, just to make sure we're not doing all this for nothing."

I tilted my head and gave her a look. "Well...not for nothing. I mean, we're pretty good at it."

She rolled her eyes at me, then pulled me in for a kiss. "I gotta go. Long day today."

Long day. Got it.

She went to the fridge and grabbed the insulated lunch box Chef had packed for both her lunch and dinner.

We walked to the door together and then, locking it behind us, headed across Bay Island toward the parking garage on the other side of the little bridge. I glanced around at our neighbors' perfectly kept yards and the common spaces and for the first time, realized that there were no children under high school age that lived here. Either people purchased later in life or lived a child-free lifestyle, but it was a definite that this didn't seem to be a place that people deemed appropriate to raising kids.

I wondered what they all knew that I didn't.

As we crossed the bridge to the peninsula, Emilia turned to me and picked up the thread of the conversation. "So, if everything on my end checks out, you know what that means, don't you?"

"Hmm?" I said, still distracted, still deep in my own musings.

"It means you're going to have to get checked out, see if your swimmers are up to snuff."

I made a face. "My swimmers can snuff. They are very good at snuffing."

I opened the gate at the end of the bridge and motioned for her to walk ahead of me while I shut and locked it with the keypad.

"There are a lot of factors...motility for one, ability to penetrate—"

"I think I've more than proven I can penetrate."

She sighed and rolled her eyes dramatically. "Somehow, I knew you were going to say that even before the words left my mouth. I guess, though, since you're such a strong manly-man you'll be up to undergoing the tests necessary. Even the one with the giant needle they stick up your—"

"*What?*" I turned to her, alarmed.

She started laughing. "Kidding. The tests for men are easy and absolutely non-invasive. And, spoiler alert, they involve some alone time with you, a specimen cup and a few dirty magazines."

"Sounds like a very exciting Saturday night," I drawled as I pulled the helmet off my bike and shoved my laptop case into a saddlebag. Emilia pulled a face and froze beside the driver's side door of her Tesla.

"Why are you taking that thing to work?"

I glanced at my bike, patting the saddle. "She didn't mean it, honey. She's just jealous because you are *also* a sweet ride."

Emilia blew out a breath. "Very funny."

"What's wrong with me taking the bike? You aren't still worried about safety again, are you? I think I've proven that I'm a safe—"

She pointed to my crotch. "I'm worried about *their* safety. If you insist on smooshing them up against your body, then that will affect your count and—"

Christ. This was really starting to get old. "Listen, you can tell me what to do with my testicles when I tell you what you can do with your breasts, deal?"

She rolled her eyes. "Just...be careful."

"Me and my balls will be just fine, thank you so much for caring." And with that, I pulled on my helmet.

With a thumbs-up I winked at her, then pulled down the visor. She laughed and slid into her car.

So now, aside from being the stud to provide sex on demand, I was also about to undergo laboratory testing because we'd been trying seriously for a whole two-and-a-half months.

I prayed this happened soon because I wasn't sure how much more I could take of my bound-and-determined overachieving wife anxiously micromanaging something we didn't actually have full control over.

Damn, this baby-making business was tough, orgasms or no.

But I was happy to note that me and my balls arrived at work safe and sound not twenty minutes later, none the worse off for the motorcycle ride.

A few days later, I was on my way back from the Game Developer's Conference in San Francisco, with my soon-to-be replacement in tow. We caught a commuter flight for the ninety-minute trip to Orange County. Jordan liked to call these kinds of trips a "turn and burn" because we were able to do it all in a day without having to stay overnight, thanks to an early-bird morning flight and a post-dinner return. I was tired of not being able to sleep in my own bed.

When I mentioned as much to Jordan, after takeoff and our drinks were served, he shook his head. "You know that's a sign of getting old, don't you? When you're away and all you can do is think about sleeping in your own bed."

I rolled my eyes. He was starting to sound like Emilia, dammit. "You're not so far behind me, you know." I said, eyes narrowing in warning.

"I'm far enough behind you that I can milk the fact with all the teasing I can possibly squeeze in until I enter my fourth decade."

Ugh, when he said it that way, it really did make me feel old. But that was ridiculous, like calling twenty-five a quarter-century just to make it feel older, weightier. But it meant nothing in the grand scheme of things.

"Well, I'll just plan to get even by interrupting one of your ninety-hour CEO workweeks by calling from some beach in the Caribbean."

Jordan arched an eyebrow at me. "Huh. Trying to scare me off of your job?"

I shrugged. "You already know how to do it."

He sobered. "I am concerned, though…"

"That you won't be able to fit into my superior shoes?"

It was his turn to pull a face at me. "That I won't have your humility, for sure." We laughed. "But seriously, my concern isn't about the day-to-day nuts and bolts of the job. I'm confident I can do all that. But…"

I raised my brows, following his lead into a more serious conversation.

He met my gaze before continuing. "The vision part of things."

My eyes widened. Wow...Jordan was keeping it real, for sure. "You had the vision to take the company public. We wouldn't be there at all if it weren't for you."

He bobbed his head. "Yeah, yeah. I see that. And I'm not going to pretend false modesty and claim I'm not amazing at my job, because I know I am. But that's the business end of it. What about the vision, the direction, what about the future of gaming and where we want to be?"

"Having the vision is good, but it only takes you so far. And you have people around you to help with that. Hell, you'll still have me. I'll be on the board of directors. Hopefully, they see fit to make me chairman. Plus, we'll see each other socially. Our wives—sorry, I mean my wife and your girlfriend—are going to be business partners themselves. You're stuck with me, man."

He laughed. "I cannot tell you a time when that thought would serve as a relief. There were a couple times I would have been deliriously happy to defenestrate you and finally be rid of you."

I laughed. "Thanks. But defenestration, though? Seems a messy way to dispose of a pain in the ass. Now if you want tips on how to fantasize cleaner ways to dispose of a pain in the ass, we can access *my* daydreams about dumping *your* body in the desert on a dark night."

He laughed right back. "Damn, I'm going to miss this."

"Of course you are."

"Do you know what you're going to do yet? I mean, are you going to settle down and be the househusband, fixing dinner and raising the kiddies?"

I rolled my eyes. "Don't know yet. There are too many choices. For now, I'm concentrating on handing all of this off properly and setting Draco up for success in the era of Fawkes."

He waggled his brow. "Also known as the Golden Era."

"Whatever helps you sleep at night, man."

He laughed, sipped at his cocktail, eyes drifting toward the window for a moment before turning back to me. "Speaking of raising the kiddies, I have to tell you, we had a recent scare."

I blinked. "What kind of scare?"

"Last month, April was freaking out one morning before work because she was a week late and made me run to the drug store and get a test."

I sat back. "I'm sure that had the two of you freaking the fuck out." With a twinge of shame, I remembered my own freakout when Emilia had tested positive four years ago on that fateful day right before New Years. There had been lots of broken glass involved, a grown-man tantrum and a raging migraine headache.

Who the fuck was I to judge, really?

"Nah, you know what? At first, I thought it was just me being, you know, protective of her feelings. I was strangely calm throughout it all. Went off and got her test, brought it back, talked her down from the brink of a panic attack, held her hand while we waited for the results."

I shook my head in disbelief. "Wow, your lothario reputation is now permanently damaged—"

"*Anyway*," he said with emphasis, cutting me off with a glare. "What I'm saying is I didn't feel panicked the entire time. And after it came up negative..." he shrugged. "Just between you and me—and I'm not even giving you permission to breathe a word about this to your wife—I was kind of sad. I think more than a little part of me was hoping that I'd knocked her up."

"Jeez, no wonder women think of us as cave dwellers."

"Ooga booga." He hit his chest. "I know it's crazy and it's definitely not the right time in our lives for that. She's starting a new business, I'm about to take over yours. It will be a miracle if we even see each other."

"Better put a ring on it, bro," I said with a grin.

"Still waiting for the right time for that, too. That one seems like a minor detail compared to this baby thing."

I blinked. "A minor detail? For a chick-slayer like you?"

"I'm glad that my reputation was so much the stuff of legends that people still talk about it. I've been with the same chick for well over three years and still going strong."

I nodded, and he shook the cup in his hand, now empty of everything but ice cubes. He knocked one back and crunched it before continuing.

"We can all grow and progress, now, can't we? Like you, when are you taking the next step in life?"

I frowned. "Still figuring out the professional angle."

He nodded. "Mia hasn't felt the need to, you know, try again?"

Jordan was the only one outside a few family members and Heath who knew about our previous loss and, like the friend I'd trusted him to be, he'd never breathed a word of it, until now.

I blinked. "Well, actually, you can't tell anyone—especially April—but we're sort of trying."

Unfazed, he nodded. "That's cool. Maybe your next life step is stay-at-home dad, then."

I rolled my eyes. "Gotta get the bun in the oven first."

He laughed. "Well at least that part of the process is fun."

I threw him a look out of the corner of my eye.

"It's not? What do you know that I don't?"

"Let's just say that sex on demand isn't all it's cracked up to be."

He rolled his eyes. "If you want tips, let me know."

"Fuck off," I said, leaning back. "I'm serious. It's just...different. Starting to feel a bit like work."

Then I looked at my lime and soda, tilting it this way and that, wondering if somehow someone had spiked it with alcohol when I wasn't looking. Or maybe I was just in need of getting this stuff off my chest.

Though the way he continued to tease me about it, I was regretting my choice in confidante.

CHAPTER
FIFTEEN
ADAM

THAT NIGHT, I WAS IN BED WITH MY WIFE AND—GIVEN that it wasn't a fertile day, I was off the hook for sex. I was starting to put a lot more stock in the appeal of cuddling and talking. Once this impregnation box was ticked, I was looking forward to spontaneity. God, I hoped that would be soon.

"Do you think we should move?" I blurted out of the blue as we lay in the darkness.

She shifted against me. "What? Why?"

"There aren't any kids on this island, for one thing."

"So? And that's not true. The Fredricksons have kids. Two of them."

"Aren't they teenagers?"

She hesitated. "Well, yeah I think one of them is in high school, other one is in junior high."

"No one here has small kids. I'm wondering if there's something we don't know. Like maybe this isn't a place for small kids."

She shifted against me. "Just because there aren't any small kids in this very small community right now doesn't mean we—"

"What about the drowning risk? We're right on the back bay."

"We live in Southern California. We also have a pool."

"We'd definitely have to drain the pool," I mused out loud.

She sat up to look at me in the darkness. "Wait, what? It's completely fenced off. Any pool built to code is."

"There are a lot of risks. And plus...I don't know. Do we want our kid to grow up a Newport Beach kid?"

She laughed, settling back so that her head rested on my shoulder. "Well, you might have a point there. But what's the answer to that? It's not like we can relocate to Anza or raise our kid in a small town out here. Plus, I'd could never hate my kid enough to raise him or her in Anza, anyway."

I shrugged and her head bobbed accordingly. "Anza's all right. I mean, its lack of hospital might make it difficult for you to finish your medical training or for us to receive immediate medical care."

"Adam, I was joking. We aren't moving up to the high desert. No, not the low desert either. And we can't go out of state as I'm committed to my residency for at least two and a half more years. Since I like the hospital I'm working at, I don't even want to leave the county, really. The thought of a long commute makes me gag, and I know I sound spoiled when I say that."

I sighed. "There has to be an answer."

"What are *you* planning on doing, commute by helicopter?"

"Nope, definitely too dangerous."

She snickered. "Joking, again." There was a long pause and she shifted against me, resting her hand on my chest. "Please promise me you won't get like you do about this. Don't fixate."

I sighed. "I've got too much to worry about with this whole CEO handover and the board of directors and whatnot to fixate on other things."

"Sure. Because you've never done that in the past...fixated on things in your personal life."

She had a point there. "I just think there might be better options for us, for a young family. Sure, we're deep in the heart of metropolis suburbia here but there might be options."

"Well, if you've got the time to look into it, that's fine. But you know, the baby doesn't move around much for the first year. I'm not even pregnant yet so we really don't even have to worry about any type of move for at least two years, yet."

I considered that timeline. "That gives me a little time to do some research."

I wrapped my arm around her waist. She turned her head to look up at me in the dim light. "Wouldn't you miss living right on the beach like we do now?"

"It's pretty hard to get anywhere in Orange County that's far from the coast. That's what cars—and my bike—is for."

"While we're on the subject of safety—"

Uh oh. Did I just walk myself straight into a trap? "Yeah?"

"Do you think it's safe for a potential new dad to be managing busy traffic on that crazy thing?"

"Emilia—"

"Lane splitting—"

"It's legal in California."

"Just about the only state it *is* legal in, but it's fucking dangerous."

I took in a deep breath. "I told you I don't do it…much."

"Adam…"

"Okay, damn." Fuck. Shit. How did I get myself into these situations? "Fine. No more lane splitting."

"What might make me happier is if you didn't ride it at all."

"Except on Sundays on back roads going thirty-five?"

"Yup, you got it."

I turned to look at her. "*Now* who's the one fixating?" Though I arched a brow at her in the darkness, I doubted she could see.

"Fine, but I need to know that you're doing everything to be safe." Her voice was dead serious now, no more joking around.

"I am."

"Because California drivers suck and are blind to motorcycles."

"That's what defensive driving is for." She sighed and caressed my arm, and we were quiet for a long time, just holding each other. "I'll stop doing it if it really bothers you that much."

She kissed my chest. "I don't want you to not be able to enjoy your bike. But maybe we can compromise. Like, you can check ahead and take your car when traffic is looking particularly gnarly."

"I can do that."

"And no—"

"No lane splitting, yeah, already got that one." I grabbed a strand of her long hair and twisted it around my finger. "Now I'm going to ask something from you."

"What's that?" she asked.

"I want you to keep an open mind about moving."

She sighed. "I'm going to be honest. I don't have the time to go house shopping, I'm barely keeping my life together as is with all these long shifts and the way that he's scheduling—I mean—the way that scheduling is looking going forward."

"I'll look around, do some research, get a realtor, I could weed out the stuff I know you'll hate or that I don't like and just show you the best candidates."

She laid her head against mine. "That sounds good," she said, sleep permeating her voice the way it did when I knew she only had a few more minutes left of consciousness before sacking out completely. "I just hope..."

"What? What do you hope?"

"I just hope it won't all be for nothing," she said, her voice sounding far away.

I smoothed her hair. "We've barely started trying. It won't be for nothing."

And that was the last conscious word I heard from her before her long, rhythmic breathing set in. I pulled the covers up to envelop her and kissed her hair. Then I rolled her so that her back was facing me. I promptly pulled her against me and curled myself around her body.

This right here? This was better than sex in my book. Okay, maybe it wasn't categorically better than sex, but definitely better than baby-making sex.

I inhaled the scent of her hair and a peaceful warmth took me over. My eyes closed and I couldn't imagine a better moment of my life than this.

The following morning, I called and left a message for my friend, Dom, asking for the name and number of his real estate guy.

He did me one better by calling me directly a few hours later.

"What's a busy and successful CEO like you doing not delegating phone calls to your assistant?" I asked with a laugh.

"I've got time in my schedule for other busy and successful CEOs like you."

"Well thanks, man. I appreciate it."

"So, you're looking for a new property?"

"Looking for something a little quieter. Maybe an atmosphere conducive to family life. But not too far away. I know that's a lot. You're probably going to suggest something in south county."

"On the contrary. I live in the canyons. Have you been out that way?"

"Silverado, once or twice."

"That's nearby. Modjeska, Trabuco. I happen to live in Canyon Hollow. And I know of an agent who specializes in the area."

"Hmm. Maybe I'll take a drive out there and check it out."

"It's quiet out there, except maybe on the weekends when people come in for hiking the back country. Lots of trailheads into Cleveland National Forest start out there. But there's some wildlife. Quirky but fun people. Small town atmosphere but not a long commute. To be fair, I'm biased. I grew up in Canyon Hollow."

"Even the name of it sounds like it's out of a storybook."

"I'd strongly suggest you consider it."

And with that, he gave me the name of his real estate agent and my next call was to her.

And an hour later I had an appointment to meet her the following week at the Canyon Hollow Café to have lunch. She wanted to show me around to get a feel for the community and find out my needs and preferences.

Talk about a new beginning and big changes. If the job thing and the starting a family thing weren't enough, then adding a move into the mix was probably just enough to push things over the top.

Emilia would laugh if I ever said this out loud, but she was right—I never did things halfway. Especially when it came to massive life changes.

CHAPTER

SIXTEEN

ADAM

THE FOLLOWING WEEK, EMILIA'S BIRTHDAY WEEK, SHE was booked almost solid at the hospital. But we managed to set something up. I could only pull off massive surprises like whisking her off to Paris or Italy once a year. So I settled for a smaller-scale surprise instead.

The night before her birthday, I showed up at the hospital before her shift ended. The restaurant I'd reserved was only a short drive away, in the Orange Hills, so it made sense to bring the date and prep to her instead of having her come all the way home to Newport and then turn around and drive back. Especially on a Friday night when traffic clogged the freeways.

Thus, I showed up with a duffle bag of her toiletry items— makeup, shampoo, hair dryer, hair styling stuff—and a garment bag with a brand-new dress that I'd been dying to see her wear. All packed, prepped and delivered to me at work by my housekeeper.

I got there before she finished with her duties—hoping, of course, that she'd be done on time, this time.

I found Emilia's friend, Louisa, at the nurse's station just where she'd said she'd be when I'd texted her for help.

"Mia's finishing up with her charts," she told me. "Let me pop into the residents' lounge and check on her, then you can surprise her and drop off the stuff. How fun! We had a birthday cake for her earlier."

After checking, Louisa waved me back toward the lounge a few minutes later. When I entered, Mia was sitting at what looked like a communal desk in front of her work laptop. She was wearing her neon-colored pediatric hospital scrubs. The lounge, bordered by the locker room on the other side, and with a sink, fridge and micro on the far counter, was decorated with birthday streamers, some balloons and the remains of a large birthday cake.

"Hey," she said wearily, surprise on her features. "I thought Louisa was kidding around when she said you were here. What's up?"

I blinked, surprised at her wary tone. "Is that any way to greet the person taking you on a surprise date?" I held out the garment and toiletry bags by way of explanation.

Her eyebrows rose in her forehead. "Oh...really?"

She didn't sound excited, which irritated me. Maybe she was more tired than I'd thought?

"Is everything okay?"

She blinked and smiled, then stood and arched her back in a big stretch. "Yeah, sorry. I was going to stay late and get caught up on some chart work."

I made a face. "It's your birthday. Give yourself a break. You can catch up from home this weekend."

"Well, of course I'm not going to stay late now." She finally smiled and waved in the air, dismissing my protest. "What is all this?"

"We have reservations in..." I checked my wristwatch. "An hour and a half at Orange Bluff Bistro."

She raised her brows. "Ooh, fancy. And here I thought we were just getting together with the family tomorrow."

I grinned. "I get you all to myself tonight. I'm selfish like that."

Emilia threw a glance at the other side of the lounge where a cluster of doctors conspicuously watched us from their tables. The one paying the closest attention to us looked familiar. It took me a minute, but he was the dude I'd caught staring at us during the holiday party.

I turned back to her. "Is, ah, everything okay? I hope I didn't get you into some kind of trouble."

She shook her head vigorously. "No, no. I'm going to wrap things up now and then I'll shower and get dressed. Do you mind waiting out in the lobby?" And then it was her turn to throw a glance over at that same cluster of doctors. She visibly blushed.

Something weird was definitely going on here. But instead of pushing the issue—which would have embarrassed her and made me look like a colossal asshole, I pointed to my laptop case slung over my shoulder. "Take your time. I've got plenty to keep me busy."

She smiled, pecked a quick kiss on my cheek, then sat at her laptop once more. I pivoted, staring straight at the guy who was still watching us from across the room. He met my gaze for a split second before looking away, back at the tablet in front of him.

To quote various *Star Wars* characters in various *Star Wars* movies: I had a bad feeling about this.

I left the lounge and stewed for the next hour while I waited for Emilia to get ready.

When she greeted me in the lobby in that form-hugging red dress, I just about forgot my own name—or that I not only knew this beauty gracing my presence but also shared my life with her.

She looked amazing. The dress hugged her every curve, gave a hint of cleavage—just enough to be sexy but not enough to make her feel uncomfortable or self-conscious, as I knew she often got with low cut stuff. Without good reason, I might add, but I respected her limits. She drew eyes from all sides of the general waiting room.

Given her brilliant smile, the gleaming dark hair that fell around her shoulders, and the way she stood, I could tell she agreed.

I shook my head. "You look…"

"I know, right?" She laughed and made a little twirl. "I've been wearing scrubs or sweats for so long I think I forgot what it was like to be glamorous in any way."

"Well, I'd say you clean up pretty damn well."

I escorted her out to the valet, who retrieved my car in short order. We left the parking lot, heading east for the hills of Orange.

"So what gave you the idea to bring me stuff and start the birthday celebrations early?"

I shrugged. "Just trying to keep things outside the box." I hesitated for a moment. "I didn't embarrass you by showing up at your work, did I?"

She shook her head immediately—almost too quickly. "No, no. It's all good. Just a surprise."

I braked at yet another red light, suppressing a curse. We'd be getting there just on the heels of the reservation, and we'd be okay, but it was frustrating nonetheless.

"So, what's the deal with that guy? The blond one with the disheveled hair?"

"Disheveled?" she snorted. "That's a fancy word for you."

"What, am I some kind of unwashed, uneducated slob or something?"

She gave me side-eye then grinned. "Well, you *did* drop out of college. I hold two whole degrees more than you."

"True...it's what I get for dating above my class. I promise I won't use the word disheveled anymore if you tell me what the hell is up with that guy. He was the same dude staring at us at the holiday party."

She blinked. "You have a good memory."

"You already knew that." Why did I get the impression that she was evading? "So, about this guy..."

She heaved a sigh. "He's the senior resident. He does the schedule. Don't mind him. He's just a little weird."

I paused, signaling to turn onto the narrow road that would take us up the steep hill drive leading up to the restaurant.

"I could swear that he's into you."

She let out a laugh—it sounded a little overly loud, I thought. "Don't project, Adam. Just because *you're* into me doesn't mean the rest of the female-attracted portion of the species is."

I shrugged. "Okay, maybe I *am* projecting. But he's not being weird with you, is he? I mean, you have complained more than once about scheduling, and since he's in charge of that..."

"Oh, it's just that Louisa and I don't get to be on the same service ever. We did a lot of rotations together in medical school, and it was cool when we matched with the same placement for residency. We had visions of being able to work together like we had in med school. It isn't happening as much now."

"And she's about to pop out a baby and go on maternity leave any day now."

She shrugged. "Yeah, that too. When she gets back, she'll have to finish up her intern year of residency. Not sure how much we'll be able to work together then."

"So that's it? This guy isn't being a dick or wielding his power inappropriately or...?"

She shrugged again but said nothing, which made me think that she wasn't being completely forthcoming with me. But short of tying her up and plying her with some kind of torture device—or multiple forced orgasms—to get the whole truth out of her, she didn't appear to be telling. And since that wasn't really my scene, it was unlikely that I'd resort to any torture beyond, perhaps, excessive tickling.

So...how to get to the bottom of it? Or should I even attempt it?

Emilia was a big girl and could fight her own battles. Or so I had to forcibly remind myself on a regular basis whenever that overwhelming protective instinct tried to shove its way to the fore and take over. That had caused us so many serious problems before and I'd learned...I'd learned to bury it. Mostly.

We ended up having a nice dinner. The restaurant was situated high in the Orange Hills overlooking the greater Anaheim and Orange areas. The lights and distant landmarks—Angel Stadium and the massive Honda Center arena—dominated a view that stretched out to the distant, dark sliver of ocean.

Emilia wasn't drinking any wine, and I had a couple glasses, so she drove us home and I sat back and stared at her beautiful profile. I'd already dispatched a driver to get her car and drive it home from the hospital.

When we were almost home, I finally spoke. "So tonight, I want to propose something," I started.

She glanced at me, then returned her eyes to the road. "Hmm?"

"I propose that we stop with the thermometers and the ovulation timing and all of that. That we just have sex whenever we want to and not make this whole thing into something tedious."

Her brows raised. "Did you actually just say you thought our sex was tedious?"

"Uh..." I trailed off, at a loss. Uh oh. Had I just fallen into an unseen pit trap?

She let me flounder like that for a few more seconds before she started laughing. "I got you there, didn't I? You thought you were in big trouble."

"Well, I mean, you are amazing and sexy and I do want to eat you up on a regular basis but..."

"Not on demand?"

"Yeah, sorry. I'm not a cable TV channel. I don't care for the on-demand option."

She snickered, then signaled to exit the freeway. "Well, I think it might be healthy for both of us to just take a few months off from the baby making altogether. Just kinda...go with the flow, I guess?"

I silently did the math in my head, wondering if her quick agreement had something more to do with scheduling than with actually setting the tedious shit aside. Maybe she didn't want to possibly have a baby smack dab in the middle of Thanksgiving or Christmas. Which...who could blame her?

She nodded again decisively as she pulled into our parking spot and killed the engine. She turned to me with a smile. "I like this plan."

I stared at her, my eyes traveling down to her curvy neckline before gliding back up to settle on those lips. "Okay, but not trying doesn't mean going back to using condoms, does it?"

She grinned. "Yeah, I don't think there's really a need to go back to that."

"And..."

She blew out a breath, already knowing where I was going. "Yes, it means you'll get a blowjob once in a while. Such a whiner." She opened the door and got out. I followed suit. On our way back across the bridge to Bay Island, I took her hand in mine, lacing our fingers together.

"I'm not whining. I'm just..." I gestured with my hand. She rolled her eyes and stopped at the gate to pull off her high heels while I keyed in the code.

She clutched them in one hand by the heel, a flash of shiny black with red soles. "These things look amazing but they're uncomfortable, and I'm always stressed out that I'm going to walk through wet grass and ruin them."

"Barefoot it is." Or...hmm. After letting myself through the gate, I turned back to her, bent, and swept her up in my arms to carry her across the island to our house.

"Adam! Don't give yourself a hernia."

My brows knit and I made a face at her. "You don't weigh that much. Plus, I didn't get in any strength training today. This will be good for me." She smacked my arm, laughing.

"Wow, you are feeling the romance tonight, aren't you?" she said with a flirtatious smile when I set her down gently on our porch.

I took her hips in my hands and smiled at her. She tilted her head fetchingly, gazing up at me. "It's been a while since I've carried you anywhere. Better that way then slinging you over my shoulder like a caveman."

She reached out and fiddled with my tie. "Oh, you can hide it all you want, Adam Drake, but you still have a whole lotta caveman in you."

"Me bring pretty woman back to cave, no need to drag by hair. Me ravish. Umph," I grunted, then opened the door and motioned for her to precede me.

Earlier, I hadn't had the chance to see her put on the dress, but I definitely enjoyed looking at her in it. Especially when she climbed the stairs to our room ahead of me and I got a full few of that perfect ass. And even better than that—the best, really— was unzipping it slowly and peeling that beautiful dress away from her bare skin.

I tasted her neck, ran my lips along the shell of her ear and whispered. "It's your birthday tomorrow, but I'm doing the unwrapping tonight."

She laughed, tilting her head to give me more of her to taste.

And wow...I'd almost forgotten just how awesome non-baby-making sex was.

CHAPTER

SEVENTEEN

MIA

YOU KNOW WHAT'S SUPER WEIRD? TO BE SUDDENLY forced to regret a good night out—especially for a birthday celebration with my hubby. But the Monday following our Friday night date, I was doing just that. Friday night had been a short shift day, which meant that I'd left the hospital hours ahead of those on the long shift. And they'd all seen me leave the shower and dressing room in a lovely designer dress and met the handsome white knight who had whisked me away on a dream date.

Jealousy abounded.

And I could detect a certainly chilly bent on some of my resident colleagues.

Or it may be that they'd gotten wind of just how wealthy he was and wondering why I was even here trying to eke out a medical license after four grueling years of medical school.

Even my neighbors had taken bets that I'd quit school ten minutes after marrying Adam.

There was no mistaking the weird vibe when I walked into the residents' lounge after grabbing my white coat and stethoscope from my locker. Several other residents were there—some looking worse for wear after nearly sixteen hours of long call.

They stared, bleary-eyed, and some had the decency to ask how my hot birthday date had gone. They were good-natured enough about it but there was a thread of tension in their words.

And while I liked to congratulate myself for being so fucking lucky as to have Adam as my partner in life, saying anything about it, even when asked, felt like rubbing peoples' faces in my good fortune.

Luckily, Dr. Iverson wasn't here this morning.

However, later that afternoon, as he was assisting while I took care of an IV on a pre-op patient the snark started.

"How'd the hot date go on Friday?"

I shrugged, sent a sideways glance to the patient as if giving her presence as my excuse for not wanting to talk about it.

But just outside her room, as I found the nearest station to rest my tablet to enter notes into her chart, he gravitated to me like a white blood cell toward an invading virus.

"I'm serious, that was quite a show on Friday. Your guy likes that kind of thing, huh?"

I blinked without looking at him. "My husband, you mean? He just wanted to do something nice for my birthday."

"So how long have you been married?"

"Three years."

"Huh, did you know that most divorces happen within the first five years of marriage on average?"

I rolled my eyes. "Wow, quoting statistics. How generically predictable of you." I focused on the chart notes, pulling out my folding portable keyboard and laying it flat in front of my tablet.

He was, unfortunately, unfazed. "When you think about it, our whole job is statistics. That's how medical studies are done."

"Last I checked, neither I nor my spouse are lab rats."

He shrugged. "I've made it a sound policy—and advise anyone I know who's going into medical school—not to get married until after residency at the very earliest."

"Interesting. Saves date money, in any case." He was trying to rile me up and visibly getting more annoyed the more chill I was with his prodding.

"I mean, why even get married at such a young age? Unless...maybe you had to?"

I pulled my hands off the keyboard and turned fully to him, resting an elbow on the counter. I sent him a withering glare that he could not possibly miss and when I spoke, it was in the sternest voice I could muster. "Not sure what you're insinuating, but I'm quite sure I'm not comfortable with it. You should definitely change the subject."

He shrugged, looking completely unconcerned. "Fair enough. I gotta say that it must be nice, though..."

I most definitely did not have time for his bullshit. I turned back to my chart, determined to blow him off.

"I mean..." he continued when I'd given him zero indication of wanting to hear what else he had to say. "If the doctor thing doesn't work out, you have a billionaire to fall back on."

I stiffened. So word had gotten out. I figured it must have. Adam was a semi-public personality that someone could easily discover by doing one google search and reading his Wikipedia article or a write-up from *Forbes* magazine. My co-workers already knew I lived in Newport Beach, and that wasn't exactly the low-rent—or even medium-rent—district of Orange County. But when we walked through the hospital doors every morning, we were all equals—medical doctors working under supervision of attending physicians to help people.

Which...I was currently being impeded from doing by my own senior resident.

"I don't fall back on anyone," I said curtly. "Now I've got a lot of—"

"Well, I mean, not necessarily to *quit,* but...if you screw up you could always get him to donate a new wing to the hospital or something."

My eyebrow arched and shoulders locked. "Okay, that's enough, Dr. Iverson. I have work to do, and so do you. I'm politely asking you to stop this. Now. You'll save us both a lot of time if I don't have to go to human resources about it."

His eyes widened and he looked honestly taken aback, like he couldn't even fathom where my offense had come from. "Whoa, whoa. No need to be so touchy. You know, as colleagues, we can joke around a little. Guess we all have different senses of humor. I'll let you be."

I clenched my jaw, feeling my temples bulge. I'd had plenty of fun times joking around with colleagues. Sometimes the jokes bordered on the not-so-appropriate, but within reason. But I wasn't going to argue. Fuck this guy. "Sounds great. Thank you."

He threw up his hands dramatically, as if my reaction was way over the top and out of nowhere. I didn't care. My patience had run out, especially since other people were starting to notice.

When Adam had asked about him during our drive to dinner, it had officially become the last straw.

I was done playing Dr. Nice Girl.

"What was all *that* about?" Louisa showed up at my shoulder just as I was finishing my notes and folding my keyboard back into my pocket.

"Oh, hey." I turned to her and smiled, taking up my tablet. She was at the stage of her pregnancy where she was taking extra care to prevent infection, so half her face was covered by a surgical mask. "How's your cards rotation going?" I had zero desire to go into Iverson's bullshit, especially where a nurse might overhear my complaints. "And how's baby doing?" I pointed to her heavily rounded belly.

"Cards is fine. Just working on some stress EKGs right now. I'm wrapping up the rotation next week before maternity leave. And this little tyke can come any time after that, please and thank you. I need to post an eviction notice for him or something—feels like I'm bigger than a swollen woolly mammoth." That twinge of envy I felt was only a dull pinch this morning. Probably smothered by all the lingering irritation at Dr. Fuckhead.

"So are you going to tell me why Craig just walked away looking so cartoonishly butthurt that I laughed a little behind my mask when he wasn't looking my way?"

With a sharp look toward the nurse's station, I hugged my tablet and ushered her toward a nearby hallway—and near where my next patient was waiting.

In a low voice, I addressed her question. "I told him point blank to knock off his bullshit. He was hinting that I'm just going to quit any time now because my husband is rich. I told him that wasn't appropriate."

Her eyes widened above her mask. "Damn, girl. You go. He was a year ahead of me in pre-med at 'SC and he honestly has always intimidated me."

"He likes to think he's imposing and all-knowing, but he's just a socially awkward dickhead who apparently hates women."

"He most certainly does the opposite of hating *you*, Mia. You have to know that."

My next two steps came hesitantly, then I stopped in the middle of the hallway, moving next to the wall to allow others to pass. "It doesn't matter what his motivation is. Saying that kind of stuff is not appropriate. *Ever.*"

She nodded, quickly agreeing.

"I have to get a move on. Everyone on pedes rotation has a staff meeting in forty-five minutes and I have three newborns to visit before that." I pulled my surgical mask out of my pocket and looped it around my ears.

"Aww," she said in a singsong voice, rubbing a hand over her belly. "Hopefully in two weeks, that will be my little guy, too."

"I won't be on pedes anymore, unless your little guy makes an early appearance. But you can bet I'll be visiting you every single damn day you're in maternity." We shared a grin and I silently fought the urge to reach out and rub her belly.

Her eyes crinkled above her mask. "I'm counting on that. In the meantime, good going with Senior Resident Dickhead," she whispered. I snickered, gave her a fistbump and moved on about my day.

Fortunately, Dr. Dickhead got the message. I only prayed it would last. His residency was up in a little over a year. Unless he chose to apply for a fellowship here.

The only thing worse than Senior Resident Dickhead would be Fellow Dickhead.

A week later, I started a cards rotation, which meant dealing with patients who had heart emergencies—myocardial infarctions, angina, general chest pains. I was in the ER a lot and things were fast moving.

And though we were once again on the same rotation, I saw a lot less of Dr. Dickhead.

But things felt lonelier with Louisa on maternity leave.

A few weeks after that, it was Adam's birthday, and as I had two whole days off in a row, a few days before he would turn thirty-two, I decided to snag a reservation at a cute bed-and-breakfast up in Arrowhead, in the San Bernardino mountains about an hour and a half drive from where we lived.

It was just far enough away to catch some peace and quiet, enjoy some relaxing walks in nature, some good food and a lot of quality time. We sadly didn't get much of that these days.

And though I didn't make a plan of it, we ended up having a lot of sex. A lot and a lot of it, like we were using those two days to somehow catch up on weeks of not having had any at all.

Because in order to have sex—hot or otherwise—you had to be in the same room and conscious long enough to do it. Go figure.

We slept in our first morning, missing breakfast hours, but neither of us cared. We might have gone at it last night until we passed out but when he pulled me against him first thing in the morning after waking up, he pressed his morning wood up against me. And that was enough to seduce me yet again. So, I hit the bathroom right after he did, quickly brushing my teeth and running a brush through my hair.

When I reappeared in the bedroom, he was on his back, hands under his head, staring up at the ceiling.

"Whatcha thinking about?"

"About how glad I am that I decided to take time off work to be up here with you."

I bit my lip. "Aww. You're so incredibly sweet."

A wicked grin slid over his astonishingly sexy lips. "Well, if you knew about the dirty stuff I was thinking, you wouldn't think I was so sweet."

"Oh, there's dirty stuff? That's even better." And with that, I pulled off my night shirt and brazenly tossed it to the floor. "I am now taunting you with my naked body."

His dark eyes hungrily skated over my bare skin, devouring every inch.

"Come here," he said in a husky, quiet voice. A commanding voice.

"I thought I wore you out last night. You are a year older now, after all."

His eyes narrowed at the taunt. "Don't make me chase you down, sugar baby."

I pushed my breasts together to make fake cleavage and topped it with a prominent lower lip pout. "You want some of my sugar? Do you deserve it?"

A wicked smile spread across his face. "You know I do."

I took a playful step toward him. Then another, until my legs came up against the edge of the bed. He sat up and, lightning-fast, grabbed me around the waist and pulled me on top of him.

I shrieked in surprise before laughing. "You ain't messing around, old man."

"Oh, I will be messing around plenty in this room, with *you*."

I bent and our lips locked in a ferocious, passionate kiss. Our tongues entwined and his hands came up to hold my head steady against his mouth. No need, really because I was in it as much as he was.

I pulled the covers off him and our naked bodies fused against each other, softened and melting against each other like two chemical compounds predestined to bond whenever they were mixed.

I had to agree with him. Sex when you weren't actively trying to make a baby was good stuff.

And in spite of our sexcapades last night, this morning it was *on.* I pulled back, opening my legs to straddle him. He grabbed my hips, squeezing tightly and with one quick shift, he slid inside me, letting out a long, pent breath.

"Why do you always feel so fucking good?"

I moved my hips over his slowly once, smiling. "Just lucky, I guess."

"You are the sexiest woman on the planet, and I'm the luckiest bastard in the solar system." He said tightly as I shifted over him once again. We both let out a long sigh in unison.

His hands slid from my hips to cup my breasts as I continued to move, my eyes fluttering closed, savoring the feel of him, his hands, his skin against my skin, his hard cock inside me.

For long moments, I couldn't focus on anything else. Adam was a storm—a raging force of nature that couldn't be ignored—and never forgotten. His touch was thunder and his presence, lightning. His force of will was the wind and the rain. Soon I was happily sandwiched between him and the bed as he rolled me over claiming full control that I was happy to cede for now.

I weathered and relished and savored him—his hot breath against my skin, the hard muscular body shifting against my own. The furious tempest slowly calmed to a steady, if determined, downpour. And I was the parched earth gratefully soaking up every single drop.

My legs curled around his hips, holding him close to me, even when he wanted to shift away and keep his rhythm. For a few playful minutes, we wrestled each other before he expelled a resolute breath, wrapped his fingers around my ankle and flung my leg away, freeing his movements once more.

I would have laughed but I soon forgot whatever it was I'd found funny as his rhythm changed in earnest. Unrelentingly, he bore down on me and I was gasping for air, eyes rolling back into my head and savoring that quick ascent to orgasm. The storm kept pounding as I found my climax and soon, he stilled, plunging deep and holding his breath as I felt him reach the same crisis only minutes later.

My legs curled around him protectively once more, holding him there until he drew breath again—and inhaled my exhales.

His eyes fluttered open and our gazes locked.

"Fuck," he uttered on a harsh breath. "You are incredible."

I smiled and ran my fingers through his thick dark hair as my legs tightened around his hips. "Hmm. You're not so bad yourself, mister." I leaned up and pecked his lips. "Happy birthday."

"Yeah, *happy* indeed."

And the rest of the day—most of it spent inside that bedroom until we emerged, bleary-eyed at dusk to finally get some dinner and breathe a little fresh air.

But neither of us complained. Not one single bit.

CHAPTER
EIGHTEEN
MIA

I SHOULD HAVE TOLD ADAM'S FINANCIAL ADVISOR AHEAD OF time to invest some of our portfolio in the stock for pregnancy tests, because I was single-handedly driving up their profit margins these days, testing early and often. I, who understood the medical probability of getting an inaccurate result by testing too early was still peeing on sticks days ahead of when my period was due.

I knew all of this and yet, like a junkie, I pulled yet another stick out of the package, held it under my urine stream and prayed my aim was good enough that I wouldn't end up peeing on my hand—*again.*

With that mishap averted, I set the test on the back of the toilet and hopped into the shower.

I hadn't taken a basal body temperature or charted anything in almost two months. And the sex had gotten back to the more interesting spectrum of things. Thank goodness. It felt good not to worry—at least for the next few months.

At some point, though, I needed to get that full fertility workup. But I'd worry about that later. Maybe I'd magically have more time then.

The shower was long, hot, relaxing, just the way I loved them. I slowly massaged shampoo, conditioner and a hot oil treatment into my scalp, then shaved my legs. By the time I dried off and started prepping for work, I'd all but forgotten the pee stick sitting on the back of the toilet.

And because I'd left them sitting there more than just once—to be pointed out to me later by either Adam or the housekeeper, I remembered to grab it and trash it after I blew my hair dry.

Only, after I grabbed it, I had to glance at it. And then, halfway to pivoting to toss it in the wastebasket, I had to do a double take. Then a triple take.

Followed quickly by a quadruple- and quintuple-take.

There was a second line on the test this time.

I stared at it, for far too many seconds uncomprehending, merely registering that something was different. Then suddenly and without thinking, I let out a sharp yelp. *Holy shit!*

A positive pregnancy test.

Like...for real? Was this thing broken or something? I checked the date on the package and then promptly peed on a second stick—this time not so deftly avoiding the pee-on-your-hand side-effect. I guess that's why God invented surgical soap.

As I spent the requisite two minutes washing my hands with the sterile soap, I stared at that damn stick like they tell you to never watch a pot that's supposed to start boiling. And this time, I watched as that second blue line showed up right before my eyes. Like a magic trick.

Damn.

The odds of two positive pregnancy tests taken within minutes of each other showing a false result were next to none.

The proof was incontrovertible.

I was pregnant.

But as a doubting skeptic who couldn't believe in the magic of a pee stick, I wrote up a lab bloodwork order for myself and stopped by an outpatient lab where nobody knew me. No sense in starting gossip at work and risk the news spreading before I even had a chance to tell my family. I marked the test STAT and was promised results within the next five hours. Good enough for me.

If I was going to be delivering this news to Adam, I was absolutely going to have every bit of information before he started shooting rapid-fire questions at me. The pee sticks were enough for me. But of course, when the STAT blood test came back positive with an HcG hormone level of 721 ml, any doubt that had lingered in the back of my mind, somehow determined to disbelieve the happy news, was now abolished.

Adam and I were going to be parents.

I punched the date of my last menstrual period into an online pregnancy calculator to learn that I was almost six weeks along. The likely conception date, based on the average length of my cycle was during our trip to Arrowhead for Adam's birthday.

And then it told me the approximate due date.

Christmas day.

I blinked, stunned. Of course, Adam and I would make a baby that had to be special about his or her entrance into the world and come on the craziest day of the year.

Damn...

Later during the long shift, in a moment where I got a few hours to breathe, I went to the residents lounge to catch up on paperwork. At the coffee station, I filled a mug and prepped a cup, only remembering to stop myself right before taking that first sip. With a sigh of deepest regret, I had to watch as that beautiful-smelling cup of brewed beans, along with the much-needed caffeine, poured down the drain.

No coffee for at least the next nine months, and likely longer, depending on my breastfeeding schedule. And no wine, either, though I'd been off that for a while.

But caffeine...caffeine was single-handedly getting me through the trials and tribulations of medical residency. I'd have to do a little research to come up with new, healthier strategies for boosting my energy.

The first symptom I noticed—and it was ridiculous to notice because it was still so early—but I definitely seemed to be peeing a lot more than normal. And on a medical resident's intern-year schedule that wasn't conducive to bathroom breaks, that was a challenge.

Then there was the other hurdle to get over—coming up with a way to break the news to Adam.

If I went with fanfare and something fancy and ostentatious, I'd have to enlist other people to help, like my mom, Heath, maybe even reach out to my extended friend group. And while it might be fun to get everyone involved in the great news-breaking, it inevitably meant that I'd have to tell all of them before I told Adam. That didn't seem right, since he was the one who was about to become a dad. He should be the second person to find out, after me, right?

But I still wanted to do something memorable. I wanted him to have a story to tell his friends and family. A story to tell our child when he or she grew up and was curious about that sort of thing. I wanted it to be something that would cause him to get a dreamy, far-away look in his eyes and remember when his wife was young and beautiful. When we were both full of hope before being broken down by the perils of decades of life and parenthood.

Damn, that went dark fast, didn't it?

Regardless, when I was in the on-call room trying to get a little catnap but not succeeding, I started searching social media for ideas—TikTok, even Pinterest—for any graphics or fun crafty hints. Every possibility I came across was either completely insipid or so very *not* us.

Frustrated, I finally dozed off. Only to be abruptly awakened by my work cell phone pager going off. A patient was reporting symptoms that I needed to check in on. Groggily, I left the bunk room and meandered into the lounge, stretching my arms and arching my back to get some blood flowing.

"Whoa, you look awful."

I turned. Senior resident Dr. Iverson, because of course this guy would have to show his ass up right in the middle of this long but crazy exciting day, just to pee into my cheerios. He seemed to enjoy doing that on a regular basis.

"Thanks, I call it my trendy 'resident on call' look. It will be in all the magazines next fall." I smirked, then swerved dangerously close to that damn coffee machine. The brew was fresh. I inhaled deeply, getting that fun tingly feeling I got whenever I relished the smell of fresh coffee. *Mmm.* I'd been a tea drinker for most of my life but becoming a medical student had made a coffee worshipper out of me. Dr. Pepper or tea didn't come close to being the magic wake-up drink that coffee was. Now I knew what Adam was always going on about as he guzzled cup after cup every morning.

If I could mainline the stuff, I would.

This kid better be grateful for the sacrifices I was making for them already.

I had to laugh at myself because even now I was lancing maternal guilt at the zygote that I'd just found out existed only twenty-four hours before.

Iverson moved to my side to refill his cup. I should have walked away then. But for some reason I wanted to torture myself by watching him pour and fix himself a cup.

"Where's your cup at? I can refill you."

I blinked. "Uh, no. I'm good, thanks."

"I mean, you don't look good."

"I'm just groggy."

"Hence my question. Where's your cup? I'll refill you."

I stepped back. "Gotta go check on a patient then finish my charts. See ya."

Before he could reply, watching me with an openly astonished expression, I slipped out of the lounge and high tailed it down a couple flights of stairs.

Even with a relatively calm last few hours of call, I still had no ideas.

When I got home, Adam was still at work. I hopped in the shower, got into my fleece pajamas, and inevitably, did more searches.

Eventually, I conked out on the downstairs couch.

When I woke up, it was dark outside and someone had pulled my phone out of my hand and covered me with a throw blanket.

I got up, feeling parched and fumbled my way over to the light switch adjacent to the kitchen, blinking at the brightness when the lights hummed to life.

Immediately, I grabbed a glass and went to the fridge to fill it with ice water. What time was it, even? And was Adam home yet? The house was pitch black, but that didn't mean much. Adam had the super-annoying habit of entering the house in the dark and only illuminating the room he was currently occupying. Which meant that often, I'd get home and not even realize for ten or fifteen minutes that there was another soul in the house. I had his location turned on for my phone, and he had mine. But my phone was sitting on the coffee table in the other room and I was feeling unmotivated to go get it while I replenished my poor parched body.

Of course, then I had to promptly go empty my bladder.

This was already getting annoying and I hadn't even gone through the merest fraction of the body changes I'd be enduring over the next few months.

When I stepped out of the bathroom, I was nearly scared out of my own skin by the very large man lurking right beside the doorway.

CHAPTER NINETEEN
MIA

I SUCKED IN A LOUD BREATH, FALLING BACK AGAINST THE closed door to the bathroom. "Fuck!"

Adam stared at me wide-eyed. "I'm sorry, did I scare you?"

I glared at him, folding my arms over my chest and resting my back against the bathroom door. "No, I'm just working on a new way to greet you."

His mouth curved and an eyebrow twitched up.

My eyes narrowed. "Did you seriously do that on purpose?"

He shrugged lightly. "Maybe a little. Payback, ya know."

I grabbed a handful of his t-shirt and balled it up inside my fist in a faux-threat. "I'll give you payback, you dork. That last time I wasn't even trying to scare you. You just startle easily, like a gazelle on the savanna."

He pulled me into his arms, leaned down to kiss me. "I do not startle easily. You're just too stealthy. Like ninja-level stealthy."

"Hmm well there were twenty-two years where you didn't know me. I could have done some secret ninja training in Nanda Parbat with Shado and Talia al Gul."

"Exactly. You have superpowers. The power to startle even the least startle-able man. The powers of bullet-fast snarky comebacks. The powers of seduction..."

My brow twitched up. "There won't be any seduction right now. You're safe. I'm actually starving."

He grinned. "Okay, food first, seduction later."

I patted him on the chest and sent him a smirk. "Gotta earn that, my friend."

Adam pulled out the food—a cold platter tonight and nothing terribly fancy. And though I wasn't experiencing nausea, it was always safer to go with a light meal just in case. This would hit the spot and quell my hunger without being too much. It's almost as if Chef knew...

Adam, of course, had to comment on it. "Wow, crunchy dinner tonight. Organic hummus and homemade whole wheat pita bread. This is picnic food."

"Is it not floating your boat?" I tilted my head at him as I grabbed us some plates and silverware. "We still have some of that fresh sourdough bread from yesterday. I think there's some left-over roast beef that she sliced up for sandwiches, maybe—"

He shrugged. "If I'm still hungry, I'll fix myself a sandwich. No problem."

It was a warm enough evening, so we set out the food on the table in the covered porch.

And the entire time, my mind was racing frantically trying to think of some special way to tell him our big news that wouldn't require so much preparation, since I was dying to just spill the beans.

Before drifting off on that impromptu nap, I'd found a video on TikTok that showed a woman with notes stashed all over her body and instructions for her partner to cut clothes off of her to reveal notes that led to other notes, right down to taking off her shoes and then using a nerf gun to pop a balloon which revealed the positive pregnancy test.

Oh damn, the pee sticks. Where had I even stashed those? In my blur of finding the news and then going off to work, I frankly had no idea. Had I trashed them right in the bathroom? If so, that was dumb of me, and I hoped that Cora hadn't done the wastebaskets today. Or maybe I'd just left them on the sink and if that was the case, then maybe she already knew—and by extension, Chef and the gardener and maybe just about anyone else who happened to pass by the house.

Hell, maybe half the city of Newport Beach already knew. Wouldn't that just suck—if I somehow managed to keep the news while preparing something elaborate—for him to find out from someone else?

By the time we sat down at the table, I was a seething pile of anxiety. Especially when Adam pulled out a bottle of wine and two wineglasses to go with it. It was a bottle of wine that we'd had shipped to us from Italy.

I looked up, frowning.

"What's wrong?"

"You know I'm not drinking these days." Or for the next nine months.

He hesitated. "Oh, yeah, crap, sorry." He shrugged self-consciously. "I just thought that since we aren't actively trying that you could have a glass. I haven't uncorked the bottle yet. We can have it some other time."

I stared at the bottle. What if I found an empty wine bottle and put the pee sticks in it and floated it onto the beach so he could find it, like a message sent in a bottle?

I could document it with cute pictures and put it on Instagram.

Now where to find an empty bottle—and where to launch the damn thing so that it would wash up on our beach? Fuck, was I truly considering calling an oceanographer to aid in my plans for breaking the news to my husband that he was going to be a father?

When I finally looked away from the bottle and back at Adam, he wasn't eating. He was staring at me with a highly concerned look on his face. "Are you okay?"

I blinked and rubbed my forehead. "I'm fine. Just a little tired."

"More than a *little* tired. I found you on the couch dead to the world an hour ago. You usually don't nap that hard. You were making this little snore I've never heard before. It was cute."

I dabbed a little olive tapenade onto a dry water cracker. "Lies, every last word. I don't snore, have never snored, will never snore."

"Maybe I was imagining things then." He winked and sent me a grin that flashed that dimple. That damned dimple that had magical panty-dropping powers over me. God, my husband was so fucking handsome that it stopped me in my tracks on a regular basis when noticing it.

Lucky, lucky me.

Except for when he made false claims that I snored. But for now, I'd let that pass, because he was pretty. And because he was going to be a daddy and he didn't even know it yet.

Adam turned back to his plate and began piling things on it—cut sections of pita bread, roasted red pepper hummus, a few olives. I bit into my cracker and chewed again before spearing a couple thin slices of cold turkey and some Swiss cheese for my plate.

"You know, when I was going over my calendar with my assistant today, I realized that I have nothing on my schedule at the end of the year."

I blinked. "Wow, that's a miracle." And providential, really, considering that his—and my—lives were about to completely change right around that exact same time.

"Yeah, and since we both loved Venice so much, I was thinking we could break away and go back, depending on your schedule. They have some big celebrations for New Year's with fireworks over the lagoon and parties. If you like the idea, I can reach out and book the place we stayed at last year—"

"Uh, yeah don't do that yet."

His brow quirked. "Oh, okay. No time off, or you don't want to celebrate New Year's like that?"

I froze, thoughts racing. Some kind of excuse—I needed something to put him off making plans for New Year's. My mind sped through possibilities, and I blinked, confused, and, strangely, a little panicked as well.

Adam frowned, concern clouding his features.

"Emilia, you're starting to worry—"

"I'm pregnant," I blurted, eyes bulging wide at the shock of the news exploding from my lips when all my best-laid plans were just that...plans. I honestly didn't even have any of those, either. Just ideas swimming around inside a mire of anxiety that was my current mental state.

Adam's expression didn't change in the slightest during the longest five seconds of my life. Then his brows pinched together. "Are you—"

"Yes, I'm sure. Two positive pee sticks and a blood test sure."

He blinked. "How long have you known?"

So apparently, I hadn't left the tests out where he could discover them. At least that was some small relief after the fact. The news was out now, and I didn't have to think up some cute, fun or crafty thing to document for social media—or future generations.

"Since yesterday, just before I went to work. I ordered up a blood test to confirm and have been stressing out about how to tell you ever since."

Now it was just a story about how silly I was—to plan and stress about how to tell him in a way that was so totally not us. And then, only to be thwarted by a propensity to blurt things unceremoniously.

The Clydesdale had already left the barn. No need to shut the door after it. I bit my lip, fidgeted, and stared wide-eyed at Adam, waiting for his reaction, hoping, maybe even crossing my fingers or some other superstitious nonsense.

Adam stared at a space on the table just in front of his plate, both hands resting just on either side. He didn't even blink—kind of looked like a robot scrolling through possible responses as they popped up on his inner menu. It took long minutes before appearing as if he finally remembered how to breathe. First, he blinked, then his fingers twitched, and then, the statue he'd become slowly came back to life as if someone had just stuck a magic hat on his head and called him Frosty the Snowman.

He shook his head. "This is...*wow*."

"Are you okay?" I blinked.

He ran a hand through his hair and had that weird sort of shell-shocked look on his face. "Yeah, yeah. I'm fine. More importantly, how are *you?*"

I bit my lip quickly. "I'd be better if you didn't look like I'd just shot you in the nuts with a paintball gun again."

He laughed then got up from the table and came around to my side. I popped up and he pulled me into his arms and kissed me.

"So, you're okay?" he asked.

I nodded. "I'm tired but that's probably just the on-call hours. And I have to pee a lot. That's about it."

He shook his head. "When—?"

"Well—you're not going to believe it."

"Sometime around the end of the year, obviously, given your reaction to the New Year's suggestions."

I nodded. "The online calculator set the due date as December 25th. So yeah, definitely don't make any elaborate plans for the end of the year."

He pulled me into a tight hug and held me for a long time. I rested my chin on his shoulder and waited. He obviously needed time to process this.

I was sure that when the time came for him to be able to talk about it, he'd say something thrilling and romantic and give us a memory we'd savor, maybe even laugh over fondly in years to come.

I pictured us driving back from dropping off our kid at college, turning to each other tenderly, holding hands and cherishing the moment we first found out we were going to be parents over eighteen years before...

"Well, I guess this means we don't have to go back to baby-making sex. That's a relief."

I should have known better, honestly. *Oh, Adam.*

Sigh. Well, between my blurting and his less than romantic rejoinder, we were being so typically us, weren't we?

CHAPTER TWENTY

ADAM

ONCE EMILIA MOVED OUT OF MY ARMS AND RETURNED to her seat, I stood there, frozen for a moment, reluctant to let her go, even if only a couple feet away from me.

I had this fierce, mad urge to wrap her in bubble wrap and forbid her from ever leaving the house again.

As I slowly returned to my seat and sank back into my chair, a million items began forming on a mental "to do" list. That, I think, was my brain's attempt to drown out the primal screaming happening in the deepest, darkest recesses of my psyche.

Emilia beamed at me as she chattered away about plans and making doctor's appointments and asking for my feedback on when we should tell people.

And all I could do was nod, smile, absently answer while paying the least amount of attention to the discussion possible without angering her. I was otherwise expending every other minute bit of energy to keep from losing my shit right then and there.

Because, God, that internal primal screaming was growing so loud as to threaten drowning out every other thought or external stimuli—including her.

I blinked and nodded in the right places and she either didn't notice or pretended not to. I was looking forward to holing up in my office as soon as possible just to spend some time getting my shit together so I could absorb every last implication.

But she wanted to cuddle on the couch instead.

I hesitated, tempted to give her a fake work excuse just so I could collect myself mentally, but that would be a dick move. She obviously wanted to know I was okay with this, and she wanted to feel safe. And I wanted her to feel safe too.

But I sure as hell wasn't feeling safe myself right now. Nope. I was feeling as exposed and unprotected as a naked musk ox in the middle of an arctic blizzard, to be honest.

On the couch, she sat very close, leaning against me and resting her head on my chest. I wrapped my arms around her and pulled her flush against me. As if I could be her armor. I wanted to be her armor, to shield and protect her from everything and everyone out in the world.

And that wasn't possible. Tomorrow morning, we'd part at the front door or in the parking garage, like we did almost every other morning, and she'd go her way and I'd go mine until that evening. And I'd have no control over her safety, her health.

And she wasn't even a her anymore, she was a *them*, her and a potential whole new person besides. A whole new person to shower that same worry, hypervigilance and concern on.

I'd fought hard to set aside that icy primal fear because she'd so wanted to try for a baby. Somehow, however, when this had all started, I'd expected that by the time we arrived here, at this point, I'd feel better about all of this.

I only felt worse.

Emilia didn't ask many questions, nor did she force a conversation, thankfully. After a good half hour of holding each other, she made an excuse to go do some things on her list before hitting the sack early. She was bone-tired, even after that nap.

Me? I quietly made my way up to my office and shut the door, sitting at the desk and opening my laptop. I thought I could get lost in my current coding side-project or even some hack and slash on a game that I didn't design.

Instead, I caught myself an hour later just sitting there staring at a blank screen.

Well, not completely blank. It was a long to-do list of everything we needed to get done with a sub list of questions we needed to ask the doctor on our first visit.

How would they be monitoring to make sure her cancer wouldn't come back now that she was being exposed to pregnancy hormones? Because right up until we made the decision to try for a baby, she'd been actively taking hormone blockers to prevent the cancer from coming back.

Now, not only was she off those protective measures, but she was now actively exposing her body to even more than the normal dose of hormones—progesterone, most especially.

Given all the reading I'd been doing, I was well on the way to earning my own goddamn medical degree. I was even starting to understand the medicalese—which, in my opinion, was equal to legalese in every way, though Emilia would die on that hill if we ever discussed it.

In this, at least, she was far more risk averse than I had been. Risk myself? My work? My company? Yes, I'd done those things.

Risk her in even the slightest? *No fucking way.*

I blinked, suddenly overcome with the urge to go running—or to go somewhere where I could belt out a respectable primal scream without getting the cops called or bringing out the neighborhood watch to witness my semi-public meltdown.

Or maybe I could just go for a drive, take the Porsche out to some high desert road in the middle of nowhere, and speed like a fucking demon for only the cacti and coyotes to witness.

Fuck. Anything but all this living—and feeling—going on in my head right now.

It was a dark place to be.

After realizing I'd just burned an hour staring at that screen, I slammed the damn laptop shut the moment she walked into the room to give me another long hug and a kiss goodnight.

I followed her into our bedroom and literally tucked her into bed like a child. I lay beside her for about a half hour before kissing her cheek and whispering that I needed to go for a run.

Then I got into my running clothes and, bypassing the home gym, went out to run along the deserted beach. After midnight on a weeknight, it was dead out there. And dark.

I could have gone directly to the shoreline and screamed into the face of the ocean.

But by the time I'd hit eight miles, I was too exhausted to do anything but limp home and take a long hot shower in the guest bathroom.

Hours later, I slid into bed beside her peacefully breathing form. My body—and mind—were just the right kind of exhausted that I slid into unconsciousness with minimal effort.

And yet, I knew that I wouldn't have the luxury of being able to do that every night.

Somehow or other, I had to find a way to cope, to deal with this. To be the equal, loving and supportive partner that she'd need—and deserved. I had to hold it together without making it look like I was fighting to hold it together. Day in and day out.

Because...winter was coming, as they say. And with it, a massive change that I wasn't ready for.

And yet, I *had* to be.

I chose to work from home the next day so we could spend the morning together. And when it was time for her to leave for another long call shift, I had to fight the urge to keep her from leaving the house.

She seemed so...normal. Yet nothing was normal.

I wanted to tail her like the secret service or a creepy stalker—I didn't care what the visual was, as long as she was safe.

But the truth of the matter was that I couldn't keep her safe all the time. It was beyond my power. And in order to keep myself sane, I had to not dwell on that thought.

So I welcomed every diversion I could, throwing myself into my work and accepting any social occasion I could—even when it was a martial arts class that I hadn't been great about showing up for in the past.

My cousin, Liam, had rented the studio where he practiced sword fighting and enlisted us to join him a few times a month. It was mostly a fun way to get the guys together.

In the few months since I'd last been able to attend, Liam had added a few new people from work—Lucas Walker and Jeremy Holme, both employees of Draco.

Though the others knew better than to be nervous around the boss, Jeremy and Lucas hadn't quite gotten that memo yet. I tried to ignore their worried-looking side-eye in the locker room and during warm up.

I was semi-tempted to cash in on the intimidation by allowing them to graciously let me win every bout—like I was some kind of medieval king whose subjects wouldn't dare challenge for real.

And then there was the only non-Draco employee and the least likely person to cut me any slack—Heath. He just happened to be matched up with me on our first bout. Liam was taking the opportunity, while we were warming up, to circulate among us and watch our progress. He was in his element—sword fighting and telling the people closest in his life what to do—his two favorite things besides art.

I wondered if he'd missed his calling and should have become a teacher, like his girlfriend. Though it took an entirely special breed of person to tolerate high school students all day long, and I doubted Liam was one of them.

"Adam, stop dropping your arm when you retreat. You're opening yourself up to him."

I gave a shrug and threw Heath a sly grin. "I was just giving the poor guy a fighting chance."

Heath laughed and rolled his eyes, but Liam, of course, failed to see the sarcasm. "Heath should be cutting you the slack, given that you've been missing classes."

"It's called running a triple-A gaming studio. The very one that writes your paychecks."

As I knew he would, Liam looked unimpressed. "I get my pay directly deposited into the bank. Now don't change the subject and stop dropping your sword arm like that."

"Yes, Sir William," I said with a military-style salute anachronistic for the Middle Ages.

Heath lunged at me like a man with a vendetta. At some points during our fraught relationship, I would never have trusted him with a sword around me. But lately, things had gone well. Our relationship always depended almost entirely on whatever was going on with Emilia. Since our wedding, it had been smooth sailing. I wondered, though, if he knew our secret news, would it send him lunging at me with that thing, point first?

He'd hit me before.

"What's going on with you, man?" Heath finally asked after he'd gotten his second not-so-light hit. Even with padded armor on, those unsharpened metal swords could pack a wallop.

I shrugged. "I'm rusty. It's been a while."

"It's more than that." He leaned his sword against his legs to readjust the Velcro straps holding his padded bracers in place. "You seem really distracted."

I shifted, readjusted my stance and gave a self-conscious look around me. "I have a lot on my mind, yeah. Just wanted to blow off some steam tonight."

Heath's brow tweaked up. "You should spar with one of the newbies, then. They are quick, fast, and young but lacking experience. Perfect for blowing off steam."

I gave a self-conscious shrug. "All right man, I see how it is. You don't want the competition." I grinned and winked.

"*Or*...I don't want to answer to my best friend about why her husband is covered in bruises and I had no real reason to put them there."

I replied with a laugh and ended up sparring with Liam—who had no such compunction about leaving me covered with bruises and having to explain it to my wife.

He shook his head repeatedly. "You're not focusing, Adam."

I sighed for what seemed like the twentieth time. "I am. You're just better at this than I am."

"I am better than you because I work out every single day, train multiple times per week and still attend coaching. But normally you fight at a higher level than this."

"You and Heath are ganging up on me." I sent him a grin.

"You and Heath are evenly matched," Liam replied evenly. "Normally. But you haven't been here in over a month."

"So yeah, I'm rusty...and okay, distracted."

"A bad combination. You're going to have bruises all over."

"So you've said." And just to express a little bit of irritation with him, I took a cheap shot and slapped the flat of my blade against his thigh. He let out a sharp grunt and glared at me. I shrugged, dancing back as he responded in kind, and thankfully, missed me. "Hey, might as well give you a few that you have to explain to Jenna."

"Oh, that's easy," Jordan said as he appeared out of virtual thin air at my shoulder. "Just tell her you got them at the BDSM club we all visited instead of nerd sword fighting practice. She'll find it sexy."

Liam glared at Jordan. "I highly doubt it."

Jordan shrugged good-naturedly and flashed a grin. "Well, it worked on April."

"Because you visiting an institution like that is much more believable than it would be for me."

Jordan turned to me. "I'm not sure, but I think I've just been insulted."

I laughed but our task master straightened, posture stiffening. Uh oh, I knew that look. Liam was losing patience. "Are you two planning to stand around and joke or are you planning to improve your skills?"

"I guess they're mutually exclusive at Sir William's school?" I shrugged.

Without replying, Liam pointed at Jordan. "You, go do the last bout against Jeremy. Adam, you're up against Lucas."

Jordan grabbed a towel and wiped his face. "I'd tear off my shirt but there are no women around here to impress. And Jeremy would probably put some real painful marks on me."

"I'm only allowing those in padded armor to spar. No room for injuries." Liam decreed before walking off.

For the last bout, I fought Lucas and, to my chagrin, I found that he'd improved a great deal when he left a throbbing welt on my thigh and then promptly dropped his sword in a near panic. "Fuck, man, I'm so sorry. Can I get you some ice?"

I took a deep breath, let it out, and walked around on the injured leg. It smarted but wasn't serious. "I'm fine."

"Can I get you a glass of water?"

"I'm okay, really. Let's get on—"

"We can grab the wooden swords off the rack instead of using the metal ones," he interrupted once more.

I stared him down while he fidgeted uneasily.

"Listen, I'm not going to fire you if you hurt me or defeat me but if you keep making me feel like I'm too old to fight you, then we're going to have words."

"As long as the words aren't *you're fired*." He sent me a sheepish grin.

I angled the tip of my sword directly at him. "Put your fucking sword up."

I ended up beating him at that bout—but only barely.

I vowed to come back more often.

I had a feeling that for the next nine months I was going to have a lot of steam to blow off, and be in need of a support system to help me through it.

And though the guys didn't know our big news right now, they soon would.

And that knowledge helped, too.

CHAPTER

TWENTY-ONE

MIA

I WASN'T SURE HOW MUCH MORE OF THIS I COULD TAKE. Given that I was only mid-first trimester, that was saying something. Because logically, I had months and months of this left to go.

To be fair, it had way less to do with my body changes and early pregnancy symptoms and a whole lot more to do with the man I shared my life with. Because—and yes, I'd been aware of this ahead of time—Adam was a lot.

A *lot.*

And expectant father Adam was just over the top extra.

For example, suddenly I was drinking disgusting green kale smoothies. He'd bought a special high-end blender and got the recipe from April.

We'd chosen not to tell anyone until the end of the first trimester—which was over a month away still, so I had nobody to rant to about any of this. Not even Heath, my usual go-to.

And the green smoothies? I'd choked the first one down when he'd made it for me and managed to keep it down—

miraculously. But it hadn't been a pleasant experience all the way around.

Since then, morning sickness had hit with a vengeance and keeping those fuckers down was not so easy. I'd been puking them up for days.

It had gotten so unpleasant so quickly that I'd started taking them in a to-go cup "to drink on the way to work." And then I'd promptly dump them down the drain upon arrival at the hospital. I didn't like doing it, but keeping my stomach calm was the top priority.

And what idiot had called it morning sickness, anyway? Mine lasted all day.

Most of the time it didn't go as far as my stomach rejecting its contents and was more just a constant queasiness. Happy times.

The only thing worse than morning sickness, though, was hiding it from my skittish partner.

Adam was barely holding it together over all this. He fussed over the organic and thrice-washed fresh ingredients he insisted on putting in the damn smoothies. Kale, pears, mango, almond milk, chia seeds, and banana. Just the thought of trying to choke yet another one down made my stomach do a flip.

Food was the last thing I wanted to put in my stomach. But dried ginger slices and soda water? Those were my friends.

Since it was common for women to lose some weight in early pregnancy, I wasn't worried. I also knew that the baby was getting the nutrients they needed from my body regardless of whether I was or not. In pregnancy mode, a woman's body prioritized the embryo first when it came to all survival needs.

Days and even weeks passed like this. I congratulated myself on my success in keeping my husband calm. But one day, when I was ten weeks along, I realized, too late, my mistake.

I'd been feeling off for a few days and, admittedly, not putting enough into my body as a result. I should have been taking an anti-emetic, for which I could easily call my obstetrician or even prescribe for myself. But even the thought of taking a pill, and having to keep it down, was unappealing. I'd been focusing on my patients and ignoring my own discomfort, trying to forget how miserable these early pregnancy symptoms were making me.

I was in the middle of my cards rotation one morning. Four of us residents and an attending physician stood in a semi-circle around the patient lying in bed. Dr. Smith, our attending, greeted the patient and, instead of opening the chart, like attendings normally do, turned to me. "Dr. Strong, fill us in on this patient, will you?"

I blinked, not expecting to be on the spot with the entire report rather than just the update. I rattled off a brief description, medical history, and current symptoms, monitor and blood panel results.

As I talked, I felt more and more lightheaded. By the time I'd finished my spiel, the attending had pulled up the chart on his tablet to quiz me.

Which annoyed me, even if I did know the answers and responded accordingly.

"Are you okay?" A fellow resident nudged me. "You look pale."

I arched a brow. "I'm fine. Just nervous." I don't have any memory of what happened next. Only that my legs suddenly gave out and I started tilting, making a grab at the rails on the patient's bed to keep upright.

But there were arms around me and the cold floor underneath me right after that.

And then, I lost consciousness.

I don't think it was long, but it was long enough for the residents to load me onto a gurney and wheel me down to the ER. They were in the middle of this trip when I came to, staring at the acoustic ceiling and glaring fluorescent lights above.

Dr. Ochoa—Maria, a fellow resident—peeked down at me from beside the gurney as the nurse's assistant guided us around the corners. "Hey, you feeling okay?"

I blinked. "Yeah, I'm fine. Are you taking me to—? I don't need to go to the ER." I put my hand on the railing as if that would stop this surreal ride.

Maria shook her head. "No can do—hospital policy. You need to be checked out before you're cleared. But I am calling typical intern-year resident fatigue on this one." She arched her brow at me. Maria, a ripe old third-year resident, spoke from her vast experience, obviously. "You aren't the first one this year to have gone down, so at least you can feel good about that."

My eyes rolled up into my head as I closed them. Even the motion of the fucking gurney was making me nauseous. But to have lost it so much that I'd passed out? That wasn't just resident fatigue, obviously. Almost certainly, it was due to low blood sugar.

And that was completely and solely my own fault. If only I'd choked down that fucking disgusting kale smoothie Adam had made me yet again this morning, maybe I wouldn't be here on the roll of shame to the ER.

Thinking back, I'd had little beyond a few crackers and some water in the last twenty-four-hour period. I'd obviously been neglecting my body's needs, so this was bound to happen sooner or later.

Stupid, stubborn me.

"We need to take your vitals. Then you need to go home for some rest. Someone called your husband to let him know. After—"

"*What?*" I nearly sat up then before the nurse's assistant gently pressed on my shoulder to lie back down. "No! Don't call my husband," I gasped.

Shit.

Once we got into an examination room, Dr. Ochoa brought in a medical scribe, Shelley, to handle my chart. And I had to spill the beans.

"I'm ten weeks pregnant."

Maria's eyes went wide like saucers. "First Bluth and now you? What is in the water?"

Aside from Adam, Maria was the very first person to know. And even though I knew I was protected under HIPAA from her revealing that info to anyone else, I had to make her swear not to breathe a word to anyone.

She shook her head, frowning. "Of course not. I promise. It's between you, me and the chart—and any attendings who might walk in here to check on you. I'm pretty sure Smith will probably be down here to see how you're doing once he's done with the morning rounds. He was really worried about you when it happened."

I blinked, suddenly awash with guilt.

I suspected that was going to be even worse once Adam got here. My poor husband. I could only imagine what was going through his mind right this very second.

Chapter Twenty-Two

ADAM

IF YOU CUT DEADPOOL EXACTLY IN HALF, WOULD YOU GET two Deadpools? Since he regenerates immediately from the largest piece of his remains, if the halves are equal, how would one half know to let the other half generate? I mean, if he was cut off at the waist, then you could assume the top half—the half with the brains—would be the natural part of him that would regenerate. But what if you cut him in half vertically? In two exactly equal halves?

Two Deadpools.

"No way, man. Adam, what do you think?" One of the devs turned to me and my brain came zooming back from thinking about a certain Marvel anti-hero to the present. Oh yeah, the meeting. We were now on our third argument of the morning and the meeting had only started ten minutes ago.

"If we do that, then we'd have to go back into the source code," Sara, replied.

Around here, we called her Sarah Connor after the heroine of the *Terminator* movies. She was every bit a badass as her namesake. And, given the way the male devs reacted to her suggestion to do more slog work, made it clear that she wasn't afraid of a few naysayers.

Someone entered the room while I leaned in to interrupt the discussion. I read off my important item notes to Jeremy, who was acting as secretary to record them on the digital scrum file while the dev next to him wrote the same tasks onto sticky notes for our giant departmental Kanban board.

"Adam?" Maggie said beside me, having quietly entered in the middle of the argument.

"Can it wait? I've got—" I turned to her and knew immediately what her reply was going to be just from the look on her face.

She shook her head quickly. "No, it's urgent."

I set my notes down. "Okay well, tell them to hold for just a few minutes. I'll be there as soon as—"

"It's the hospital. They were calling about Mia."

I bolted out of my chair, tossing my list at Jeremy. "Handle that."

Then I spun and followed Maggie out of the room while the devs stared after me, shock and concern easily readable on their faces.

Just outside, I shut the door and turned to her. "Tell me."

She was wringing her hands. The normally unflappable Maggie was, well, flapped, it seemed. "She's alright. But she passed out during morning rounds, and they took her to the ER to get checked out."

I blinked, icy cold clamping around my throat. "She passed out?"

"She's conscious now. Didn't hurt herself in the fall. I asked about that. But they want you to come get her. She's probably going to need to go home and rest."

I ran my hand through my hair, the other gripping the doorknob overly tightly. My heart hammered. "*Fuck.*"

She handed me my laptop case, keys and wallet. I, of course, already had my phone.

"I've rebooked your afternoon appointments and that one meeting with testing."

I breathed out a heavy sigh. "Thank you."

"Go take care of her. I hope she's okay."

No one knew about her condition. But once news of her fainting got out, they'd all think the worst and worry about a cancer relapse. Well, they could fucking join the club on that one.

Later, I'd have little to no memory of that drive—but I likely drove like a massive asshole up the clogged freeway. Fortunately, I didn't get stopped. I handed the keys off to the hospital valet parking as I wasn't about to fuck around with trying to find my own parking space. And I walked straight into the ER and the front triage desk.

When I got there, my voice was breathless, panicked. I had no idea what I'd find. Maggie had said they assured her Emilia was okay but that could mean so many things. "I'm Dr. Strong's husband. She's been taken into the back?"

The person nodded quickly, checked something on the computer. "Room A-3." She gestured past the door to intake.

The labyrinth of examination rooms in the ER was such that it wasn't easy to find the one I needed. After stopping and asking someone walking by, I finally found the one I wanted. I pulled aside the curtain that had been drawn across the doorway and slipped inside.

I wasn't prepared.

Emilia lay on a gurney with an IV in her arm and monitors that attached her to a computer.

Fuck.

The sight slammed me with a shockwave that was like a fist to the gut, taking me straight back to that night. The night she'd been so sick from her chemo that she'd passed out in the bathroom. Then, when I'd found her, she frantically demanded that I write down a bucket list for her. Then she passed out again. I'd fucking carried her, unconscious, across Bay Island to the waiting ambulance. That night, I was almost positive that I'd lose her. The worst fucking night of my life so far.

My pulse hammered in my throat and cruel fear dug its icy claws into my heart. I relived it all in an instant, as if it'd happened fucking yesterday.

Emilia's eyes landed on me, widened and she blinked, pushing to sit up. "Adam!"

"Lie down," I snapped too harshly. Without hesitation, she complied, frowning as I approached her.

She looked up at me, wide-eyed. "Are you okay?"

I blew out a breath, eyes darting to the IV bag hanging up on the pole above her head. "I should be asking *you* that."

She stared at me for a long moment, then she seemed to snap out of wherever her mind went as she said. "I'm fine. It was just low blood sugar."

"How is that possible? Those breakfast smoothies have plenty of—"

She sighed, eyes down like a scolded child. "I haven't been drinking them. I haven't been eating much."

I closed my eyes and rubbed at the spot in between my brows, trying to will the irritation to pass. It was illogical to be angry with her and yet, I inexplicably was. "*Why?*"

"Morning sickness. It kicked in hardcore a few weeks ago. I didn't have the heart to tell you that I started puking up the smoothies."

I swallowed. "*Weeks* ago?"

She bit her lip. "More or less."

I folded my arms across my chest. "And you're only telling me this now because...?"

She shrugged. "Because I didn't want to worry you."

I gestured to the IV bag. "Yeah, *this* is so much better. Thanks for that."

Her brows came down. "Adam, I didn't do it on purpose."

I ran a hand through my hair, rubbed the back of my neck and walked in a circle waiting for the anger to abate. It wasn't working. "You were hiding from me the fact that you were sick. Why?"

"Because I know how worried you are about all this. I didn't want to burden you any more than—"

I spun and faced her. "*Burden* me? Emilia, we are a team, this is bullshit. You can't fucking hide this from me."

She blew out a breath, eyes widening. "Adam, chill, please. Enough with the swearing and yelling. We're in a hospital—and not just any hospital, but the hospital that employs me so would you—"

I clenched my teeth and lifted a finger to point at her. When I spoke, my voice was as low as I could manage. "We'll talk about this later, then. And you'll tell me everything."

A few minutes later, her doctor came in. He addressed Emilia by her first name, leading me to assume that she'd worked with him before. "Your bloodwork is fine, but you're dehydrated. The IV had an anti-emetic along with helping you hydrate. I'm prescribing some in pill form for you—which, you know, you could have prescribed for yourself." He turned to me as if sharing some funny aside. "That took some getting used to, knowing that I could prescribe myself medication if I needed to."

I might have smiled and played along but I was in no mood, lurking in the corner of that exam room like a storm cloud, stiffly propped against the wall, arms folded over my chest.

"Mia, I've told scheduling to give you a couple days off, and no long call for a week—"

She sat up. "But—"

I stiffened and it drew her attention immediately. She was going to argue with her doctor? No way, *no fucking way.*

The guy spoke up before I could say a word, thankfully. "Doctor's orders, Mia. Don't perpetuate that old stereotype about doctors being the worst patients, okay? Once you've got the nausea under control and can keep fluids and nutrients down, you'll be back in fighting shape and ready to heal other people."

"My patients—"

"You heard your doctor," I said and flashed her a look of warning. Her mouth thinned but she didn't make any more protests.

Soon her IV was removed, and she was asked to stand if she could without feeling lightheaded. She immediately wanted to use the bathroom, and I helped her with that. Her prescriptions were sent to our pharmacy, where I'd pick them up later. She was discharged from the ER shortly thereafter but not before she was visited by at least four other doctors in the same shorter white coats of residents, and one in a long, full-length coat whom I surmised, based on their discussion, was her current attending physician.

A few hours later, I was asked to wheel her to the car and a hospital orderly accompanied us so she could return the wheelchair. Emilia mostly fiddled with her phone, and we didn't talk until she was loaded into the car.

Oh right, her car.

"Where did you park? I'll have someone come get your car."

She glanced up from her phone. "I can Uber back to work tomor—I mean whenever I come back."

I took a deep breath and let it go, fighting the rise of that heat again. "*Or*...you can tell me where you parked so it won't have to sit there for a week."

"A *week?*"

"Or whenever your obstetrician tells you it's safe to go back to work."

"My obstetrician doesn't know—"

"*Yet.* But you're calling her immediately to tell her what happened, right? And if she wants to see you, you're going in to see her."

Before backing out of my parking space, I sent a text to my driving service, asking them to stop by the house in an hour for her keys so they could fetch the car and bring it back. Emilia quietly stared out the window as I exited into a side street, heading for the freeway entrance.

Tension simmered in that car between us, but I was in no mood for an argument. I cued up a stupid podcast and we listened to it in silence. I had no idea what they were even discussing and was paying more attention to the traffic while thunderclouds coalesced into a storm inside my head.

Nothing was said until she reached up and turned down the volume. "Can we...talk about this?"

My eyes stayed glued to the road. "Not feeling too chatty at the moment."

"Why are you pissed at me?"

I let out a long sigh while I signaled to change lanes. Though it was late afternoon, the traffic going in this direction, from City of Orange toward Newport Beach, wasn't terrible this time of day. The other direction, however, was a bumper-to-bumper parking lot in the making.

"I'm not pissed at you, but I *am* frustrated with you. I need you to take better care of yourself, and I need you to not hide things from me when they aren't going well. You could have been seriously injured today."

She took a deep breath and gestured with her open hands. "It came from a place of love and concern for you, Adam. I know you, ah, have some trauma around my being ill last time. Naturally, there are going to be times during this pregnancy when I'm not doing well. I just didn't want you to—"

I shook my head, tightly gripping the wheel. "Don't you do that. Don't you put this on me. What you did was irresponsible. You repeated that mistake—from last time."

When she'd gotten sick, she'd hid it from everyone except for Heath and gone through a huge part of her treatment alone while pushing everyone else away, including her own mother. How had it not occurred to her that this would be a massive issue for me?

She paused for a long time, staring straight out the windshield. Her hands were folded tightly in her lap. "Agreed. I screwed up. I'm sorry."

I took a deep breath and let it go. That eased a little bit of the tension, but it didn't fix this. Was this how my life was going to be for the next eight months? Starting at shadows like a tasty prey animal in a jungle packed full of apex predators?

I readjusted my hold on the steering wheel the moment I realized my knuckles were aching from gripping it so hard. "I can't protect you if I don't know what's wrong. And I can't help you if you won't help yourself."

"But—"

"No, Emilia. No arguments. For fuck's sake, I—" Then I cut myself off, not wanting to go off on her again. I shook my head vigorously. "Goddamn it. I can't do this."

Her head swiveled to me abruptly. "Well, it's a little late for that, because it's happening whether you want it to or not."

I sent her a heated look out of the side of my eye. "That's not what I meant. I mean I can't do *this*..." I gestured between the two of us. "You may not like how I'm being right now. I sure as hell don't like it either, but you did some stupid fucking shit because you thought it would be easier for me, and quite frankly, you made it worse. I need you to promise to be open and honest. *And* that you're going to call your OB and tell her what happened. *And* that you aren't going to argue with your orders to stay home and rest for the next few days. *And* that you are going to take your medication and eat and drink and take good care of yourself. I need to be assured of these things—and to be able to trust you—or it's going to be a long fucking nine months for both of us. Way too long."

She was silent for a long time. I signaled to exit the toll road on our off ramp, my gut tied in knots from this entire situation—and subsequent conversation about it.

She might think I was exaggerating or blowing things out of proportion. But the truth of the matter was that the gut-freezing fear inside my chest since seeing her on that gurney hooked up to an IV and monitors hadn't thawed even now, hours later.

I made a quick stop at the pharmacy to pick up her meds and then drove to the house. Not another word was said between us until we parked. She stayed seated in the car until I came around to open it for her. She slid out of her seat and stood in front of me, then grabbed my arm when I turned to go.

Emilia pulled me into a hug, her arms slipping around my waist. "I fucked up. I'm sorry. I promise I'll tell you what's going on, even when I'm feeling shitty. I promise I'll talk to my doctor and take my meds and eat. But I need you to promise that you aren't going to hover, and you aren't going to worry or freak out."

"I'm not sure that's something I can promise."

She let out a long sigh. "Okay, well I guess we'll work on it, then."

She made no protest when I hooked an arm around her waist and pulled her close as we walked back across the island toward the house. I watched her closely. Though pale, she seemed to be walking and acting normally.

I still insisted she spend the rest of the day in bed and thankfully, she didn't argue. I brought up her dinner and we ate on trays together in bed and watched some TV. I tried to be subtle about it, but I low-key monitored every fucking bite that went into her mouth.

Was there enough protein, enough carbs, enough fiber, enough nutrients? She definitely wasn't eating like she used to, measuring every single tiny bite and waiting minutes between each one. But clearly, the anti-nausea drugs were helping because she seemed less hesitant about her food. I cursed myself for not having noticed before. We hadn't eaten many meals together in the past few weeks due to our clashing schedules, but when we had, she'd taken extremely small portions and then returned most of the plate untouched.

I hadn't even paid attention.

And if ever we had to be on the same side, it was now. I wasn't bullshitting—we were a team. So, if she'd promised to be honest to me, I had to trust that she would.

But that didn't mean I wasn't going to watch her every second that I possibly could.

She said nothing when I informed her that I'd cleared my schedule and would be working from home for the rest of the week. She said nothing when I handed her phone to her the next morning and hovered while she called her obstetrician and told her what had happened the day before.

She was easy and pliant and went along with all my demands. She even ate snacks when I brought them to her, stayed in bed for the first day when I asked her to. Everything.

Not one argument.

It was like she'd transformed into a Stepford wife. To be honest, if she'd become an android, I wouldn't have to worry about all this health bullshit.

But it ate away at me regardless.

CHAPTER
TWENTY-THREE
ADAM

AS EMILIA WAS GETTING OVER HER DEHYDRATION AND inherent weakness, I was plunging deeper into my own private dark world. One of hypervigilance over her—I had to know where she was all the time, had to keep a close eye on the amount she ate and drank. Had to make sure she was getting enough sleep—while I neglected my own.

After she fell asleep every night, I was up walking the floor of my office or running it off in the home gym until exhaustion set in.

Anything to avoid the racing, intrusive thoughts that seemed to creep into my every conscious minute where I wasn't otherwise over occupied with something.

But when they were denied residency in my conscious mind, they came out to play in the form of bad dreams. Dreams about going somewhere and forgetting all about her for days, coming home to find her unconscious or dead.

It was a dark place to be, and I was getting deep enough into it to know it soon would be hard to find my way back out again.

Which was why I decided, with Emilia's permission, to talk to my Uncle Peter about it and seek a little guidance. But asking Peter to keep this news of her impending grandmother-hood from his wife would be asking too much. So, this meant we would tell her mom and Peter earlier than we'd planned.

So, we invited them over to our house for lunch that weekend. It was a gorgeous day in late spring and chef served us personally on the picnic bench by the beach. Peter sat beside me and our wives sat directly across from us. My uncle stared at the yacht bobbing in its slip.

"When are you going to take her out again? I miss going out on the ocean and my fishing pole is getting dusty."

I glanced at my wife and then back to my uncle. "You tell me. How about you two clear a long weekend, and I'll get the captain to take you out to Catalina or down to Rosarito for the weekend?"

"Oh, that's so sweet. But it would be nicer if all four of us could go," Kim said, eyes lighting up. She'd been pushing for us all to go on a short trip together for a while but none of our schedules—or, apparently, the stars—ever aligned for it to happen.

Emilia looked noticeably green at the prospect of going out on the boat, as I knew she would. The anti-nausea meds had been helping, but she still felt delicate and even during the best of times, she wasn't super excited about going out on the yacht for long periods of time. I guess I had our honeymoon and the few days of rough seas we'd endured to thank for that.

"I don't think I'll be wanting to go out on the yacht for a while," Emilia piped up. "But you guys should definitely take him up on that."

Kim blinked. "Why not? Don't you like the yacht?"

Emilia bit her lip, then glanced at me as if seeking reassurance that this would be a good time to break the news. I nodded. Kim's eyes flitted from her daughter to me and back again, sharp as a whip, like her daughter.

"What's going on?" she finally asked.

"Well," Emilia said, adjusting her fork on the table so that it was perfectly parallel to the knife, as if she were adjusting scalpels and other medical instruments on a tray in preparation for surgery. "I haven't been feeling so great lately because—"

Kim sucked in a breath, hand going to her chest. "Oh no...*no*. I was wondering because you've been so pale. Please, don't tell me you're sick again."

It was like Kim had just cast a dark blanket over the entire table and Emilia's eyes widened. That fear wasn't far from any of our psyches and none of us had quite healed from it. My wife blinked guiltily at her mother. "I'm perfectly healthy. And I'll be feeling much better soon. Nine months, to be exact."

Peter caught on first while Kim stared at her daughter silently as if stuck in loading screen mode.

He reached over and put his hand over Emilia's. "That's wonderful! Congratulations."

Kim frowned, then blinked, then slowly the implications dawned on her. "What...?"

Peter turned back to her, laughing. "You're going to be a granny!"

Now he was slapping me on the back.

Kim glared across the table at her husband. "If you ever call me 'granny' again, it's going to get ugly." This made Peter laugh even harder.

Kim grilled us for details—due date, everything we knew about Emilia's health, whether we had informed her oncologist and gotten his okay. At one point Peter sighed heavily at Kim. "You do know you're dealing with Adam, right? I don't think there's a single stone he would have left unturned."

Kim's eyes widened. "Well, how should I know? It could have been an accident."

My wife leaned forward conspiratorially. "Adam doesn't make mistakes, Mom. You should know that by now." Emilia threw me a pleased-with-herself, teasing look. I narrowed my eyes at her, and she smirked in response.

We talked for a little while longer, but when Kim started going into detailed plans for baby clothes, the nursery and decorations, Peter threw me a look that was clearly a call for help.

"Wanna go stretch your legs with me?" I asked him.

He raised his brow. "I thought you'd never ask."

And with that, we bid goodbye to our lovely ladies, who barely noticed our departure.

We walked across the island and from the bridge onto the peninsula, crossing Balboa Boulevard toward the beachfront. As it was a beautiful day in early June, the surfers were out in full force and the sand was packed with sunbathers and clusters of families huddled under colorful Easy-Ups. I made a left turn to move down the paved Newport-Balboa bike trail eastward toward The Wedge. Bikes whizzed past us at a regular rate.

Peter seemed to sense the inner turmoil I was experiencing along with the happy situation because he cut straight to the chase. "So, how's it going? Are you still sane in there or have you overthought all this about seven million ways to Sunday?"

My uncle knew me well.

I stuffed my hands in my pockets and glanced at him. "Well...yes to all of that. I've overthought and rethought every angle but not necessarily for the reasons you're suspecting."

Peter tilted his head, giving me a questioning glance without saying a word. I took a deep breath and continued. "Last week we had an...incident." He nodded, remaining silent. Honestly, Peter was the best listener. "She got really sick. Fainted on the job because of low blood sugar and she'd been hiding her extreme nausea from me for weeks."

He blinked, mouth thinning. "Hmm. That's not good, especially her feeling the need to hide things from you. I'm sure it took you right back to when she was fighting cancer."

I let out a long breath. "Exactly. I'm just—" I cut myself off, shaking my head. My hands, inside my pockets balled into fists.

Peter put a hand on my arm. "Adam, take a breath. It's not happening again. I'm sure you talked to her."

"More like I yelled at her."

He nodded again. "Understandable."

I shook my head. "Understandable, yes, but not acceptable."

Peter laughed. "Every couple yells at each other once in a while. No one's perfect. And Mia's a quick learner. I'm sure she understood, when pointed out to her, that she was repeating the same pattern as before. She won't repeat her mistake."

"I mean...I understand where it comes from. She feels like she has to protect everyone at the expense of herself and her own health, but that runs exactly contrary to my needs—protecting her and keeping her safe. If she won't let me in, I can't do that. And I gotta say, it's two strikes now."

He blew out a breath. "But this isn't a ball game. You've got a trust issue, true. Do you feel like this is going to lead to something serious, like a marital breakdown?"

I shook my head vigorously. "No, no. I mean, not this direct issue. But if I don't trust her, well, it worries me."

Peter shrugged. "I'm happy to give you my advice, for all that's worth. But honestly, I think at this point, you might consider talking to a professional."

I took a breath, turned my head to gaze out at the rolling waves slamming against the shore and dissolving into white foam, bringing body surfers and swimmers along with them. A breeze kicked up scented with coconut suntan lotion, salty air and pungent, drying seaweed. I'd been afraid he'd suggest therapy. Quite frankly, that thought had crossed my mind, too.

Clearly, I was still harboring some issues from before. And, honestly, given my past, there was a whole heaping mess of issues buried deep in there. Was I ready to confront all that? My shoulders slumped.

"It's not that bad, Adam. I saw someone for a couple years after my divorce. It helped. I honestly recommend it."

I gave my uncle a long look. "Am I broken, Peter?"

Without hesitation, he laughed. "You're the strongest man I know. But everyone, even the strongest, sometimes needs to offload some of their burden—and work on themselves as a person. Not only are you dealing with the past, but you're also facing a massive life change. I can't understate how enormous this coming bend in the road will be for you two."

I nodded. "Yeah, I worry about that too."

"What are you worried about?"

I shrugged. "I wonder if I'll even be a decent dad. I had no example of what that even meant during the first twelve years of my life until I moved in with you and the cousins. And the one parental example I did have...well, you know how wonderfully that went."

Peter's face clouded for a moment as if he was remembering something from that time, maybe even about my parents, that he was debating sharing with me. Instead of pushing him on it, I followed his example and waited. It was weird, really, to have this kind of conversation with Peter but a bit of a relief, too.

He took a deep breath, and I looked straight ahead. "You're miles ahead of them, Adam. And you shouldn't let them haunt you. Your dad..." he cut himself off and squared his shoulders. I could always tell that talking about my dad brought up emotions for Peter. As brothers, they were close. I'd picked that up, too.

Peter continued, "He was the best man I know. But your parents' marriage was failing well before it even started and I know that's on your mind, too. You and Mia have been through the gauntlet, really. You've already faced things most married couples never have to face—and you've come through brilliantly. I couldn't even dream up a fictional woman better suited to you than Mia is."

He sent me a reassuring smile and when I nodded for him to continue, he did without hesitation. "The key to bringing a new life into the world, what makes it so much easier to do, is the foundation of a good partnership with the co-parent. They don't have to be married, or even together romantically. I've seen divorced couples and never-married parents alike put aside their differences to be amazing parents to their shared kids. But clear communication is the key. And this burden isn't all on you. But talking to someone, learning strategies on how to deal with—and in some cases—educate your partner for what you need will go a long way in helping you tackle these challenges."

We walked on for a few yards. Then he cleared his throat and spoke again. "Your present isn't doomed by your past, Adam. What happened between your parents isn't even a part of your story. That was their story and quite frankly, it was a tragic one for all of you involved. But that doesn't have to define your future. I once heard someone say that almost every person has two parent-child relationships in their lives—the one we have as a child with our parents, which is the one we have much less control over. And the one we have, as an adult, as the parent with our children, which we have so much more control over. You can think of this as your do-over and with a little help, some conscious effort and support, I think you're going to knock fatherhood out of the park as well—or better—than you've met every other challenge in your life."

I blinked, absorbing that.

Not long later, we turned around and walked back to the house, mostly in silence, stewing in our own thoughts. We spent a few more minutes chatting with the ladies and then said goodbye. Peter gave me a long hug, slapped my back and said, quietly. "You've got this, Adam."

I only wished to feel as confident in myself as he seemed to be in me. But he had given me a lot to consider. And I intended to do just that.

Chapter Twenty-Four
Mia

WEEKS PASSED, AND IT SEEMED LIKE EVERY DAY brought some weird change to my body. I started to develop a baby bump, though only if I was looking closely in the mirror while in my underwear. In addition, my breasts had started to feel sore, which made for awkward bear hugs.

The nausea stayed mostly under control, though sometimes felt a little like permanent seasickness. However, I managed to keep food down. My husband side-eyed every single thing I put in my body in his presence, and I could all but hear the clicks and whirs of his mental calculator as he computed every last calorie I ate. He'd even ask me about it in the evenings—what I'd eaten for breakfast, what I'd eaten for lunch—did I have any snacks? I humored him because I felt guilty for the scare I'd put him through.

The PTSD was obvious. I could sense his underlying anxiety getting bigger by the day. So I played along, giving him the reassurance he so obviously needed. He consumed books like crazy. *What to Expect. What to Expect when She's Expecting. The*

Pregnancy Encyclopedia, Handbook, Wiki, Ultimate Database for the Anal-Retentive Control-Freak Husband. How to Be an Authoritarian Taskmaster When Your Wife is Carrying your Unborn Child. I may have made some of those up.

Instead of getting short with him or expressing outright exasperation, I decided, instead, to have a little fun with it.

I made up shit for him to do. For example, I made him talk to my tummy every single night for thirty minutes and if he didn't want to talk that long, then he could do ten minutes of singing. When I proposed it, he gave me one of his looks.

I raised my brows at him, folding my arms over my chest. "Dude, if I'm going to jump through all those hoops for you, then I need you to do some things for me. Our son or daughter needs to hear from their father."

His brows furrowed. "But they don't even have ears yet. I read in that fetal development book that—"

I held up a hand, raising my brows. "Vibrations. The *vibrations* of your voice. There've been scientific studies done about this." I gave him the sternest look I could manage, trying hard not to crack up at his obvious irritation.

Like a trooper, he finally complied. The first night, he started talking about a bunch of stuff that I was almost certain was bullshit, but it was hard to tell because I could barely understand it.

But I loved the way his large hand spread over the slight curve of my abdomen as he talked. "The first step is conceptualization, where you define the purpose and establish themes. Then you have to introduce gameplay mechanics and challenges that align with the quest's theme and objectives. Things like combat encounters, stealth segments, dialogue puzzles, or platforming sequences. But it's always necessary to establish a balance of difficulty, because—"

I sighed. "I think it's going to be a while before the baby can follow in daddy's footsteps."

He shot me a sly grin. "It's never too soon to start the indoctrination."

"And what if the baby wants to follow *my* footsteps and go into healthcare?"

He shook his head. "Not a chance. They've got to support us in our old age in the style in which we've become accustomed. Doctors don't make enough for that."

I smacked his arm. "Very funny."

Mischief gleamed in his dark eyes as he adjusted his hand on my belly. Then, he dipped his head to land a kiss there and started talking to the bump again. "One last thing—I'm about to do some naughty things to your mom, so please cover your eyes. You're too young for that."

All he had to say was *naughty things*, and everything inside me lit up like Clark Griswold's house in *National Lampoon's Christmas Vacation*. We hadn't done much of anything in the bedroom for over three weeks—since even before the incident at the hospital, as I hadn't been feeling well then. And he'd never even approached the subject since the infamous incident. I'd made a move on him once I started feeling better, but he'd politely rebuffed me.

But tonight, it was clear that this extremely sexy daddy-to-be needed some stress release and I was down for a little release of my own.

Just as he moved to lay beside me and pull me to him, however, I started snickering at that thought—mid kiss, even. He pulled back and gave me a questioning look. "Am I somehow tickling you by osmosis?"

"No, no." I smiled, then laughed again. "I'm just thinking about how hot a DILF you are."

"No...no, we're not going there unless you want me calling you a MILF."

"As long as I'm the Momma *you'd* like to fuck, I'm down with that."

"Oh, you are right now, *very much.*"

He hadn't lost his touch—my panties were whisked off me in seconds flat. Adam kissed me deeply on the lips before pulling away and working his way down my body, avoiding my too-sensitive breasts without me even having to remind him that they were still sore. Nope, he bypassed that area completely to work his way quickly south, tracing the meridians of my body with his soft, determined lips.

And with sighs of pleasure and anticipation, I relaxed in his arms.

Adam's mouth traveled down to the apex of my thighs, his lips softly encircling my clit as my back arched and my toes curled. It had been a while since I'd felt sexy and having this much attention lavished on me quickly had me gasping and climbing my way to release.

"Don't. Stop," I gasped. And though he could have teased me by stopping, he didn't. His moves were urgent, resolute. Undeterred from his goal which had me clenching my thighs around his head, screaming his name when I came. Brain officially fried.

By the time I was able to catch my breath and became aware of the world around me again, he was lying beside me once more.

"Fuck, that was...amazing." I blinked, still seeing colors I had no names for like fireworks behind my eyeballs. My body felt lax, soft and wrapped in a deep, warm glow.

"It's been too long, hasn't it?"

I reached over and palmed his straining erection. "It definitely has. I think we should make up for lost time."

He sucked in a breath as I confidently wrapped my fingers around his length and slid them down his cock. "I'm greedy though. That was an amazing orgasm, but I need some D."

"Some D?"

"Yeah, D as in dessert. As in do me, baby."

He rolled onto his side and pulled me against him, his mouth enveloping mine. "Your wish is my command."

We kissed for long moments while I hooked a leg over his hip and pulled him to roll onto me. He came quickly, willingly, but hesitated right after, as if realizing what was happening.

"Is it...?"

I laughed. "It's okay. It's more than okay. It's what this doctor ordered."

He grinned wickedly. "Time to fill your prescription, then."

"Oh man, fill me. Definitely fill me."

He snickered as he rolled onto me and settled his hips between my legs. Without another word, he slid into me, and I locked my legs around his hips. He brought his face back to mine and we lay like that for long moments, bodies and arms locked together, staring into each other's eyes.

Those dark eyes had the ember of arousal and a hunger deep inside of them that sent my anticipation soaring. My greedy, greedy body wanted more, and I was here for it.

"You are so fucking beautiful," he whispered with a hushed awe, like a priest at the altar, deep in prayer.

My eyes fluttered closed and I couldn't imagine any moment between us more perfect than this one. We'd collected so many perfect moments throughout our years together.

I was so fucking lucky.

Then he started to move and my eyes rolled back in my head and my body swayed in time with his, making music together all our own.

His movements were slow, gentle and his mouth opened to lock around mine, his tongue slowly sliding in and out of my mouth in time with the rest of his body. He took his time and though tonight I was wound up and craving a quick, hard pounding, I didn't pressure him to change pace.

It occurred to me that he was probably holding back, probably forcing himself to be extra gentle because of the baby, or my recent illness, or some other reason that was purely Adam. But I was here to enjoy this, enjoy him. His hands, his mouth, his cock sliding inside of me as his breath hitched and tightened.

Despite his care to go slow, it didn't take much time for us to climax, since it had been a while. When he stilled, hovering over me and holding his full weight on his elbows, eyes squeezed tight, I hooked my arms around his neck and arched into him, feeling the rush and contractions of my own orgasm topple over the edge of his own ecstasy.

When he finally sucked in another breath, his skin was coated with sweat and stuck to mine in a way that I relished.

Gently he eased himself off of me and pulled me against him. He kissed my temple.

"Damned hottest MILF I'll ever want to fuck. Lucky me."

CHAPTER
TWENTY-FIVE
ADAM

As WE PREPARED FOR EMILIA TO RETURN TO WORK, I was slowly gaining confidence that she was being honest with me. But I wasn't all there yet and had to remind myself not to be a dick to her when my anxiety spiked. I took that as my cue to start some online research, make a few phone calls, and set an appointment. I was a little too self-conscious to let my assistant in on the fact that I'd be seeing a mental health professional. And while I was unsure of which way things might go, I was also simultaneously hopeful that this might be a good thing for me—and for us.

And, if I was being honest, my heart harbored no small amount of doubt that this was going to help the fucked-up feelings, the dark, icy fear that now resided deep in my gut twenty-four-seven.

I found a therapist who looked promising. A woman whose office wasn't far from mine in Irvine. I bit back my own fear and forced myself to make the appointment. Then I had to come up with something not-embarrassing to pencil into my calendar to block off the time so Maggie wouldn't double-book me by accident. That took some thinking, but I finally settled on TR, which stood for Temporal Reduction, a fancy way of saying head shrinking. I'd have to switch it up every month or so, maybe juggling lessons next?

And it was about as weird as I was expecting. At least at first.

Her office was upscale and streamlined, all white and glass and chrome. And thankfully, she didn't have the cliched therapist couch.

"Mr. Drake, great to meet you, come in and sit down." I chose the white armchair facing her, thankful that it was more comfortable than it looked.

The therapist was kind and professional—about Kim's age, I'd guess, with close-cropped copper-colored hair and a tiny frame. I'd be surprised if she stood much taller than five foot even.

"I'd prefer you call me Kendra. My pronouns are she/her. And how would you like me to call you?"

I cleared my throat, fidgeted a moment, and returned her gaze. "Adam's fine. He/him."

The first part of the appointment was a standard questionnaire where I replied to her rapid-fire questions with clipped, concise answers.

Then came the point where I was on the spot.

"So why have you decided to pursue psychotherapy, if there is a specific reason?"

Ugh. Not twenty minutes into this and I was inwardly cringing and regretting my decision already.

I blinked, taking far too long to answer the question as I shifted in my seat.

She seemed to sense my unease but gave me the time to formulate my reply regardless.

"I'm facing a bunch of massive changes in my life...in the process of them, really. And I just need to get rid of these dark feelings going on inside. I don't even know if that's something you can help with."

Her mouth quirked up at the corner and she tilted her head. And then she nodded. "Yes, yes, that's exactly what I can do."

I left the office more assured. Yeah, it had only been an intake appointment where she'd asked me a lot of questions and took a lot of notes. But I felt like I could work with this person.

The next challenge would be keeping this a secret for now, even from Emilia. I felt mildly hypocritical about that. Especially since I'd berated her for withholding her morning sickness from me. But despite coming out of this initial appointment feeling generally positive about this course of action, I didn't want to get Emilia's—or anyone else's—hopes up in case I ultimately failed.

And in the same vein of self-improvement, we enrolled in parenting classes. Because our schedules were so crazy busy, we'd opted for online courses with consultation from an on-site personal parenting coach at different stages throughout the course.

And as usual, we turned working through that course material into a game between us, competing against each other based on our progress through the modules or our automated quiz scores to check comprehension.

And when the course material—like the videos—got boring, we opted to do those together, sometimes heckling the video presentations *Mystery Science Theater 3000*-style.

The other big project at hand was the question of the house, and I'd done the majority of the footwork on that. Connecting with the realtor Dom had recommended, I looked into the canyon communities that Dom had suggested, reading up on this idyllic-sounding Canyon Hollow place. From its description, it seemed like a tiny quaint hamlet, an island surrounded by the rushing sea of some of the densest suburbs in the country.

Well, we could start looking there, and if Emilia hated it, we'd turn our search to other areas of the county.

Our first approach looked promising, after exiting the freeway and taking the long road that narrowed down into a two-lane highway. The not-quite-rugged Santa Ana Mountains grew on the horizon as the road followed the land, snaking around old growth groves of California Live Oaks which arched elegantly over the road. They created a dim, green corridor all around.

It felt like traveling to another world, really. One that was close enough to commute to work. "It's beautiful," Emilia breathed. "I don't think I've ever been back here."

The road curved up again briefly before dipping back down and we caught an uninterrupted glimpse of the iconic twin peaks of Saddleback Ridge, a prominent landmark that towered over inland Orange County on clear days. The drive itself was relaxing—a scenic stretch of hills and valleys and wooded areas tucked into giant pockets of undeveloped backcountry that made up the eastern edge of the county.

Canyon Hollow was a community adjacent to the Silverado and Black Star canyons and not far from neighboring Modjeska and Trabuco, named by Spanish explorers who made their way through these parts hundreds of years ago.

Meeting us at the mouth of the canyon and escorting us in, our realtor gave us a rundown of recent and local history of the tiny communities. We drove by hodgepodge and mismatched homes, some mostly hidden behind high hedges, others littered with eclectic and unusual yard décor and nonfunctioning automobiles.

There were giant, gorgeous new homes near tiny dwellings that looked like they were once weekend cabins built during the turn of the century. They were all over the place.

Our realtor had four homes to show us, and while I could see, with some work, any of them working, Emilia did not care for them at all.

"I have one more place. It's tucked up right against the Cleveland National Forest. The property needs some TLC, but we can swing by if you're interested in having a look."

We glanced at each other. "Why not?"

The mail carrier, a middle-aged, stocky man was just finishing putting mail in the neighbor's box when we got out of the car. He turned to us with a wide smile.

"Hello there," he grinned widely.

We replied with a smile and a wave and that was enough for him to walk over and start a chat with us. He knew the realtor already. "Hey, Alan. You catch that latest picture? A stunner, isn't it?"

"Oh hey, Miguel. How are you doing today?"

"Pillars of Creation—better than Hubble's shot from '95, of course. Incredible." Our realtor, Alan, seemed to want to herd us away from the mail carrier but before he could, the amiable-seeming mailman turned to us. "You two follow the James Webb telescope images?" He shook his head. "They caught one in the Eagle nebula 6,500 light years away. Stunning photo."

Alan threw us each a sheepish glance. "Miguel is our letter carrier, and he's also an amateur astronomer up at the observatory."

I quirked a brow, suddenly interested. "There's an observatory?"

"It's actually not far—up the hill from the wildlife sanctuary. This property butts up against the sanctuary, just across Saddleback creek."

"We don't get many dark skies out here anymore, with civilization encroaching," Miguel added.

Observatory. Wildlife sanctuary. Creek adjacent to the property. Quirky local populace. I was liking this place more and more. I threw Emilia a sideways glance. If she didn't like any of these existing houses, maybe we could purchase some property and have one built.

But that would take time, and the baby was going to be here in less than half a year.

But it took just one look at the house—which had been vacant for a few years—to realize that the property was unique.

"It's going to take some work to fix up. And update." I said looking around and sending a glance at Emilia. It was once a lovely home, large, built in the 1920s with beautiful details and built-ins. But it had been neglected and the fixtures were old.

But the property it sat on was where it truly shone. It was nearly two acres of wooded clearing bordered on one side by the creek far below—and just far enough away that there was no concern for flooding.

We toured a part of the property and stood at an overlook above the slow-moving creek. "Kinda small, even for a creek," I remarked.

"It's southern California, and this is dry coastal chaparral climate. The creek is just a trickle now, but the winter and spring weather makes it a respectable body of water."

"It sounds relaxing just standing here listening to it," Emilia said in a quiet voice. She seemed affected. Could this be the right place for us?

What clinched it, however, was when, just as the sky was darkening and the sun had sunk below the high canyon walls. Alan hushed us suddenly and said in a quiet voice. "Look up but don't make any sudden movements."

And just across the creek, near the base of the steep canyon wall, a mother deer and two fawns grazed peacefully in the brush, paying us no attention at all. Wow.

Emilia looked at me and I saw it, then. It was cinched—this was the place, as far as she was concerned.

We wrapped things up shortly after that and I told him I'd be in touch.

But within twenty-four hours, we submitted an offer on the house.

My next calls were to a contractor that Jordan knew and trusted whom I hired to do the home inspection and start the process of the renovation. We hired a decorator, too.

Soon, we'd be leaving the beach to become canyon dwellers, and I was here for it. Because, as some famous dead philosopher once said, the only constant in life was change. And when the Drakes did change, they did it in a big way.

CHAPTER TWENTY-SIX
MIA

WHO WOULD HAVE THOUGHT THE FUN NEVER STOPS when sitting in a frigid examination room wearing nothing but a paper gown that opens in the front. Those oh-so-wonderful chrome stirrups gleamed at me mockingly from the end of the exam table. Ugh.

It was moments like these, when I was forced to be a patient, that I took the opportunity to mentally record for myself. As a physician, it was so easy to forget that the patient on the exam table was a person with fears, anxieties and general discomfort with all things paper-gown and metal stirrup, for example. These were the moments I needed to force myself to be present, to remember and internalize in order to become a better doctor.

Instead, I was being forced to listen to the nervous chatter of my husband while his leg bobbed up and down at a million miles a minute. If I asked him why he was nervous, he'd staunchly deny any sort of discomfort or anxiety. So instead, I humored him, which definitely wasn't conducive to living in the moment.

"What do you think of the name Ada?" he asked.

I pulled my gaze from the holes in the off-white ceiling tiles to look at him. "Name for what? A new character in Dragon Epoch?"

His dark brows twitched together. "No. For the baby, if she's a girl."

I wrinkled my brow at him. "Where the hell did you get Ada from? Did you just take the M off your name, so she'd be named after you?"

He brightened at the thought. "Actually, I hadn't considered that angle but that makes it even more of a plus. The idea is actually because of Ada Lovelace. She lived in the nineteenth century and was considered a key figure in modern programming. The government named a programming language and there's even hardware named after her."

I raised my brows. "And now…our baby, if you get your way?"

"Ada Drake. It sounds nice, doesn't it?"

I laughed, amazed he couldn't hear it. "Everyone's going to think you just wanted the feminine form of your name and named her after you. So what do you want a boy to be, Adam Drake Jr.? If I decide to give the poor kid a middle name, he wouldn't be a junior, right?"

He shook his head vigorously. "Nope, no junior. I went to school with a kid who was a junior—and people called him junior instead of his actual name. He was a total asshole."

I sighed, turning my attention to the settings on the ultrasound machine. This early in the game, I'd have to have a transvaginal ultrasound, which included the dreaded wand. I wasn't the biggest fan of that.

"How does this contraption work, anyway? Sound waves?" he asked.

"Ultrasound waves." I pointed at the wand. "This is a transducer. It sends out a beam of sound through the body. They are totally harmless, which makes this process much safer than an X-ray. The sound waves bounce off or move through the body, depending on whether it's going through soft tissue or bone. So the echo—"

"What about Grace?" he cut in.

I heaved a sigh. "Adam, you aren't listening. You asked me a question and I was trying to explain how this whole process works. It's really quite fascinating what you can see using this technology."

But he wasn't listening. "She's another programmer. Grace Hopper."

"Well, I guess Ada and Grace are better than something like Padme or Mon Mothma."

He quirked a dark brow at me. "Well, I'm going to resort to Star Wars names after I've exhausted possible programmers."

"Resort right on to something else."

"No Leia?" He looked at me doubtfully. "Okay, what about Galadriel? That's a lovely, elegant name for a powerful, kickass woman."

I sighed. "I don't think her ears will be pointy enough for that name. Besides, Galadriel Drake sounds like, I dunno, a dragon hunter or something." I stared at the door. "Damn, I have to pee. When is she coming in?"

"I'll wait here, go use the bathroom. It's right next—"

I shook my head. "No for the external ultrasound, I need to have a full bladder."

He gave me a look. "Do I want to know why?"

I laughed. "No, it's just anatomical stuff. It puts my organs in the right position—"

At that moment, thank goodness, my obstetrician, Dr. Weir, showed up, greeted us with smiles and made a little small talk. Once she had the transponder on my stomach and got measurements, I was finally able to use the bathroom before moving to the next step in the process.

This part, I knew, would be more interesting for Adam. And sure enough, not ten seconds after the transponder was in place, the familiar whoosh whoosh whoosh of a fetal heartbeat resounded on the speakers.

"So Mia, do you want to show Adam?"

My husband blinked, then stared at the screen, obviously completely at a loss for what he was looking at. Which was understandable, because to the non-initiated, ultrasound imaging must resemble the constantly scrolling green code in *The Matrix*. But in this case, I was Neo. I put my finger just below the slight flutter inside the dark circle. "This is the fetal pole on the embryo and see that little flickering motion right there? That's the heart. The tissue starts that flickering motion, emulating a heartbeat, at five to six weeks."

Adam leaned in, squinting. "Yeah, I see it. That's so cool."

"The tissue starts pumping like that very early on."

He blinked, tilted his head and blinked again. Then, without a word, pulled out his phone. "Can I get a video?"

Dr. Weir intervened. "Oh, I can send you a video clip. We don't normally do that but Mia's in the business so I can make an exception. I'll just pull your email address off your chart and send you a snippet."

I smiled at her. "Thank you. That's very kind."

She grinned. "No problem." Then she turned to Adam. "And I have to tell you that my daughters love your game. In fact, they love it a little too much. The youngest had to have her gaming time restricted because her grades were starting to tank."

Adam gave her a sheepish look. "Sorry but...not sorry?"

She laughed. "Somehow I knew you were going to say that."

I raised my brows. "But she's okay now? She managed to pull her grades up?"

Dr. Weir nodded. "Oh yeah, yeah. Everything's just fine now."

Adam said, "Well maybe when she's on a school break, you could bring them down to the campus and we'll do a tour, if that interests them."

She laughed again. "Are you kidding? I think they'd flip out."

"Maybe put it out there as an incentive for her to get her grades up," I said.

The doctor considered and nodded. "That's a really good idea. I have a feeling you're going to be a natural at this mothering thing, Mia. Already thinking like a mom."

When I looked back at Adam, he seemed distracted, as if he wasn't paying attention to what we were saying. On closer inspection, he appeared pale. But he seemed to bounce back quickly and by the time we were alone in the car, he was his old self again.

I sent him a stealthy look under my lashes and tried to make the inquiry as casual sounding and off the cuff as I could. "Everything okay? You seemed a little, um, distracted there at the end."

He pressed the button to start the car. "Hmm? Yeah, just thinking about all the stuff we need to do before the happy event.

Making a mental list, you know. The stuff to get, the classes to schedule, writing up the birth plan—"

I put a hand over his. "Adam, don't put the cart before the horse. We have many months left. We're good."

"Yeah, about that. Why does everyone think that a pregnancy is only nine months long when it's actually forty weeks?"

I laughed. "Well forty weeks if you're counting those first two weeks where a woman isn't actually pregnant. I guess we stick with tradition—even if it's based on bad math. Or maybe women didn't like the idea of calling 40 weeks 10 months. I'm sure I'll be wanting it over and done by the end, just like everyone else."

"Maybe it's just another one of the great medical lies we've been fed all these years," he teased, as he was so fond of doing, knowing how much that medical conspiracy stuff got my back up.

I arched a brow at him. "Listen—" And when he snickered it only made me more annoyed. "Fine, you join the medical conspiracy camp. I'll sign up for the flat earth society."

CHAPTER
TWENTY-SEVEN
MIA

AFTER OUR FIRST CHECKUP AND THE ULTRASOUND, Adam and I decided that it was safe to start telling our friends. I started with Heath, of course, for so many reasons. First, the excuse to hang out, since our schedules didn't allow that often these days. And also because if ever a person, besides my husband, had been through it with me, Heath had. In the true definition of "ride or die" friend, he had won the first-place ribbon. We met up for frozen yogurt on a day where I had a few hours to spare, still technically on call but unlikely to be called in.

"So, what's new with you these days?" he asked after I'd listened to him complain about a client he was currently working with and, in turn, he'd sat through my bitching about the long hours at my work.

"Well..." I arched my brow and plunged my plastic spoon into the salted caramel frozen yogurt, stirring vigorously. "I do have some news."

"Hmm? You finally decided to leave that bum and make a new start in life?" he smirked.

I rolled my eyes. "You love him almost as much as I do, so I don't buy it. And anyway, you have more reason to love him because he's the soon-to-be father of your nephew or niece."

Heath stared at me blankly, blinking. I could all but see the gears turning in his head as he tried to puzzle that out.

I bit my lip. "What I mean is...*you* are going to be an uncle. Since you're my brother from another mother." I waited patiently for it to sink in.

After one more awkward second of him staring and blinking, he finally blurted, "I'm going to be an uncle!" He popped up out of his seat and moved over to squeeze me into the tightest bearhug—more powerful than words for conveying his excitement, that hug.

I couldn't help but laugh, unfettered joy fizzing in my chest on warm, feel-good bubbles. "That is literally what I just said. You're just repeating me."

"Oh man, this is awesome." He finally let me go and moved back to his seat and his quickly melting yogurt. Nevertheless, he ignored it and just stared at me.

"Uncle Heath—has a nice ring to it, doesn't it?" I beamed at him.

He smiled. "It sounds amazing to me. So what do you want? A boy or a girl?"

I frowned and stirred my yogurt that was growing softer by the moment. "I have no idea, actually. I think either would be fun."

His blond brows bobbed. "Or equally as tough, depending on your glass is half full, half empty status." He grimaced. "Sorry."

I smiled. "No I get it. It's definitely not going to be easy."

"So how are you going to pull off a whole pregnancy while trying to become a doctor?"

"Well, technically speaking, I already am a doctor. But the residency is so I can get my license to practice medicine. It's doable but, admittedly, also tricky."

He gave me a reassuring smile. "You're the queen of doing hard things, Mia. In fact, I'm convinced you do better when things start out tricky."

"Uncle Heath is so wise."

"Yes, that's perfect. I've always wanted to be the wise uncle. So we'll have to indoctrinate the kid that Uncle Heath is the wise one."

"The wise, eccentric uncle."

His eyes narrowed and he shook his head. "Eccentric will be William's angle. I'll be the fun uncle."

"The fun uncle, huh?" I arched a brow. "The *Funcle?*"

He belted out a laugh. "Yeah, that's my official title now. Funcle Heath."

I returned that wide grin, absolutely confident that he was not only up to filling the role, but he was excited about it. And the biggest relief? Not a single bit of expressed worry about my health.

That was refreshing.

After I'd returned to work, things proceeded as if my little episode had never happened—aside from a few colleagues asking if I was feeling better. Enough intern-year residents had neglected their own sleep and eating schedules to not make my particular struggle something to stand out. Thank goodness, my condition was still safely secret at work. Louisa was still out on maternity leave and the two doctors who had treated me during my episode weren't about to violate HIPAA to spill the news.

Thanks to the anti-nausea medicine I was mostly back to my old self—if my old self got tired easier and had to go pee a lot more. But my secret being safe didn't mean I was safe from his assholeness, Dr. Craig Iverson, senior resident.

I didn't actually cross paths with him until my third day back—the day of my first long call of the week. It was early in the shift, and I had twenty-eight hours to go.

I was at the nurse's station looking over a chart before dipping into a room to check on a patient. He pulled up right beside me, setting his own tablet down to enter some notes into it.

Without looking up he said. "I trust we're feeling better?"

"Yep," I said shortly as I scrolled down to check the latest set of vitals. I knew the patient was going to again push me to discharge her, so it was important to know what her latest panels read.

"Yeah, it was all over the floor that day. When I came in that night for long call, people were still talking about it."

I studied the blood panels—there were still a few fields outside the normal range, but in general, showed positive improvement. I'd have to consult with my attending regarding when this patient could be discharged but things were looking good for tomorrow morning.

He was *still* talking. "Gonna be a long road, you know, if you faint at the sight of blood."

My eyelids fluttered. What an asshole. "Oh, it's not so bad," I shot back. "I can always become a radiologist instead and read x-rays all day."

With that, I scooped up my tablet and without another word to him, I pivoted and crossed the hall into my patient's room to get on with the day. I was officially done with that dickwad and his bullshit. And his little comment was going in my little file of documentation as soon as I had a moment to do it.

My next opportunity to tell a friend our exciting news came a few days later.

April walked to my house and we set up our laptops and notebooks on the table in the covered patio area overlooking the Back Bay, bustling with activity. Duffy boats and sailboats motored by, people called out to each other between the shore and the boats. It wasn't the quietest place to live, and I was starting to anticipate the quiet and calm of the surrounding canyon at our new house.

Adam and I had visited a few times over the past month, walking the floors, speculating on décor, and trying out paint swatches on the wall. I'd also had a meeting there with the interior decorator and she'd helped me choose color schemes.

Due to my time limits, she was going to run with my styles and preferences as I continued to pin pictures to a shared board to give her ideas. Which suited me just fine because moving and redecorating was extremely time consuming.

It was two in the afternoon, but April let out a long sigh as she spread out her paperwork, all ready for us to work on the company vision and mission statement. "Is it too early to pop open a bottle of wine? I mean, I know we're doing business but...it's been a *week*."

I served her a glass from the bottle we had open in the fridge and fixed myself a glass of soda water with a twist of lime. When

I came back to the table, April's brows knit as she took in my drink. "So, I'm drinking wine all by myself at two o'clock?"

I laughed. "Don't worry, I'm not judging you. I'm just not going to join you, though I've had a week too and I'd love to join in."

She blinked. "What gives? Are you on call tonight?"

"No, I have the next three days off, actually and I can't wait to sleep in late every day and binge watch at least two seasons of *Ted Lasso*."

"Oh, okay." She hesitantly reached for her glass. Just before she was to sip it, she squinted up at me over the rim. "Either you're aware of some recent and obscure medical research that labels wine as deadly or you're pregnant. Which one is it?"

My eyes widened in shock.

She seemed amused by my reaction, studying me closely with a head tilted to the side. "I've actually suspected for a while now. You looked pale and sickly the last few times I saw you. But it could have also just been due to sleep deprivation from your highly demanding job. But you definitely weren't acting your normal self, so I pegged pregnancy as a high possibility."

I tilted a brow up. "Well, then you've just spoiled my quiet humble-but-with-gratitude announcement."

She clapped her hands together, grin widening. "Oh, I'm so happy for you two." She popped up and came around the table to give me a hug. "Congratulations! When?"

"December twenty-fifth."

She burst out laughing.

"I know, I know. Worst day of the year to have a baby."

"I feel sorrier for the kid than I do you, though. What a shitty birthday."

"I was thinking maybe we could celebrate his or her half-birthday on June twenty-fifth or something."

"Well, whenever they happen to be born, this is going to be one lucky kid. And with yours and Adam's genes mixed together in one human, gorgeous as fuck, too."

I pretended to preen, batting my eyes. "Why thank you." We both laughed and I answered a few more questions about details until we decided we needed to get down to why we were there— our business venture. And the deeper we waded into the necessary paperwork and vision and mission drafting, the more grateful I was that April was in this with me.

"This is going to be amazing." She looked up from her screen once we'd finalized the vision statement. "A clinic especially for women and children of lower income."

"I've been thinking, what with the tendency currently in our country to limit women's reproductive rights, would it be possible to create a safe haven for women in states where their rights are limited or even nonexistent?"

April smiled sadly. "We are fortunate to live in a state that will never restrict those rights." She shook her head. "It makes me angry and also a little hopeless that not every woman in our country is guaranteed that."

I nodded. "Me too. And to think that those state governments are making illegal threats to arrest a woman who travels out of state in pursuit of her own reproductive rights. And some are dying from not getting essential medical treatment. So I was thinking, maybe we can have a, I dunno, what we'd call it. A stretch goal?"

April nodded. "An expansion plan, and yes, absolutely. I'd love that. Maybe we could even provide lodgings and set up a transportation fund for women who have to travel across state lines."

I clasped my hands together excitedly. "That would be amazing." I blinked, considering. An abortion had likely saved my life—or at the very least, greatly increased my odds of survival. And though I'd always have a mixture of emotions around it, I'd never regret exercising my right to put my own life first. To make it that much more likely for me to survive and become a mother at a later time.

To many women, such a thing was a theoretical, but to me it had been reality. And in some little way, I'd like to help others in a similar position who'd had that right torn away due to laws made by old men.

After all, this clinic, our special project, was about medical justice for those who too often didn't receive even the most basic care—women and children.

Our little team of April, Lindsay, and me—and hopefully those who would join us as our journey proceeded—couldn't change the world, but we could improve our corner of it just a little bit.

And for that, I was both proud and excited.

CHAPTER TWENTY-EIGHT
ADAM

ONE DAY IN MID-JUNE, JORDAN AND I WERE DRIVING back from the Los Angeles Convention Center, where we'd spent one of the days at the Electronic Entertainment Expo. This event, also known as E3, was the biggest event for gaming on the west coast along with Pax West and the San Diego Comic Con. And it wasn't lost on me that this would probably be my last one as the CEO of Draco Multimedia Entertainment.

I was still experiencing that weirdly dizzying and slightly lost feeling whenever I'd contemplate the future. Sometime in the next six months, Jordan would be taking the helm as CEO, and I'd just be the Chair of the Board of Directors. It was still a powerful position from which I could influence the direction of the company. But I would be completely hands off on day-to-day decisions. That would be Jordan's job. And he was clearly excited about it.

I couldn't have chosen a better replacement, in terms of enthusiasm and general competence. But that reassurance did nothing to quell the strange cocktail of aching loss, the uncertainty and thrill of the open road in front of me.

As if echoing my thoughts, Jordan, who was driving us today in his huge Rivian SUV, turned his attention briefly from the road to glance at me. "You okay over there, champ? You've been quiet today."

For some reason, a slight irritation flared up at him for noticing.

At my prolonged silence, he adjusted his grip on the steering wheel. "Are you having second thoughts? Because I'm fine with that, you know. We haven't gone so far we can't back up. I just want to put it out there that I won't be upset."

I glanced at him. Maybe on the surface he wouldn't be disappointed, but I was certain that deep down, he'd resent it. Besides, reversing the decision wasn't something I'd even contemplated. It was my style to follow through on a decision once I'd made it. And my gut still told me this was the right thing to do.

I shrugged. "No, no. We're not reversing this. I may just be jittery about an uncertain future. I've always had a goal and been driven to pursue it. Now I just have a vague sense of need to do good in the world."

Jordan nodded. "You could hop on the AI bus. With your knowledge, you'd probably blow the rest of those emerging generative AI companies out of the water."

I darted a look at him. "Messing with AI at this stage is a bit like sewing together a bunch of corpses, exposing the resulting monster to a shit ton of electricity, and *then* worrying about what to do with the animated creature you've created. No one knows where any of this is going to lead or how it's going to affect our world as a whole. And it seems that no one wants to take it slow, just in case."

He shook his head in amazement. "Adam Drake taking the conservative route. Never thought I'd see the day."

I shrugged. "With great power comes great responsibility. Some of the most powerful aren't behaving as responsibly as I'd like. AI can be a great force for good, but there are so many unknowns."

"Are you hoping to get more involved with XVenture Space? You could guide them into private sector space exploration. Wouldn't it be cool to get private astronauts on the Moon, maybe Mars someday? You could beat Musk to it. Send him a private greeting by drone in Valles Marineris when he finally does show up."

I laughed. "I like the way you think. Yeah, I'll probably continue working with XVenture. Not sure in what capacity. I'm seriously considering a sabbatical from all work during the first part of next year."

"A *sabbatical?* Hmmm. So, you're going to be the stay-at-home dad? Better start working on those diaper-changing skills, bro."

I blinked and cranked my head toward him. "Wait, you already know? I was leading up to breaking the news."

He laughed again, shaking his head. "Dude, the deed was done last week when Mia told April. You had to know she wasn't going to keep from spilling the beans to me, didn't you? I don't think Mia asked her not to."

I laughed. "I should have known. Who else has she told?"

"Oh no one else. She just figured it would be safe—or that you'd both assumed she'd be telling me."

I sighed, a chuckle forming from my exhalation. "Well, I guess that makes breaking the news to you a lot easier."

"Yup. It's already done." He shot me a smile. "Congratulations on the happy news. But please, for the love of God, promise me one thing."

"What's that?"

"Well even if you're a stay-at-home dad for a while, promise me you'll never wear one of those damn baby slings on your chest. You know, the ones that tell the world without even speaking that your balls are in a jar on a shelf somewhere in Mia's office."

I shook my head. "Goddamn, you're a sexist."

"In cases such as these, it's about the bro code. Bros don't let bros wear their babies like clothing accessories."

And though his pronouncement made me roll my eyes at such a typical Jordanism, the visual made me laugh regardless. I had more than just diaper-changing skills to work on before the big day arrived. Thank goodness for those parenting classes. And therapy, because I had to make sure I was the best me I could be so I could be an even better dad.

To be honest, I'd never realized I'd gotten my vision of what therapy would be like from Looney Tunes. Typically some idiot character like Daffy Duck or Elmer Fudd would step into a wood paneled office to find a bespectacled Bugs Bunny, complete with large bushy mustache smoking a long pipe, sitting in a giant padded leather chair and ordering his patient to lie down on an equally old-fashioned looking leather couch while he took notes, puffed away on his pipe and asked his patient to "tell me about your childhood."

Real therapy wasn't remotely like that, which was a good thing. I didn't need Freudian Bugs breathing over my shoulder and conking me over the head with an oversized mallet whenever I tried to get up from my seat.

Or maybe I'd just watched too many fucking cartoons in my childhood, which was a definite possibility.

Unfortunately, the childhood subject did come up because, as it turned out, that shit ran deep, and I hadn't healed from it.

After a particularly harrowing session while talking about my sister, Sabrina¬¬—harrowing enough that I'd even shed a few tears—I had to laugh at myself. Kendra smiled and asked if I felt comfortable sharing what was funny.

"I was just thinking that I'm glad my wife isn't here, or she'd be gloating about the fact that she was right."

"What about?"

"Well, she's the only other person that I've ever told all that to, and though I felt most of the time, that all that was behind me, she suspected more."

Kendra tilted her head at me, nodding knowingly. "She's a natural healer, as you say. Her chosen profession is healing the body, but she had to learn about that mind-body connection in medical school. She's probably done a psych rotation."

I nodded. "Yeah, that's when she first brought up the subject of my going to therapy. Right after she finished that rotation. She didn't mean it in an insulting way, but I'm afraid that's the way that I took it."

Kendra nodded. "It can be a sticky subject. There's so much onus around mental health. It's difficult, especially with male-presenting patients. For some reason, it's been deemed 'unmanly', when in reality, it takes a monumental amount of strength to come to terms with seeking mental health healing. Things are changing now, though slowly. But they *are* changing. Does Emilia know now that you're not angry at her for that suggestion?"

I fidgeted—literally squirming in my seat. "I, ah, she doesn't know about us...I mean, about *this*." I laughed at myself for making it sound like some kind of secret affair or something. "I mean, no one knows."

She laughed. "You might want to break the news before she finds you keeping secrets and suspects something worse."

"Have you ever heard of someone getting in trouble for going to secret therapy?" I laughed.

She quirked a brow. "Stranger things have happened, Adam. And believe me, if I could tell you about them, I would."

I stopped by the canyon house afterward to check on the renovation progress and it was coming along nicely. There'd been some difficulties getting the necessary materials up the twisting canyon roads and the long driveway, but they'd managed, and were moving fast.

I was impressed.

And it gave me an idea. A devious, very Adam-like idea.

It was something I had to run by the general contractor. I had a feeling he'd be resistant, but I was prepared to wave a nice fat bonus under his nose until I got what I wanted.

Sure enough, it worked. And Emilia, who so loved to complain about my penchant for surprising her, would probably enjoy this one so much that she'd forget to complain.

Chapter Twenty-Nine
Mia

MY WORK UNIFORM OF LOOSE-FITTING HOSPITAL scrubs under the three-quarters length white coat of a medical resident helped camouflage my steadily growing baby bump. If the weight gain showed in my face, then most would put it down to typical intern-year resident weight gain.

I'd just wrapped up my intern year, as a matter of fact, but still had two years of residency to complete. Which meant, basically, more of the same, except there were new interns in our program now, and I was a PGY-2, which stood for post-graduate year. It put me about a half step above peon.

Work continued to pile on the challenges, which I mostly enjoyed, like puzzles to solve. Especially as I started my emergency room rotation. I also navigated my share of scut work and long call hours. I got deft at evading the senior resident but congratulated myself too soon on my good luck.

Because we then spent two rotations in a row on the same service. That was *no bueno*. At least I'd now crossed the threshold into the second trimester and no longer needed to be on the anti-nausea medication. Admittedly, however, a strange smell or sight would occasionally trigger me out of nowhere.

In fact, I seemed to have developed the keen sense of smell of a backwoods bloodhound. Not the superpower I would have wished for, especially when given all the not-so-wonderful scents a hospital could offer up.

"Wow, Strong, you still haven't gotten your iron stomach? Are you sure you're in the right profession?" Iverson drawled one day, catching me just outside a door to the exterior of the hospital where I was literally taking a breather.

We'd just finished a morning in the ER and a patient in intake had power-projectile vomited all over the examination room. Even the orderly who had to clean it up hadn't appeared thrilled. And me? I'm quite sure I'd gone as green as a Shamrock Shake and fought my own dry heave. Unfortunately, Dr. Iverson had walked in on that. Great timing, as always.

But instead of blowing him off, today I felt snarky in my own power. "If you're done berating every other resident out there about their choice of profession and lording your superior stomach over everyone, know that there are many more facets to this job that make a person an excellent physician without involving the strength of their gag reflex. I'll do rounds around you any day of the week and I'll win. And I'll be a professional about it because I don't need to put down others just to feel better about myself."

His eyes widened, mouth half open in exaggerated shock. I'd rarely found it worth it to bite back at him. But it seemed that today, he'd picked the wrong time to poke this bear. Because this bear was now secretly a mama bear and no fiercer creature existed in the wild. And she was fighting back now.

He scoffed at me. "It was just a little good-natured teasing, Strong. You should learn to take a—"

"Oh, I can take a joke. I work with you, don't I?" My face flushed hot, and I mentally willed myself to rein in the anger. I was perfectly capable of dressing down this idiot while staying professional.

Or maybe I wasn't, because the hormones, they were a-raging, which made it difficult to keep my emotional reactions in check.

He blinked. "No need to get like that."

"Maybe that's what you need to be telling yourself just about every time you open your mouth to speak to me because, quite frankly, your attitude is crappy. I've tolerated way too much of it as it is. But I'm hoping that, by being straightforward with you now, you'll be smart enough to catch a clue and check yourself."

His eyebrow arched. "Check myself before I wreck myself?"

I smirked. "Yeah. Something like that."

He held up a hand, again in that passive *I'm the victim here* gesture. "Okay, okay, Dr. Strong. I see I got you on a bad day, so...." he backed away, shrugging.

"No, you got me on a good day. A day where I finally feel willing to say what I'm thinking. Be better, Dr. Iverson."

He raised his brows, eyes bulging in indignation, and spun on his heels. I stared after him with narrowed eyes. Somehow, this wasn't over. And now that I'd thrown down the gauntlet, that meant that the gloves were off. And the big decision loomed on the horizon. Either he'd catch a clue and take my advice, or I'd have to escalate this to a step that would be uncomfortable for both of us.

But fuck it. Why didn't men have to worry about this shit? I'd been documenting, as my mom had advised. So, I pulled out my phone, grabbed a quick seat and typed in the date and time and a general description of the conversation—and my response.

Then I blinked back a few uncharacteristic tears of frustration. Staring up at the ceiling for a moment, I blew out a breath and tried to muster the strength to go back to the resident office to update my charts and make some phone calls to specialists.

As I sat there in the stillness of that moment, it happened.

At first, I thought it might be indigestion, or even a muscle spasm, this weird sort of fluttery feeling just to the right of my navel. It felt like butterflies' wings and the tickle of a stiff wind in tall grass. An ephemeral, fleeting moment of existence, demanding my notice, before retreating just as quickly.

Instinctively, my hand shot to my belly. Was that...? Did I just seriously feel what I thought I felt? I was at eighteen weeks today with my belly rounding noticeably deep under my hospital scrubs.

And just when I was starting to doubt what it was, it happened again.

I blinked. Holy crap. It *was* the baby, finally making himself or herself known.

I pulled out my phone, wondering if I should call Adam. He'd be on the way to work right now, probably lane-splitting his way up the 73 freeway—though he swore to me up and down and sideways that he didn't do that. *Your days on that bike are numbered, mister.*

I debated whether to tell him now, via text, or to wait until tonight in person. I opted for tonight, but opened another note file on my phone and wrote it down under my pregnancy milestones list.

Then I pushed out of my chair and headed back to the resident office to do my job, annoying senior resident and tiny, kicking passenger notwithstanding.

Chapter Thirty

Mia

Turns out, I didn't see Adam until bedtime that night. He had a dinner meeting that he swore he'd told me about, but of which I had no memory. Maybe it was a case of mommy-brain or resident-brain or a toxic combo of the two.

Just to reassure myself of his schedule, I double-checked our shared calendar. There it was again, that weird block on his calendar. Unicycle training lessons? I'd have to ask him about that, but I'd probably have to go about it in a sneaky way. Knowing Adam, he'd clam up about it if I took the direct approach.

I took the extra spare time to review messages and sample images the decorator had sent over. She had some amazing ideas and a wonderful computer program that laid out the rooms and inserted her furniture and color scheme ideas.

By the time Adam got home, I was already washing up for bed. To my surprise, he came upstairs and changed into his

"

pajamas while I stepped out of the shower and started my skincare routine.

He entered the bathroom just as I was rubbing moisturizer cream into my face. When he was about to land a kiss on my face, I turned away. "I taste like moisturizer." So, he aimed for my neck, instead.

Then he stood behind me, wrapped his arms around my waist and rested his hand on my curved belly, sliding his fingers under my top. "And how was your day, beautiful lady?"

I leaned back against him, savoring the pure bliss of being in his strong arms. "Mmm, it was great except that my handsome prince wasn't around for dinner, and I had to eat alone."

His mouth curved up. "Might've been for the best. I bet you were hangry beforehand and eating for two."

I grinned at him in our reflection. "It's true that I tend toward the hangry end of the spectrum these days. And do you know what your kid did to me today?"

His brow twitched. "Uh oh, you're already calling them *my* kid. That's not a good sign."

"They *kicked* me."

His eyes widened. "What, really? You felt a kick?"

I bit my lip to keep from grinning like a stupid fool, just to see that reaction from him. The baby was still just an idea to him. Just the thing we talked about.

Unfortunately, for him, that would last a little longer. "I felt the fluttering, yes."

"Are they kicking now?" He palmed the bare skin of my belly with both hands.

I slowly shook my head. "No, and even if they were, you wouldn't be able to feel it yet. They're only the size of a large apple." Fortunately, there was no clear disappointment on his face but just in case, I added. "It should only be a few weeks, though, before you'll be able to feel the kicks, too."

He smiled again, then leaned in to land a kiss on my neck before releasing me and pulling away to grab his own toothbrush. "That will be a trip."

He bent over the sink to start brushing his teeth as I continued with my little routine, rubbing lotion into my hands and arms and elbows—and now, my belly, in the odd hope it would help with the stretch marks that I knew were coming. As I did so, I watched him—my sexy husband.

Yum. I mean seriously, yum. Had he been working on his arms? The sleeves of his t-shirt hugged his biceps which bulged with the motion of him brushing his teeth. My eyes flew to his face, the hint of dark whiskers peppering his jaws with a five o'clock shadow. Adam didn't like going scruffy but, damn, it looked so good on him. And even with his mouth full of foamy toothpaste somewhat resembling a rabid dog, he was still the hottest guy I'd ever laid eyes on.

And tonight, I really wanted a piece of that.

Adam finished up in the bathroom before I did, mostly because I decided to do a quick impromptu leg shave for...reasons.

When I entered the bedroom, he was sitting in bed propped up on a pillow and reading his tablet with those reading glasses he'd been prescribed to help prevent headaches. *Quadruple yum.* The prodigy genius looking nerdy and hot as fuck. The man was downright mouthwatering.

From my side, I plopped onto the bed and simultaneously did a weird sort of awkward roll so that I landed half across his body.

"*Oof*," he grunted loudly.

My jaw dropped as I stared at him. "Did you just *oof* at me? What's that supposed to mean?"

His dark brows twitched together. "It means that you just landed on my gut and knocked the wind out of me."

My eyes narrowed at him. "*What* did you just say?"

He gave me a wary look. "You just jumped on me. How the hell else am I supposed to react?"

I tensed in irritation. "Maybe I was seeking a little *affection* from my hubby. But after he's seen fit to remind me that I'm not sexy anymore, I guess I'm not in the mood."

He frowned. "Emilia, you just jumped and landed on my stomach. That wasn't a commentary on your weight or some sort of low-key body shaming."

I pushed off him, suddenly blinking back tears. "Okay, if you say so."

I rolled back to my side of the bed and started to crawl under the covers. Maybe there was a convenient hole in the ground somewhere nearby that I could temporarily inhabit.

He set aside the tablet and pulled off his glasses. "Hey...what did I say wrong?"

I sniffed, suddenly feeling those tears strangely close. What a stupid thing to cry about, but in the moment, I felt powerless to stop it. Hormones be damned. "You *oof*ed."

He reached for me and pulled me up against him. "It just meant that you missed your aim."

I sniffed loudly. "So, I'm a big ol' clumsy oaf, then."

"Wrong on four counts." He wrapped his arms tight around me to keep me from squirming away from him, which I was attempting to do now. "You are neither big, nor old, nor clumsy, nor an oaf."

Tears wetted my eyelashes. "So, I'm just wrong and stupid then."

His face twisted with real concern. "Emilia..." I turned my face away when he tried to land a kiss on my cheek. "What's going on? Are you tired?"

I swiped at my eyes, suddenly feeling deflated. "You don't find me desirable anymore."

He hesitated, mouth still open, cautiously considering what he was about to say. "I don't think I can win, here. Because saying that's not true will make you wrong and calling you wrong made you upset. Please tell me what I can say that won't make it worse."

In spite of my sudden spate of tears, I found myself laughing a little. But still emotional enough that more tears spilled onto my cheeks at the same time. And when I laughed, snot shot out my nose which...damn.

All I wanted was some love, affection, and sexy attention from my hot husband, and this evening was suddenly melting into disaster.

"Emilia." His voice held true concern now. "Please tell me how I can make this better."

I shrugged. "I have no idea why I'm crying right now. I....*fuck.*"

So, he pulled me tighter against him and rested his chin on my shoulder and waited it out while I sniveled and, finally, let my body relax against his strong, solid form, melting into his solid arms. I calmed under the awareness of his body wrapped around mine and enjoyed the sense of security it gave me.

We lay there like that in calm silence for long minutes, And you know what? It was exactly what I needed. No lectures, no cold shoulders, no long-suffering eye rolls. As I let out the long breath I didn't know I'd been holding, he landed a kiss on my neck and whispered, "I'm sorry."

I raised my hand and rested it on his sandpapery cheek. "No, *I'm* sorry. You didn't do anything wrong. You *oof*ed, and that's not a crime."

"I'm so relieved. I was already trying to figure out how to never *oof* again."

My laughter brought more snot and he reached over, grabbed a wad of tissue off his nightstand and handed it to me. I mopped up the mess of tears and snot. Jeez, I was so the very polar opposite of sexy right now. And I said as much.

He sat back and made a face at me. "At the risk of making you upset again, you're wrong. To me, you've never been sexier."

I froze for a brief moment, hope flaring. "Really?"

Unmistakable heat flared in his eyes. "I want to pull that nightshirt off you right now and have my way with you."

I blew my nose and finished wiping up my face. "Hold that thought. I'll be right back."

I pushed out of bed, trotted to the bathroom to wash my face, then ran back to bed, taking extra special care not to land on Adam's stomach lest we repeat the cycle that just took place.

And wow, did he ever show me just how sexy he still found me. Though I did convince him to spare the nightshirt from ripping.

He lavished me with tenderness, taking his time to explore me as if he'd never seen me naked before. He was careful of my overly-sensitive breasts, but still spent some time there, kissing them lightly. I closed my eyes, threading my fingers through his thick, dark hair.

"You are so fucking beautiful," he murmured against my skin as I arched my back to meet his kisses. His hands smoothed over my skin. "So soft."

Then he landed kisses on my rounded stomach, smoothing a hand there, too. "Even more beautiful than before, with my baby inside you. How could I think otherwise?"

I opened to him, preening under his lavish attention. My hand smoothed down his solid body. "You gorgeous, delicious man, tell me more."

He laughed, his mouth pressed against my skin. "Can't you tell how much you turn me on?" He pressed his very-ready erection against me. "All the fucking time. Even when I'm too exhausted to act on it. You're the most amazing woman in the world to me. The perfect partner. And you're the mother of my child, the cherry on top. I'll never find you anything but ridiculously, magnetically beautiful—inside *and* out. Sometimes, it's almost too painful to pull my eyes away from looking at you."

His head came up to meet my mouth with his and our lips and tongues intertwined, creating the vortex of a building storm—of connection, of arousal—the center of a tiny world we now inhabited, just the two of us.

Centuries and civilizations and worlds could crumble all around us and we'd never know, in here, in our sphere. Just the two of us—just the *three* of us—locked in a universe of our own making.

He matched his palm to my palm, our fingers splaying wide, pressing together. His lips continued to tangle with mine and waves crashed, dark clouds raged, and we rode this storm.

"Fuck me," I whispered into his mouth, and I could almost feel his knowing smile against my lips.

"Oh, I will. I will, but before I do, I want to worship you."

He made me come twice before ever entering me—once with his delectable mouth, once with his hand. When I was riding the afterglow of that second orgasm, he rolled onto his back and pulled me to straddle him.

"I want to look at you. I want to see all of you while I'm inside you."

I shifted my hips over his and he slid inside me easily. A perfect fit—a metaphor for our whole life together. There might be friction sometimes, there might be missed timing but ultimately, our union only took us to higher levels of joy, happiness. As I moved on top of him, our hands clasped each other tightly, fingers intertwined for long moments before he released his grip.

His large hands smoothed over my breasts, my belly, my hips as I continued to move, slowly, relishing the feel of him inside of me, the sound of his rushed breathing mixed with my sighs of pleasure.

"You are so fucking incredible," he breathed, his hands clamping onto my hips to urge me to move faster. "My perfect mate."

I leaned forward, and my long hair fell over my shoulder, draping across his chest. He sucked in a breath, and I purposely turned my head to do it again. One of his hands left my hips to twine through my hair and I felt that familiar climb to climax.

My breathing changed and he grunted hoarsely. "Yeah...that's it. I want you to come again. I love making you feel good."

I moved faster, bracing my hands against his hard pecs. "Oh, I feel good. *Very* good."

I quickened my pace again and he was breathing deeply now, as if trying to fight off the inevitable. I felt him come just as that tension crested toward climax. My back arched and my head fell back, and the wash of ecstasy skated over my skin, every muscle in my body. The intensity with which it hit—a full body orgasm.

I think I felt it in my scalp and my fingertips.

Just as he grabbed my hips to still me, I collapsed against his hard chest feeling only semi-conscious when I landed there.

He held me against him as we basked in that afterglow. Our faces pressed together, and his whiskers scraped my cheek in that way that I loved. I relished the feel of his body, so different from my own, pressed so closely against me.

"I think I already love the second trimester," he said. "The first one, not so much. I was too worried all the time. But this? This is fun."

I snorted, slowly sliding off of him to lie beside him. "You just like it because I'm horny as a goat."

He laughed. "Well, I'm not going to deny that I'm enjoying that part. But you, with all your energy, and you just—when I look at you, you *glow*."

"And I'm horny and you are the beneficiary of the horniness."

"Okay, okay. You're hornier than ever before and I'm not going to deny that this sex is lightyears above baby-making sex."

"That's not a stretch." I laughed.

His hand came up to smooth my cheek. "It feels good, to hear you laugh. To see you happy. And so healthy."

There was a long pause as we held each other in the dark. I cleared my throat, giving voice to the unspoken thought. "You aren't still afraid, are you?"

He took a while to answer and when he did, his voice was a little quieter. "Sometimes I am, yeah."

I pressed my cheek against his chest, relishing the sound and feel of his heartbeat beneath his skin. "Thanks for being honest with me."

His fingers found the edge of my hair, grabbing a thick strand and twirling it around his index finger. "The not knowing. The fact that the cancer could have come back, and we might not even know."

I stilled his hand by wrapping my fingers around his. "We do blood tests every month. So far, everything is good. I know that's not the absolute certainty you need, but nothing is ever certain, you know? I worry about you every damn day on that fucking motorcycle."

He sighed. "You have hated that motorcycle since day one."

"Well, it's a big bugaboo for me. Consider it my version of worrying about you. Besides, dads don't ride bikes."

"Cool dads do."

"You're already a cool dad, without the bike."

He was silent for a long time, so long that I thought he might have drifted off, until he spoke once more. "Tell you what. When the baby's here, I'll stop commuting on the bike and keep it for a fun ride here and there."

I ran my hand across his lightly hairy chest and kissed his hard pec. "That sounds like a great idea. I'm on board with that."

"Good. We have a deal then. You stay healthy and keep taking good care of yourself—even after the baby is out."

I sighed. "For as much as my schedule will allow that, I will. Eat healthy, get as much sleep as I can, and exercise."

He threaded his fingers through mine. "Sounds like a plan."

He leaned down and kissed me then, a long, lingering kiss on the lips. It was full of passion, and I almost wondered for a minute if this meant round two was coming up. To be honest, I was too exhausted for round two.

But instead, Adam sighed, warm breath against my face and he said, "You said nothing is certain, but that's not true. Some things are certain. This present moment. It's real. What I feel for you is certain—and more rock solid than the Sierra Nevada. And..." his hand moved down to smooth over my belly. "It's certain that I love you both more than I ever thought it possible to love another being."

Chapter Thirty-One
ADAM

EMILIA WAS AT TWENTY WEEKS WHEN IT WAS TIME FOR more cryptography, that was how I liked to think of the so-called big ultrasound.

I took the afternoon off work and met her at the doctor's office. She was working on her laptop in her scrubs, having just come off a short call shift, all while sipping at a small bottle of orange juice, not her usual beverage of choice. I frowned. "What's that all about, you aren't getting sick, are you?"

She shook her head. "No, it's for the ultrasound. I have to have a full bladder again, but juice has a lot of sugar in it, and it will get the baby moving. Just don't want him to be so shy he won't show off his bits."

I arched a brow. "Or lack thereof. If he's a she, there won't be any bits."

Emilia nodded. "Fair. But either way, I've heard of people getting their ultrasound and the baby is quiet and keeps their legs closed the entire time and they don't end up finding out what they're having 'til the baby comes out."

I smirked. "Ah, the old-fashioned way."

"Yeah, I don't want the old-fashioned way. I want to know. This is the modern age and this is modern medicine—"

"And your mom is dying to know how to decorate the nursery."

She nodded, running a hand over her curving belly. Her scrubs were still loose but it was starting to get obvious at certain angles that her body was changing. I flicked a glance up at her. "Are you telling people at work yet?"

She shook her head, gaze flicking away. "Nope, not yet. Soon. Maybe after we find out the gender of the baby."

I narrowed my eyes at her. "We're not doing one of those kooky parties or TikTok videos, are we?"

Her dark brows arched. "Are you kidding? Neither one of us is into social media BS since I dropped my blog. The thought of throwing a party right now makes me beyond exhausted and we're not even in the exhausting trimester yet, so, no. No party, no fancy firework show that threatens to burn down half the state of California. Nothing that will wreck the environment or make us look foolish for all the world to see."

Well, that was a relief, at least, though I hoped she wasn't too tired for the surprise baby shower that her friends had twisted my arm to cooperate with. But that wouldn't be for at least a month.

"Nobody's got time for that shit, especially when we're taking graduate-level parenting classes."

She started laughing. "That last test was crazy. I have a medical degree and I still missed a question!"

"Yeah, you have an unfair advantage."

"Oh?" her brow arched. "What was your score?"

"I passed my first-aid certification, thank you very much," I said indignantly. I'd never in a million years tell her how many times I had to retake the damn test to do it, though.

We were assigned to a different room this time, and instead of the obstetrician, we were seen to by the ultrasound technician. This appointment took a long time because the technician was doing a close look at organ development and taking measurements of the different bones. Emilia watched closely and made a few comments, noting the baby was within all the standards of growth milestones, and on the upper end, at that. A big baby.

And at least, this time, I had a better idea of what we were looking at, at least after Emilia pointed out the baby's cranium and long bones, all four chambers of the baby's heart that seemed to be beating regularly, et cetera.

As all the clicking and measuring came to an end, the ultrasound tech asked, "Do you want to know what gender your baby is?"

Emilia smiled wide. "I already got a peek."

I narrowed my eyes at her. "You mean you know already, and you didn't tell me?"

She shrugged. "I know what I'm looking at."

My eyebrows climbed in my forehead. "Okay, well, then, let me in on it. Are we having a son or a daughter?"

Her grin widened and she turned back to the ultrasound screen, pointing to a certain area. "Right here is where we're looking. What do you not see?"

I rolled my eyes. "Emilia, I have no idea what I'm looking at and you really don't have to use this as a teaching moment, just say—"

"There's a vulva here. No penis," she stated matter-of-factly.

"My son doesn't have a penis?" I blurted, alarmed for about two seconds before I realized how stupid my words sounded. The ultrasound technician immediately burst out laughing.

Emilia grinned at me. "No, your *daughter* has a vulva."

I blinked, mouth dropping open, my eyes flew back to where Emilia was pointing. I'd just have to take her word for it because computer inner-workings and multiple programming languages were a whole lot easier to comprehend than this stuff.

"She's sucking her thumb, did you notice?" The tech said. "Awww, so cute."

Emilia glanced up, then bit her lip and turned to me with tears in her eyes. She grabbed my hand. "You ready to be a girl dad?"

I took a big, deep breath and squeezed her hand tight while looking back at that incomprehensible screen. "Is any man ever ready to be a girl dad?"

She laughed. "If you suggest Alloreah'ala for her name, I'm vetoing it instantly."

"Eowyn?"

"Nope."

"Daenerys Khaleesi?"

"Absolutely *not* that one."

The next morning, I left the bike in the garage and drove the car to work.

Because now, I had not one, but two women in my life to protect.

About a week after finding out that we had a daughter on the way, we were lying in bed reading. I was on my tablet, and she was reading a paperbound book with a book light clipped to the pages—another pregnancy book. This one, by the looks of it, was from a more hardcore medical perspective, given all the Latin words strewn about when I glanced over at the pages she held open.

I was reading for pleasure for once, a fantasy novel that was immersive enough to catch my interest. It had been a long time since I'd picked up a novel, having preferred long, epic history books about the Roman Empire and the like. But this novel was good enough that I was sucked in. I didn't notice until her tossing and turning jostled the bed for the third time how restless Emilia was.

After her twentieth explosive breath and fifth turning from her side to her back to the other side and returning to her back, I looked up from my tablet. "Everything okay? You seem uncomfortable."

She sighed heavily. "Not uncomfortable, per se, but she's kicking like crazy. She's been doing this a lot lately. She's quiet during the day, but at night, I can feel her moving around in there like she's playing Dance Dance Revolution or something."

"Are you automatically assuming our daughter is going to be a gamer girl?"

She rolled her eyes. "Please, she has no choice. Look who her parents are. It's already in her DNA."

"Don't put our baby in a geeky box. She can be anything she wants to be."

"Yeah, well right now she either wants to be a ballerina or a break dancer. Maybe even a soccer player."

I couldn't resist the temptation to put my hand out onto her rounded belly. "Where is she kicking?"

Emilia grabbed my wrist and repositioned my hand high on her stomach. "She likes this spot a lot, but I'm not sure if she's big enough for you to be able to feel it yet."

I waited for a minute and we looked at each other but nothing happened. "Are you feeling something right now? Because I got nothing."

"No, she suddenly went quiet. Maybe it's stage fright or something."

I sighed. Oh well, there was time yet. I kept my hand where it was but pressed the button on my tablet to reactivate it and continue reading.

Emilia seemed to get comfortable and settled in that position, propping her head up on her arm so she could keep reading her book.

A few minutes later, a muscle on her stomach twitched. She sucked in a breath and looked at me wide-eyed.

"Your muscles are twitching," I said.

"Uh, no. That wasn't me. That was your kid. She's back at it again, apparently, after her two-minute nap. She must be nocturnal."

I blinked, adjusting my hand so it stayed on that exact spot. "That was the baby?"

"Yeah, you felt it. She's kicking or head-banging or something."

I shifted my palm on her stomach, putting a little pressure against the surface, instantly enchanted. "C'mon, you can do it. Give me another kick."

Almost as if she'd heard me, there was that sensation again— what I'd mistaken for a muscle twitch.

Emilia's eyes widened. "Did she just do exactly what you asked her to do?"

I grinned. "Yep. That bodes well for the future, doesn't it?"

She shook her head, marveling. "She's not even out yet, and she's already daddy's little girl."

I grinned, then set my tablet on the nightstand, fantasy novel now forgotten. "Roll over," I said, and when she had her back to me, I pressed up against her, spooning her, placing both my hands on the spot where the baby was now kicking relentlessly. "Does it hurt?"

She shook her head, her fragrant, soft hair falling against my nose. I inhaled deeply. She smelled so good. My lips sank automatically to her neck, kissing her there.

She sighed happily. "I think Daddy has something else in mind besides going to sleep?"

"I'm not sure whether I'm liking you calling me Daddy in bed."

She snorted. "I'm not calling you Daddy like *that*. Or are you saying you want me to?" When I didn't answer, she rolled over to face me. "Are you?"

I blinked. "It's not a known kink that calls to me, no. But maybe I can see the appeal—under the right circumstances."

She screwed up her face as if truly contemplating that. "Don't you and I both have too many daddy issues to explore that, though? Wouldn't that just drive us straight to therapy?"

I blinked, suddenly feeling defensive and not realizing why. "Is that a bad thing?"

She frowned. "Seeking therapy? No, not at all. I was just joking around but...." She shrugged almost self-consciously.

"Nothing wrong with going to therapy. It wasn't an appropriate joke."

"I mean, you've done therapy before, so I was just wondering."

"Yes, therapy helped me. I was just saying it to be funny. And not everyone who has daddy issues—or a daddy kink—needs therapy. Did I...did that joke bother you?"

I blinked. "Not specifically, no. But..." I took a deep breath while she looked at me expectantly. The baby kicked again and this time, with her belly pressed to mine, I felt it right in my abdomen. Impressive, little Miss Drake. Very impressive.

I met her mother's gaze and suddenly we were grinning like fools at each other. After a moment, her smile faded. "I'm sorry. I hope my joke didn't offend you."

I sobered. "It didn't. It just got me thinking and realizing that I have a confession to make."

She looked mildly alarmed. "What's that?"

I swallowed. "I've been seeing a therapist for the past few months."

Her brows knit as she stared at me, probably trying to discern if I was pulling her leg or not. Then, she suddenly laughed, as if she had concluded that I was cracking a joke. But when she saw that I wasn't laughing along with her, she sobered. "Oh, sorry. I thought you were joking. I—sorry. I'm processing." She bit her lip and frowned briefly. "Every time in the past when I've brought up the subject of seeing someone, you seemed resistant—sometimes very resistant. I'm stunned that you made the decision to go on your own and then decided not to tell me about it."

I sighed. "I'm sorry. I wasn't keeping it secret more than I was just...managing expectations. In case it didn't work out, I didn't want you to be disappointed if or when I decided to throw in the towel."

She nodded slowly, appearing to understand. "I get that, but it's not for me to be disappointed. It's for me to be supportive of your journey. And if I didn't know, then how—" She cut herself off, as if having a new thought. Her brows knit then a look of pure amusement crossed her face. "Unicycle lessons, circus training, underwater basket-weaving class and that weird TR one."

I laughed, realizing what had just crossed her mind. "Well, I had to put something in that time slot on my calendar so that Maggie wouldn't double-book me."

She giggled again and the baby kicked twice as if echoing her mother's amusement. "What does TR mean?"

"Temporal reduction."

She burst out laughing. "Head shrinking. Clever."

I smiled. She got me. This amazing, smart, beautiful, clever woman really got me. Even when I made stupid jokes on my calendar. "I didn't realize that you were looking at my calendar that much these days."

"For all these baby appointments and our crazy schedules, I've had to. Your calendar is a scheduling nightmare of Tetris-style time-slots, and we have parenting classes and checkups and on and on."

"Exactly, so I needed to put something in that block, and it really isn't any of Maggie's business that I'm doing therapy."

She tilted her head. "But it *is* my business." She smiled sweetly and put her hand against my cheek. "And now that I know, how can I support you?"

"Well, maybe we could go together in a few months. My therapist suggested that as something we should do in a little while."

She nodded. "Okay. Just let me know and I'll put it in my not-so Tetrised calendar."

I shook my head. "You are in denial thinking that your schedule is less crazy than mine, Dr. Strong."

She studied me for a long time. "So, would it be okay if I asked what prompted you to go to therapy?"

I thought for a minute, acknowledging the brief surge of my pulse as a familiar fight-or-flight response to her wanting me to open up. I acknowledged it, understood where the feeling came from, and reminded myself that I was safe here. With her, I was always safe. Huh, curious. Was this evidence that the therapy was working?

My hand went to her stomach. "I'm doing it for her. I want to be the best dad I can possibly be. But I also want to be the husband you deserve."

Her eyes widened and she blinked rapidly, her mouth softening. "Oh, Adam. You're already pretty damn terrific."

I cracked a smile. "Still not what you deserve. But I'm getting there."

She shook her head slowly. "Well, you're setting that bar pretty damn high tonight, mister." She leaned in to kiss me and the baby kicked multiple times as if echoing her mom's emotions. This woman in my arms, our baby safely tucked inside her, between us. I was the luckiest fucking man on this planet.

I kissed her deeply and she returned it with fire on her lips, her tongue. When I drew back slightly, she let out a pleased sigh and leaned in, deepening the kiss. "I am so turned on right now, Adam Drake. You better watch out."

And as she pushed me onto my back and did wicked, delicious things to my body I could only bask in this happiness and appreciate this for what it was. This present. This moment. I was overwhelmed with gratitude for what I had and I'd fight like a questing knight to keep safe what was precious to me. And if that meant wandering into the mysterious, unknown regions of my psyche with a therapist as my guide to do it, then I would, as I had been. Sometimes those regions resembled the Fire Swamp and sometimes it was like fucking Mordor in there.

But I wouldn't quit.

Because I wanted to become the man she deserved. That *they* deserved.

CHAPTER
THIRTY-TWO
MIA

I GUESS NEVER EXPLICITLY STATING YOU DIDN'T WANT A baby shower was not the best way to go about avoiding one. I should have suspected something when Adam suggested he take me out for Sunday brunch at a nearby resort hotel. When I gave him a weird look, he'd said something about meeting my mom and Peter there. That seemed more credible, so I went with it without any further questions, probably because my tired brain couldn't muster up the energy.

But here we were now, on a private patio overlooking the ocean, with my friends and colleagues, pink flowers, balloons and centerpieces everywhere. So much pink.

My girlfriends—April, Jenna, Alex and Katya—the enthusiastic co-hostesses, each accosted me with big hugs and fawning pats on my growing belly.

Alex jumped up and down, wide-eyed. She challenged me accusingly. "You didn't ever tell me you were friends with celebrities."

I frowned. "Who do you mean?"

"Well, he's a big hero, I guess maybe you don't think of him as a celebrity," she hastily corrected when I met her with a blank stare.

"Oh," Kat leaned in. "She means Commander Ty. I just walked by him. He remembered me from the demo I did for the astronauts a couple years back. That was cool."

I turned back to Alex. "He and Adam are friends. They've known each other a long time."

In turn, I greeted him and his adorable fiancée, Dr. Gray Barrett, a nerd girl after my own heart.

"Congratulations," Gray said, punctuating her earnest words with a tight hug. "I'm so happy for you two."

"Way to go, Adam." Her hunky, national hero boyfriend, Commander Ryan Tyler, slapped my husband on the arm with a wide grin. "It's yours and Mia's duty to populate the planet with brilliant people."

I met Adam's gaze and though he smiled, I could read it at the back of his eyes. He wouldn't willingly put himself—or me—through this again, so that re-populating thing was probably out of the question.

Before I could say anything, Adam fired back. "You've gotta help out with that burden, Ty. We definitely need more astronauts in the next generation."

Ty's brows twitched. "That would require me admitting I was getting old and needed a replacement."

"Come on, we're holding up the line," was Gray's only response to the male bravado about repopulating the planet. The planet was plenty populated as it was, so we were good.

Next came Lindsay with her boyfriend and a big hug, pointing out how much fun it had been to shop for baby stuff for us.

"Adam, I had no idea that you were friends with Dominic Fischer. Why did you never introduce me to him?" she said semi-jokingly while her significant other had moved on to put their giant gift on the gift table. Typical Lindsay.

Adam appeared extremely amused. "You seem to have done very well for yourself. You don't need my help."

"True, true. I'm quite happy but still, you're full of surprises, aren't you? Ever secretive, Adam Drake."

I bit my lip, covering my own amusement. He was so much less so now, at least with me, but I could see where Lindsay was coming from. Adam didn't share, as a rule. He kept things buried deep and close to the vest, which had me wondering again how things were working for him in therapy. Ever since he'd dropped that little bomb last month, a day had seldom gone by where I hadn't thought about it.

How on earth did that poor women get him to open up when he was like Fort Knox buried deep under the Lonely Mountain with practically everyone else in his life?

I didn't envy anyone trying to pry things out of him that he didn't want to give up. She might as well be deep-earth mining for rare diamonds in South Africa. But the fact that he'd gone on his own without being cajoled or coerced said a lot. Maybe he was ready, now.

The reception line was getting a little tedious, but it was nevertheless wonderful to greet more friends. Louisa, Josh and their beautiful son, Wilder, were in attendance.

Louisa giggled. "Maybe Wilder and your baby girl will go on a date someday."

The man beside me practically bristled with paternal defensiveness. "A little soon to be talking about dating."

I sent him a look. *Down, boy.*

Josh laughed. "Someone's setting her dating age at forty-three, then, huh?"

"More like a hundred and forty-three." Adam grinned back at him.

This poor baby, when she hit teenagerhood and started dating. Either she'd have to go on medication, or her father would. I bit my lip. Perhaps we'd have to work slowly on getting him used to the idea well before that point, but we had over a decade before we'd have to worry about it.

Jordan came next with April to give us both yet another hug. Jordan gave Adam a vigorous handshake and kissed me on the cheek with genuine congratulations.

Then he said the most Jordan-thing ever. "There any booze?" Adam and I burst out laughing.

April smacked his arm with the back of her hand. "It's a baby shower, you idiot."

He sent her a look. "So...not even beer? Beer comes in bottles. Bottles are baby things."

April pulled him away, apologizing profusely with laughter in her eyes. Those two laughed a lot, I imagined.

Dom Fischer came next. Adam stepped forward with a big grin. "Wow, glad we could catch you when you weren't up north."

He smiled back. "I'm trying to spend more time down here. Family obligations, you know."

"Thanks so much for the gift. Your assistants notified me that it was dropped off at the new house yesterday but neither of us have had the time to go over and see what it is."

Dom Fischer was a strikingly handsome man. Tall, dark-haired, gray eyes, strong physique. I could almost feel all the single women's eyes on him—and some of the men's, too. He smiled mysteriously. "I completely understand a busy schedule. But I hope you like it. Or more importantly, I hope *she* likes it." And he made a gesture toward my stomach.

I smoothed my hand over the generous swell of my belly and smiled. "Whatever it is, I'm sure she will."

"I have to check in at work today, so please don't think I'm being rude when I duck out early. I apologize in advance."

"I've never heard that one before," I drawled sarcastically, shooting a look at my husband. In response, he shrugged sheepishly. "We completely understand. No need to apologize."

With all our guests greeted, we settled in at tables in the adjacent dining room, ate brunch, listened to live music and chatted. In other circumstances, I might have been too busy to notice that Jordan was obviously up to something. But damn, he was being so obvious, walking up to people I was sure he didn't know and whipping out his phone every five seconds.

I made a note to ask April about it but she was busy running the stupid baby shower games I would have rather avoided.

Most notably...the notorious candy bar diaper game. Gross.

My co-hostesses passed around numbered baby diapers containing melted chocolate bars that party-goers were then asked to guess the type of candy bar contained therein.

The first time someone pulled a diaper up to their face to get a big sniff, my stomach did a somersault. Ugh. Next someone would be asking if they could get a taste.

Before that happened, I made my great escape.

I nudged Adam and gave him a pointed look without saying a word. I then awkwardly pushed out of my seat and excused myself to the bathroom, making sure to throw another pointed look at my husband in case the subtlety had been lost on him. His head tilted slightly, as if indicating he'd got the message that he should meet me outside.

I was stretching my back in vain when he joined me.

Adam swaggered up with a devilish, devastatingly handsome grin on his face. He pointed to the nearby swimming pool. "Hey, sexy lady. Wanna go skinny dipping with me?"

My eyes narrowed. "I don't flirt with strangers. My husband would rough you up if he knew."

He smiled. "Sounds like a mindless brute." Then, he hooked his arms around me and pulled me in for a kiss.

"Can barely get your arms around my waist anymore, can you?"

He shook his head. "Not true. My arms fit perfectly around you and your gorgeous body."

I let out a long sigh, feigning irritation. "Stop flirting. You're distracting me."

His brows knit. "From what? I thought you just wanted an excuse to get away from the gross baby poop game."

"It was gross, but it was also a great excuse to sneak off so I could talk to you about something."

"What are we talking about?"

"Jordan."

Adam frowned. "What about Jordan? Is he being inappropriate? Should I go rough him up or—even scarier for him—get April to do it?"

I shook my head. "No. He's fine. But he's acting weird. Keeps approaching people and walking out of the room with them. It looks hinky, like a multilevel marketing scheme or something."

Adam gave me a skeptical look. "I wouldn't put that above Jordan in normal circumstances, but definitely not at our baby shower."

"Maybe you could find out what he's up to?"

Adam shrugged. "I'll try. But you never know, maybe he's planning some kind of nice surprise for us or the baby or both. We wouldn't want to spoil that, would we?"

I gave him a look. "You're Adam Drake. You hate surprises, remember? Even the best ones."

He nodded, blowing out a breath. "That's fair."

We parted ways not too long afterward when Jenna came looking for me because my participation in the next activity was mandatory.

Not too long later, as I was legit headed toward the bathroom, however, Adam found me again. This time the look on his face was one of exasperation.

"I solved the Jordan mystery. He's got a betting pool going on. Dates and times for the birth."

I blinked. "What the...*what?*"

"People are laying down money and the closer the date to the actual due date, the lower the odds. Higher odds for more than two weeks out on either side of the due date. Lower odds around the full moon in December because of statistics. He's put some real thought into this shit."

Despite my shock, I burst out laughing. How very Jordan of him to turn the impending birth of our child into a moneymaking scheme. I'd be disappointed with anything less.

"He actually asked me if I wanted to buy in on a slot on New Year's Day. I said you'd murder me if you found out I was betting on you being that overdue."

"You aren't wrong. I'd make myself a widow and a single parent in one fell swoop."

"Yeah, so on the basis of self-preservation, I declined. But the way he's got it all figured out shows he did some research and put a lot of thought into it, so there's that at least."

"God help April when and if they ever decide to have a kid because...*wow*. That's about as intense as your disgusting kale shakes."

He held up a finger. "Don't diss the kale shakes. They are completely healthy and good for you. So, they're a little disgusting and made you nauseous but that's beside the point."

I peered at him through narrowed eyes. "Not for me, it isn't."

He laughed and pulled me into his arms, kissing me on the top of my head. That's how Jordan found us.

"Get a room, you two. I'd also say get protection but it's too late for that." He threw us both his signature sly-charming grin. Sometimes, through all his bravado, I could see what the ladies who fell at his feet like dominoes saw. But most often I found him endearingly annoying. Like right now, for example.

"So, what's this about a birth date pool?" I folded my arms across my chest, resting them on my prominent baby bump.

Jordan looked like the proverbial deer in the headlights, throwing my husband a glance that said something like, *et tu, Adam?*

"Hey, dude. I had to blab. You know the adage—or may understand it very soon, anyway—happy wife, happy life."

"Yeah, but happy best friend happy—oh I don't know, I'm not as witty as you two. Just know that someone's going to make a lot of money off the impending arrival of your sweet little girl, and it will most likely be someone you love."

"Not if you're the winner," I quipped back with a teasing smile.

Jordan put a hand over his heart and deadpanned in the most sincere-sounding voice, "Mia, you wound me, you honestly do."

I smirked at him but moved up to give him a hug anyway. "I'm quite sure that I have not affected that black heart of yours in the least."

He belted out a laugh, then leaned down and kissed me on the cheek. "Do me a favor and pass every bit of that snark down to your daughter. It will do me good to know that Adam is constantly being dressed down by his women at home."

On further discussion, I discovered that nearly everyone had bought into the birth date pool—including my own mother. Though no one would tell me what dates they'd placed their bet on for fear of jinxing it. As if I had any control over the situation. Though I had half a mind to foil them all and pick a time no one had bet on to schedule a c-section.

And did my eyes deceive me, but when he thought I wasn't looking, I saw Adam hand Jordan a twenty. I decided not to ask about it. But he better not have bought into that New Year's slot.

After managing the transfer of gifts with the hotel coordinator, which was, really the only task we were left to do since our hostesses were that good, we made our way to the hotel exit. We were moving slowly, exhausted and ready to hunker down for the rest of the day at home.

Before that happened, however, Louisa ran into me on my way out. Josh had already taken Wilder to the car.

Her expression was serious enough that I paused and asked Adam to supervise loading the presents up for transport. Then, she led me back out on the patio where we had privacy and lowered her voice so we wouldn't be overheard by the cleanup crew.

"I know you're about to go on maternity leave soon, but I wanted you to know that I walked in on a really upset nurse who's on my psychiatry rotation."

Iverson was on that rotation with her. I mouthed his name to Louisa and she nodded slowly, giving me a look. He'd been keeping his distance from me, not even speaking or looking at me since I'd announced to my colleagues that I was pregnant.

I'd counted myself lucky and hoped it meant the end of his weird inappropriate behavior. Perhaps he'd moved that to some other target, however.

"She feels like no one's going to pay attention to a nurse complaining about a doctor—even if he's just a resident. You know how patriarchal shit gets in a hospital—especially with white, male doctors."

I took a deep breath, let it go, and glanced toward the inside of the hotel to make sure my husband wasn't remotely within earshot. "I should say something, so they take her complaint seriously."

Louisa watched me carefully. "It would absolutely help her case. I think he's been really forward with her and may have even asked her out."

I blinked. "That's not even remotely appropriate."

"No, it's not. If he goes unchecked, think about how shitty he's going to be to his own staff in the future, if he's this bad as a goddamn resident."

I clenched my jaw and relaxed it. "Okay. Go ahead and tell her she's not alone. I'll file a complaint. I was prepared to do it but I kept second-guessing myself because this guy is like death by a thousand cuts. No one thing he's done or said was enough to complain but adding it all up makes it something more."

"Hostile workplace at the very least. His future colleagues and staff would thank you for it, if they ever knew, which they won't."

I nodded, inhaling deeply and feeling a new conviction settle in deep inside. "Okay...anything to help out my fellow female healthcare workers."

Louisa leaned in and pulled me into a hug. "I love that you're so brave, and I'm not sure I would be, in your place."

"Thankfully, in this instance at least, you've been spared." I returned the hug and stepped away. Louisa met back up with Josh and Adam was waiting for me by the front desk.

He cast me a questioning glance and I just shrugged. "She had some words of advice for me." I rubbed my belly to misdirect his thoughts. None of that was a lie, and he didn't need to go into beast-mode husband by knowing all the details.

I had no intention of giving the father of my daughter a reason to get thrown in jail before she was even born.

That night, I pulled out my laptop and composed my email describing Dr. Iverson's behavior. A cold lump of dread formed in my stomach as I briefly described his words and actions, consulting my documentation file. And I honestly wondered why I'd waited until now to do it, in support of someone else instead of feeling this indignation for myself.

It seemed I had a lot to learn and as a woman in a still patriarchal world, I doubted this would be the last time I'd be in a position like this, unfortunately.

I only hoped this would do some good.

Chapter Thirty-Three

Adam

THE DAY BEFORE CHRISTMAS EVE, EMILIA WAS CRANKY as fuck. And antsy all day—unable to sit still. We were scheduled for an induction the day after Christmas, as the baby was getting big and she'd be overdue at that point. But that was two long days away.

For this reason, we'd planned a very quiet, easy-going Christmas and made no promises to relatives. In the meantime, I bit my tongue and strived to do her every bidding while not speaking because apparently, the sound of my voice inexplicably enraged her.

I'll never understand pregnant women, apparently—and I'd spent the last nine months living with one, so that said a lot.

I'd been working longer hours to onboard Jordan into the CEO position, but this last week I'd been mostly at home in anticipation of my wife going into spontaneous labor. Unfortunately for her, it hadn't happened yet, and she was done being pregnant. Jordan and I had decided to have the birth become the line of demarcation between my leadership and his.

Or as he called it, his *soft launch* as CEO. As far as the employees and the public knew, this was my paternity leave. But for us, this was proof of concept. He'd be running the company and when our daughter was three or four months old, I'd go back to work long enough to pass the baton officially, make the public announcement, and ceremonially endorse my best friend.

Jordan was willing, he was ready. And by god, was he eager. And my feeling was that he'd anticipated this, at least over the past year or two, and had prepared accordingly. I'd chosen well in my replacement.

The night before Christmas Eve, after not getting enough sleep for weeks, I crashed early and—unusually—before Emilia. She'd been opting to sleep in the guest room most nights and I'd tried not to be offended by that. In a brief, non-cranky moment, she'd explained that she was worried about waking me with her tossing and turning.

However, when I woke up at 2 a.m., I found her sitting on the end of our bed, slumped over and breathing heavily.

It took me a minute to process what was happening. I pushed out of bed, hit the bathroom, blinking as I turned on the light. I was mid-stream during a long piss when I realized what that heavy breathing and slumped posture might mean. With a start, I finished up, washed my hands and rushed back out to her.

"What's happening? Are you alright?"

It took her a minute to answer, so I sank down on the bed beside her and wrapped an arm around her shoulders. She immediately shrugged my arm off. "Don't touch me—" she snapped, then took a breath. "I'm sorry, I didn't mean that harshly."

"It's okay. Are you okay?"

"Yes and no. I'm in labor and it hurts like fuck."

"You're having contractions right now?"

She let go a long sigh that told me I'd said the wrong thing. I braced myself, prepared to be the villain in her story for the next few hours. I'd read about it and was fully prepped to don thick skin. "Yes, Adam. That's what labor means. Contractions."

"Okay, so how far apart are they?"

"I don't know. I haven't been timing them. I've just been breathing through them. They definitely aren't close enough together to worry about yet—oh—" her voice tightened. "Here comes another one."

I popped up from where I was sitting and went to my side table, scooping up my phone. "I'm gonna time the next few, just to be safe."

She rubbed her belly, rocking and inhaling deeply. A minute or two later, she seemed to breathe normally again. "We have hours, yet, before we need to go to the hospital."

And she was right. Currently, they were eleven minutes apart. I knew enough from the birth classes we'd attended that we were only at the beginning of this journey.

By five a.m. the contractions weren't getting closer together. I'd put on my glasses now and was carefully searching every birth site I knew of to find out if early labor typically progressed this slowly. As in not really progressing much at all in three hours.

And, not to worry, many said a *primiparip*—the weird medical term for a first-time mother—typically had long labors. It looked like Emilia would be joining them.

But when she came back from the bathroom, she had a startled look on her face and a hand pressed to her swollen abdomen. "I'm pretty sure my water just broke."

Before even saying anything, I recorded the time in the file on my phone, then looked up. The bottom half of her night shirt was wet.

I jumped off the bed, stuffed my phone in a pocket and grabbed the bag with our clothes and items that we'd packed the previous week.

"Let's get you dressed—"

She waved me off and went toward her closet. "I can dress myself. I'll be right out."

"Okay, I'll load up the car and bring back a golf cart from the bridge. Do *not* come down those stairs without me."

She heaved a sigh. "I can walk downstairs by myself, Adam."

"I know you can, but I'm going to help you anyway, in case you slip or get a contraction mid-descent or something."

She rolled her eyes but didn't say anything, disappearing into the closet.

I reminded myself that this attitude was only temporary and instigated by discomfort and pain. And to help her get through it, I was willing to be her figurative—and maybe even literal—punching bag.

After loading the car, I parked the golf cart on our front step and reentered the house, leaping up the stairs two at a time. I got her down and loaded into the cart without incident.

"Walking to the car would be good for progressing my labor," she protested mildly.

"Save your energy. You're going to need it later," I insisted, and she didn't argue. If my suspicions were correct, this was going to be a long ass day for both of us.

Eventually, with the help of medication via IV, Emilia was able to progress quickly into active labor. And God, though I knew this journey was necessary, it was tough to watch her go through it. In fact, I fucking hated it and wished there was a way I could take on the pain myself.

Throughout all of history, I'm pretty sure I wasn't the only man to wish that. We, whose instinct was to protect, could only stand back helplessly and watch while nature took its course. Thank all the powers that be, we lived in a time when childbirth was so much safer than it had been in past centuries—even for a woman who'd previously had significant medical challenges.

I sat beside her, replacing a cold wet cloth on her forehead when she allowed it. And promptly leaving the room when she demanded I do so. Though this time, it wasn't in anger. She was worried about me not eating.

But I'd vowed not to eat again until she could.

"You're being ridiculous," she said. "Go down to the cafeteria and eat something nutritious for God's sake."

"But—"

Her gaze sharpened. "If it's any comfort to you, I have zero desire to eat. If you're in here and starving by the time the next contraction hits, I'm kicking your ass. I mean it."

I obeyed her, but ended up waiting just outside the birth room, unwilling and unable, really, to leave her despite her harsh orders. A nurse took pity on me and sent an order slip to food services.

I stood near the coffee station, about fifteen feet away, and downed a grilled-cheese sandwich in what felt like five gulps. Not the healthiest way to nourish myself but it was 1 p.m. and I hadn't eaten a bite since the night before, so I was ravenous.

The nurses sat at their nearby station and watched me, whispering to each other and laughing quietly. I realized that I either looked like a starving animal or a caveman gulping down his meal before being attacked by a Sabretooth tiger. But I wasn't about to go back in there with food in hand to eat in front of her. Not when her stomach was just as empty, and she still had hours before she could eat.

One of the kinder-faced nurses approached me. "Mr. Drake, you can eat in the birth rooms, you know. Or we have our break room with a table just around the corner."

I swallowed the massive bite I'd been chewing and turned to her, wondering how she knew my name. "I'm just about to polish this off and I don't really want to eat in front of her."

She smiled, nodding. "I get that but, let me assure you that right now, she's not really thinking about food. What's happening is all-encompassing. She's tired and hungry but neither of those things are registering right now."

I paused, mulling that over. "Yeah, I know that's supposed to make me feel better, but it doesn't. Besides, she insisted I go down to the cafeteria so if I go back in there with the uneaten food, she's going to know I didn't, and I'd really rather not cross her right now."

The nurse laughed. "Hate to break it to you, Mr. Drake, but the fact that you exist is bound to cross her today."

I flashed her a grin. "I've prepared for that."

Just then, her labor and delivery nurse exited her room, and I caught her eye. "Where are we at?" I asked.

She gave me a slight smile. "She's made a little progress. Six centimeters, and definitely in active labor now. So, things should start moving a little faster. Her mom's in there with her. Why don't you go to the cafeteria?"

I shook my head and went back into the room with the can of soda, making sure to set it away from her direct line of sight. She might be thirsty, and I didn't want to rub it in. Which reminded me... "Would you like me to grab you some ice chips?"

She grunted. "Fuck your ice chips." Clearly, she was in the middle of another contraction, so I shut my mouth and shot a look at Kim, who grimaced.

She'd be rational again in just a few minutes and that would last a few minutes.

But damn, things were moving way too slowly for my tastes. This baby girl was being a diva already, apparently, and taking her own sweet time to make her appearance into the world.

CHAPTER
THIRTY-FOUR
MIA

I WAS BARELY AWARE OF ANYONE AROUND ME THROUGH the haze of pain that came with each contraction. Every muscle in my body squeezed tight, sucking the breath from my lungs. I was trapped in an invisible vise, and it was tightening all around me. Sweat matted my hair against my forehead. The nurse and sometimes the doctor milled in and out of the room. Adam never left my side and yet... I only perceived these circumstances at the very periphery of my awareness.

For these past few hours, my whole world had become the pain.

I'd opted for an epidural but since the labor had progressed so slowly, they waited until active labor started, which made the process so much more difficult.

Nevertheless, I sat slumped over on that bed, attempting to stay as still as possible and hoping another contraction wouldn't overtake me while the anesthesiologist had a needle inserted in my spine.

But the epidural brought the known side-effect of slowing the labor's progression. So, the pain relief didn't last. They ended up turning down the numbing agent in the interest of hopefully spurring the baby along.

And thus, after being awake for over forty hours and experiencing contractions for well over sixteen of those hours, I was a virtual zombie.

The only thing that got me through it? Knowing that on the other side of this, I'd be seeing my baby girl. I'd be holding her. Smelling her. Feeling her soft skin under my lips when I kissed her head. Would she look like me or more like Adam? I fought like a tiger to keep these questions in my mind as the labor progressed and things got nasty.

And I was quite sure that I was probably a rancid bitch to my poor, exhausted husband, but given the fact that he held my hand, even when I squeezed it hard, I was pretty sure he wasn't holding it against me. After all, it was his kid I was pushing out of my violence-wracked body, right?

When the time finally came to start pushing, I was exhausted beyond comprehension. Sure, I'd been awake for this long—and longer—before. Medical training was no joke. But I'd never stayed up this long while actively managing the unrelenting contractions of one of the most powerful muscles in my entire body and dealing with the pain that came along with it.

Sixteen hours was a long time to be in pain.

But this wasn't the light at the end of the tunnel I'd been hoping for.

After an hour, I was sweat-soaked and nearly incoherent. And the baby was no further down the birth canal than she had been when I'd started. After a particularly heinous contraction, while the doctor checked the baby's position, my eyes drifted out the window. When had it gotten dark again? What time was it? My eyes flew to the clock on the nightstand beside me. It was well after nine p.m.

"The baby is at zero station, Mia." My obstetrician told me with sad eyes.

I let out a breath of exasperation, rolling my eyes upward. "The nurse just said she was at plus one."

"She was incorrect. The baby's head is swelling, so she thought that meant the baby had moved down the birth canal, but she hasn't."

I banged my head against my pillow with a huff of frustration. "*Fuck.*"

She sighed. "The baby has been in the birth canal for a while with very little progression. I think it's time to consider a cesarean section."

I shook my head as tears prickled my eyes immediately. I didn't want to go through major surgery. Especially after going through all of this. The recovery from surgery was hard enough—and painful. And unfair, after also enduring the full pain of labor for the better part of a day.

Adam moved to my side. "Emilia, I think the doctor might be right."

"I don't want surgery. It's not fair!" I yelled, repeating my own thoughts on the matter. Some misguided people judged mothers who gave birth by c-section as not having experienced true birth, but they were idiots. Birth was birth. What I didn't want was a large, painful incision in my lower abdomen to have to recover from while caring for a newborn.

Adam reached up to dry my tears.

It was such a sweet gesture, that I really needed. My eyes found his and he gently pushed the hair away from my sweaty face and locked gazes with me. There were tears in his eyes, too. "I'm so proud of you...you're a fighter. But I think the doctor's right. What do you think?"

I swallowed, feeling myself slump against the bed even as another contraction came on. When I grabbed my leg to start pushing, the nurse gently put a hand over mine. "Just breathe through this one, Mia. Let's not push for a bit. You can take a break while you make this decision."

"The baby...?" I asked without completing the question.

"She's not in distress right now. But that can change quickly. You've been pushing for nearly an hour and a half and she's not budging. I suspect she's coming out the wrong way."

"Sunny side up?" I asked.

Adam frowned. "What does that mean?"

The nurse answered Adam's question as I breathed through the contraction. "A baby is usually born face down. The shape of the head is more conducive to navigating the birth canal in that position. But not all babies get the memo, and some even come bottom-first, which is what we call breech. Yours isn't breech but she is obviously struggling. Or she may just have a head that's too big to get through Mia's pelvis."

My eyes drifted closed. I could almost drift off to sleep if it wasn't for these damn contractions that came every three minutes. I swallowed, forcing moisture into my throat so I could talk. "Do it, then."

"I'm sorry, I didn't catch that?" the doctor replied.

"Go ahead and prep for c-section. I'll sign the papers."

"Okay." The doctor nodded. "I'll send someone in. Meanwhile, I'm going to get an OR ready. And some pediatricians from the children's hospital."

And miraculously, all that was done within thirty minutes. I was wheeled into an operating room where Adam met me in full surgical garb. I'd just breathed through a particularly heinous contraction, fighting the almost instinctive urge to push.

My husband smiled down at me from behind his surgical mask. "How are you doing?" he asked gently.

"Better now. You look sexy in surgical scrubs."

He laughed. "I think you just have a doctor fetish."

"Well so do you, or you wouldn't have married me."

His eyes crinkled at the corners as his smile widened. "Fair point."

Not long after the surgical and pediatric teams joined us, their work started. I was asked to spread my arms out at a right angle from my body, helping to position my organs correctly for the birth. I'd assisted in several c-sections in med school during my obstetrics rotation, so I knew the drill from the other side of the divider that separated my line of sight from the work they were doing on my lower abdomen.

Even as my OB narrated what she was doing, I knew what to expect. The outer incision, the inner one, the tugging on my body as they reached in and delivered the baby and the placenta.

Since I had nowhere else to look, I watched Adam's face. Watched that transformation as he became a father. He didn't watch the work the doctors were doing, and that was understandable. Few people really wanted to see their spouse's innards on display. But once the doctor held up the baby for him to see, I watched as his eyes widened before they lowered the baby again to take care of the umbilical cord.

I was pretty sure that I'd resent him for life for being the first one of us to lay eyes on our daughter. But it would only be a matter of seconds before I saw her too.

Even if I wouldn't be able to hold her for several hours yet.

But fair enough....

She was quiet when they lifted her quickly just above the partition so that I could see her. I stared into dark blue eyes. Her little head had a light dusting of black hair. And—oh my god— even now I could see it. She was Adam's mini-me. She looked exactly like him.

Just as quickly as they flashed the baby to me, they whisked her away again to be examined by the waiting pediatric team and cleaned her up while the surgical team worked on me.

Adam left my side to approach the table where they examined the baby.

But he drifted back almost as quickly with a prominent frown.

"What's wrong?"

"They're putting a tube down her throat."

I blinked. "She must have swallowed some meconium." I reached for his hand. "She'll be okay. It happens sometimes with long labors."

Sure enough, after they'd worked on her for a few more minutes and cleaned her up, they brought her to us. She was this tiny red-faced bundle, swaddled in a hospital blanket. Due to the two hours of pushing, she had a temporary cone shape to her head. The nurse gently placed her in Adam's arms.

"Here she is. Baby Girl Drake," the pediatrician beamed, then turned to me. "She *was* sunny side up and had to have her airways suctioned but she's good now."

I nodded. "Thank you."

"She's still not crying." Adam stared down with open wonder at the tiny bundle in his arms.

"She's just taking it all in." I said. "She's staring right at you. See? She's saying, 'hi Daddy, here I am.'"

He took a shaky breath and watched as her mouth stretched. "She's beautiful," he said. "Just like her Mama."

"Yeah, she looks nothing like me." I laughed.

He turned to look at the baby even as a nurse appeared with a rolling hospital bassinet to take her to the nursery. "We're going to put her under a warmer while you're in recovery and then she'll go to your room when you're transferred."

I turned to Adam. "Go with her. They have to monitor me while the anesthesia wears off, so I have to stay in recovery for an hour or so."

I'd never seen a look like that on his face. All wonder and amazement and a little lost. He nodded and followed the bassinet out of the OR.

Me? I succumbed to my exhaustion and dozed off. Ninety minutes later, I was declared ready to be discharged to my room and I couldn't wait to finally hold my sweet baby.

A half hour after that, I was in my own room and she was wheeled in, this time wearing a tiny diaper, a soft knit cap and her swaddling blanket.

Like a seasoned pro already, Adam lifted her out of the bassinet and now, at almost midnight after the longest day of my life, my little girl was finally in my arms.

"Oh, my goodness, you are precious," I cooed at her as Adam slid an arm around my shoulders and gazed down at his daughter over my shoulder.

He leaned down to kiss my hair. "She sure is."

I perched her in the crook of my left arm and reached my right hand to touch hers. That tiny fist immediately closed around my finger. That was all it took for my heart to plunge irrevocably in love. "What's her name?" Adam asked. "We never resolved that issue."

But now, after seeing her, in my heart, I had no doubt what her name should be. "Her name is Sabrina, if you agree."

Adam was quiet for a long time and the air was thick with this special, poignant emotion. We were enveloped inside a cloud of love, this tiny, brand-new family. Tears prickled the back of my eyes and I knew that Adam fought his emotions similarly, though because of the angle and where he was standing, I couldn't see that struggle.

Finally, with a swift wipe of his eyes and a gentle clearing of his throat, he said quietly. "I think it's perfect. Sabrina Eloisa?"

I shook my head, laughing. "No gaming names, no matter how much we're tempted. I was thinking of naming her after your sister and my mom...Sabrina Kimberly."

"That's perfect, because Kimberly is also your name."

I nodded. "Yeah, it works. It's her name."

"Sabrina Kimberly Drake." His large hand came down to reverently palm his daughter's nearly bald head. "The most beautiful little princess in the world."

And that moment? It was magical. I wished hard that I could freeze it in time. Just the three of us here, alone and cloaked in love.

But it didn't last long.

Because the lactation consultant entered the room, and I was faced with the challenge of getting the baby to nurse for the first time with some strange lady tugging on my boob to get the baby to latch and help the whole thing happen.

But in the end, Sabrina and I learned together, and it was all good. It took work and I was beyond exhausted but before I knew it, she was eating like a champ.

CHAPTER THIRTY-FIVE

MIA

THE HOSPITAL STAY—PROLONGED, NOW, BECAUSE OF the c-section, was almost as exhausting as the labor. We had a reprieve the first day after she was born because not many could break away from Christmas day festivities anyway and we enjoyed the silence. But after that? The parade of family and friends streamed through my private room during visiting hours like it was a national holiday.

Most of them brought gifts but they weren't for us. The baby got all the loot. Heath showed up with a giant stuffed dragon— almost as big as he was—as an homage to her gamer heritage. Jordan and April came by with a huge, gorgeous bouquet of light pink hydrangeas. April asked to hold Sabrina and picked her up like a pro, like she'd been handling babies for years.

When she caught my surprise, she shrugged. "My sister and brother are twelve and fourteen years younger than me. I've handled babies before."

William and Jenna came every day, bringing me fast food whenever I begged them for it. On day two, Adam's cousin presented me with the most exquisite pencil sketch he'd done of our baby girl.

"William," I said, jaw dropping as my eyes pored over the likeness. "This is incredible."

"It's just a pencil sketch. I brought it to see if you like it so I could do something more permanent."

I blinked. "Of course I like it. I *love* it. I want this sketch, too. I'm greedy."

"I'm going to need her exact time of birth so that I can do her star chart," Jenna said with a dazzling grin. I avoided meeting Adam's gaze as I knew he didn't believe in astrology. I most likely didn't either, though I hadn't fully made up my mind yet.

And Jenna, herself, had a degree in physics and taught it in high school. But that only pushed her further away from the skeptical scientist stereotype. She'd be the first one to launch into the relationship between the metaphysical and quantum physics, when asked. I don't think I'd ever known someone as open-minded and as accepting as Jenna.

Mom, of course, spent hours a day with me at the hospital just gazing dreamily at her granddaughter and chatting with me. When Adam had wandered home to grab something or to check in with the office briefly, she was there for me. In fact, during my stay in the hospital, I was never alone.

Ever.

And that, in and of itself, was exhausting.

At night, Adam stayed beside me on a convertible bed that folded up into a couch during the day. But neither of us got much sleep. As soon as the baby stirred, he'd pop out of bed before I could so much as move—or even, sometimes, before I'd wake up. He'd change her diaper like a pro. I had yet to do one myself, in fact. Then he'd gently hand her to me after grabbing the nursing pillow and I'd do the feeding, of course, since he lacked the proper equipment.

It was two in the morning on day 3 and later that day I'd, hopefully, be discharged. Adam had just propped the baby onto my nursing pillow and settled back down on his temp bed. Though he clearly looked as exhausted as I felt, he merely propped his head onto his hand and watched us while she nursed. I almost drifted off, mid-nursing, myself, but when I shook myself awake, I found him gazing at us, a tired smile on his lips.

"Go to sleep." I told him. "I can put her back in the bassinet when she's done."

He shook his head. "Nope. It's my job and I take it seriously. Besides, I like to watch you two together. You're so beautiful and such a good mom."

I arched a brow at him. "It's way too early to tell. I've only been a mom for three days."

He shrugged. "I can already tell and I'm an excellent judge."

"And totally unbiased, too." I grinned.

"Yes, of course. It is my completely impartial opinion that I'm in the room with the two most beautiful ladies in the world."

I knew I may not remember long stretches of this new time with just the three of us alone together as a brand new, tiny family. But I was completely and fully aware, even in this present moment, that I'd cherish every second of what I would hopefully remember with fondness someday.

But for now, it was no crime to wish for more sleep.

When it came time to leave the hospital. Adam hired a driver in a completely sanitized SUV to take us home so that we could all sit together in the back. I was surprised until I saw the phone in Adam's hand taking all manner of photos and video of the occasion. Baby's first car ride. Baby's first car seat. Baby's first burp in the car. Baby's first nap in the car. Followed quickly by Mommy's first nap as well. I have no doubt that he snapped pics of me slumped against the car window, blissfully unconscious.

When I stirred, it was because we'd exited the freeway, and the lull of the road was no longer hypnotizing me. But I was disoriented. I had no idea why I was looking at rolling hills and the approaching ridge of the Santa Ana Mountains instead of the flat stretch of the bluffs leading down toward the coast and our home.

click

Adam's phone was in my face, snapping another photo. I grimaced at him. "What's going on? Does this guy even know where we live?"

"Yep."

"Then why are we out here headed to the—oh, are we going to the new house? Are you signing off on something?" The renovation wasn't scheduled to be finished for another month. We'd be moving in soon after.

"Yeah, I have to sign off on some of the work on the house. I hope you don't mind the detour."

"If she stays asleep the whole time, I'm totally fine with it. Might do me some good to walk around a bit."

"Are you still in pain?" he asked.

I shrugged. "The incision is sore, but it's fine." It was more than a *little* sore, but I wasn't going to tell him that. I'd be dealing with pain for at least a week or two. But beyond that was the sheer fatigue of my body spending ninety percent of its energy on either manufacturing breast milk or healing from the surgery.

I didn't say so, but I was longing for a long nap in my own bed. Oh well. At this time of day, this detour, if it went fast, wouldn't be much longer than forty-five minutes.

After a short drive through the canyon, we pulled into the long driveway that wound up toward our new house. The first thing I noticed was the lack of trucks. Maybe the workers had taken the day off. But why request that Adam sign paperwork today when they weren't even working on site?

When the car came to a stop, however, Adam reached into his pocket and produced a key. He handed it to me. "Welcome home."

I blinked, still a little slow on the uptake—I blamed the pain meds for that. "I don't..."

Adam reached for the car seat and unlatched it, taking hold of it by the handle. He nodded to my car door. "Go have a look. I've got her."

I got out of the car and left them behind while I made my way up the front walk toward the door. There were young trees and decorative potted plants out front—the landscaping was new and in that fresh stage that looked a little bare but promised to become utterly stunning in the next year or so. I blinked. So, they'd finished the outside early, but what did that mean for the inside?

I opened the front door and pushed it wide with a gasp. The work on the house had been completely finished—right down to the warm eggshell shade of paint on the walls that I'd selected months ago.

The house was exquisitely furnished—but not with furniture that I recognized. It was like someone else lived here in the same

California ranch style and color scheme—terracotta, sage green, soft marigold—that I'd chosen.

The hardwood floors had been completely refinished and the carpeted rooms had new wall-to-wall carpet. I'd been corresponding with the designer here and there when I could and had answered all her questions but had never dreamed she'd take what I'd given her, the color schemes I'd selected and created a gorgeous, elegant but cozy home.

"This is staged." Adam explained when he caught up with me. "We can buy the furniture and décor as it is, or our designer will make any adjustments and changes we want. But I wasn't going to bog you down in details with all you had going on."

I blinked, shaking my head. "It's incredible. She really captured our style but also the feel of the canyon and the nature surrounding us here. I'm floored."

He grinned, quite satisfied with himself. "And this way, we didn't have to move our old furniture over, so I could set up the whole thing without you even suspecting."

I threw him side-eye. "You like doing that way too much."

The baby stirred and Adam lowered the car-seat onto the couch, unbuckled her and gently lifted her out. "I'll get her settled again. She's not due for a feeding for at least an hour and ten minutes."

I bit my lip, reminding myself not to be surprised that he'd already set up a schedule in his head for the baby. He was even making notes about when she pooped and how often she wet her diaper—to stay on top of any danger of dehydration, of course.

I moved into the kitchen—perfect, large, and with every brand-new appliance I could think of. Then down the hallway into the rest of the house—his office, mine, a den. No fancy theater room yet but that was what he called "Phase Two" of the remodel—a nearby outbuilding for the fun stuff and guest accommodations.

Adam caught up with me about two minutes after I'd crossed the threshold into the nursery. I turned to him, wide-eyed with wonder. "I was stressing out because ours wasn't done and she was coming home to a generic room instead of her pretty storybook-themed room I wanted so badly. But here it is...like magic."

He grinned. "Some have suspected me of being a secret wizard, it's true. Remember a few months ago, I was asking you some weird questions? They were from a secret questionnaire our decorator had sent me.

All of my childhood favorites were represented: *Chronicles of Narnia, Winnie the Pooh, Anne of Green Gables.* And his—*The Hobbit. Charlotte's Web. The Secret Garden.* Not only did the lovely little freestanding bookshelves on the wall house special leather-bound embossed editions of these books, but the artwork featured special prints and quotes from the books in colors matching the décor of the nursery—dusty pink, beige, and bone.

Adam had Sabrina safely nestled in the crook of his arm. He followed my gaze around the room smiling. That's when I noticed it. Spelled out on the wall in giant dusty-pink wooden letters, the baby's name.

"How—how did you do that? We didn't even know what we were going to name her when we went to the hospital."

Adam gently laid the baby down in her gorgeous wooden crib swathed in bone-colored tulle. Apparently, she'd promptly fallen back asleep. Then he came over to me, wrapped his arms around me from behind and pulled me flush against him. "There's this amazing invention called the telephone, if you recall. You tend to be very salty about my relationship with it."

"Hmmm," I said, my head falling back to rest on his shoulder. "Is this all the work of our magical decorator?"

"Indeed. She was very motivated to finish early, given the approaching holidays. And she used all your suggestions. Our other house is completely intact except for all our personal effects which were moved over while you were in the hospital. The old furniture is still in the house and any pieces you still want will be bought over. But we're sleeping here tonight."

I let out a long breath of relief. "You don't know how glad I am that I don't have to pack and unpack boxes."

"No way. Not on top of everything else you've got going on—feeding a hungry baby 24/7 while recovering from major surgery."

How on earth did I get so fucking lucky? I had no idea. "So why did you decide to rush the job and have us move in now?"

He was quiet for a moment, then he slowly shifted us both so that we were now looking at our sleeping daughter. "I wanted the princess to be brought directly to her shiny new castle. She deserves a room that is all ready to receive her."

"It's only been three days, but you're one hell of an amazing dad. This little girl is very, very lucky. And so is her mama."

Neither Adam nor I'd had the chance to know our fathers. But I was quite certain that I was right in my judgment, for every new thing that Adam took on, he did it with gusto, with his full heart and energy. And the pure love I could feel emanating from him whenever he looked at her... Well, this girl was going to grow up fully loved—and knowing it—every second of her precious life. Lucky, lucky girl.

"This is perfect." I sighed. "This is *home.*"

He kissed me then, and we left the sleeping baby in the nursery. For the first little while, we were going to do co-sleeping but she could take naps in her special room. Adam led me into our new master suite, and I was stunned again. It was beautiful, decorated in a way to immediately make me peaceful and calmed, sage green and cream and full of greenery. The perfect sanctuary in which to decompress between long shifts as a medical resident.

But I didn't have to worry about that until maternity leave ended in three months. Until Adam returned to work, we had time to bond together, just the three of us in a sanctuary all our own.

And start an exciting new life here, together.

CHAPTER THIRTY-SIX
MIA

ADAM WENT BACK TO WORK FOR A TOTAL OF FOUR hours a day when Sabrina was four weeks old. It was good for us because, frankly, being together all day, every day without a break was starting to get a little old.

And he was now dealing with the press releases, the official announcement, and the working transition over to Jordan as the new CEO of Draco Multimedia, while Adam made his own transition to the chair of the board of directors.

That gave me a few hours on my own each day. Sabrina was still sleeping a lot, though not yet sleeping through the night, requiring two feedings in the early morning hours, which kept me semi-sleep deprived. But I was attempting to learn how to use a breast pump to give me a break at night. It was a slow process, but parenting classes, and a medical residency had helped get me ready for early parenthood. In general, life was good.

And Mom was a massive help, taking over for a few hours in the early afternoon while I caught a nap. As it was January, the inn was closed, and Peter was the busy one. Come the springtime, they'd relocate to Anza and open the B&B back up for the busy season while Peter switched to working remotely.

And as Adam was only working half days, he left late morning and arrived back from work just before dinnertime.

A week into Adam being back to work, we'd had a particularly hard night with the baby, taking turns walking her around until she finally slept, then dealing with her feeding just a few hours later. That day, Mom was only able to spare me an hour break due to an appointment.

By the time Adam arrived home, I was too exhausted to think about eating. I just wanted him to take the baby so I could crash before the whole thing started again tonight.

But he was also exhausted. When he headed to the bedroom to change and didn't re-emerge after twenty minutes, I went in search of him.

He was unconscious, face first on the bed, still in his work clothes.

"Were you going to eat dinner?" I asked loudly without preamble.

His eyes fluttered open, face still pressed to the bed. "No, I'm good. Just need to crash for a bit."

I gritted my teeth and folded my arms over my chest. "Well, that sucks because I really wanted to crash, myself."

He still didn't move. "Your mom didn't come over today?"

"She had to leave early because she had a dentist appointment."

"Hmm."

I waited for more. Nothing came. That's all I got. *Hmm.*

I tilted my head and watched him, then noted the pattern of his breathing. He'd fallen asleep again. The asshole.

"Hey, I'm tired, too. It's not fair that you just come home and literally pass out face first in the bed and make me deal with this."

"Hmm," was his only reply.

My blood was beginning to boil.

"Adam," I muttered between my teeth, and he didn't move. What the fuck? "*Adam,*" I belted, a little louder.

He startled awake with a loud snore, blinking. "What, what happened?"

"You fell unconscious. Again."

He rubbed his eyes through his lids. "Mmm, yeah, that was amazing."

I blew out a breath of disgust. "If only I knew how amazing. I get more sleep than this on a long call shift. Maybe I should go back to work early—so I can get more sleep."

He blinked and turned on his side but not quite enough to look straight at me. "Are you mad at me for something?"

I clenched my jaw, heat rising to my cheeks. How could he possibly be this clueless?

"I can't possibly think of what I'd have to be mad at you about," I uttered while I could practically feel the steam coming out of my ears.

He rolled onto his back and stared at me. And god, he did look awful. Pale, dark circles under his eyes.

In spite of my irritation, I let out a breath. "Did you get *any* sleep last night?"

"No. I couldn't get back to sleep whenever you took over with the baby."

"Well, that's your own fault, buddy. In this environment, it's every man for himself. Don't expect me to stay awake when you're with her because that ain't happening."

He ran his fingers through his hair and stared up at the ceiling. "We need to recognize who the true enemy is, here. The one who's depriving us of sleep. She's a monster," he uttered on a long sigh. "She's enforcing sleep deprivation torture on her prisoners, so we'll turn against each other. We're playing right into her tiny little hands."

In spite of myself, I laughed, rubbing my forehead. "She's a criminal mastermind. A diminutive Dr. Evil, right down to the bald head."

"I vote that we start referring to her as The Puppetmaster—or better yet, Baby Palpatine."

In my sleep-deprived state, I found that hilariously funny. "Baby Palpatine! Palps for short."

And almost as if on cue, her wails came across the baby monitor in my hand.

"Her Imperial Highness demands her dinner," I said with a sigh.

"I'm so sad I can't be involved in that. So very, very sad."

"Fuck you," I sneered with a laugh still on my voice.

He pushed up to a sitting position. "If you give me an hour or two to nap, I can stay up with her tonight until she needs to be fed again."

I was already half out of the doorway. "Deal." And I flicked off the light so he could get a head start on that nap.

For days after that, we referred to the baby as Her Imperial Highness or Baby Palps. Adam even ordered a black, baby-sized hooded cape for her to wear, to complete the effect.

But things got better. We had a night nurse come in to give us a break once she started taking pumped breastmilk from a bottle. At eight weeks postpartum, I started feeling a little more human. The incision had healed, and I got my strength back. I also took pains to monitor my own mental health, as postpartum depression was a common threat to new mothers. Fortunately, I was able to avoid most of it.

One night, we were even feeling up to a little gaming. So, we invited Heath and Kat over to dust off the old DE characters and run around the game for a little bit, just like old times.

Those days seemed like a thousand years ago, to be honest, back when I didn't know who FallenOne really was, and Kat was just a voice coming over the internet from Canada.

Now we were all here together in the same room, one of the spare rooms designated as a gaming room, sitting around a table with our laptops propped up in front of each of us. But no headphones tonight as we were all together in meatspace.

"Okay so we have a solid two hours before Sabrina needs to eat again. Let's get into something good."

Heath frowned, sorting through his character's quest log. "Well, there's that fucking annoying boss—The Slayer—that we've never managed to get, but he's got some amazing loot on him."

I sighed. "Isn't that the dude that caused us to wipe out, over and over again?"

Kat nodded. "Yeah, we tried that asshole every night for nearly a week. He's impossible." She darted an unreadable look at Adam who looked away quickly.

My eyes narrowed. "Wait—Kat, how do you not know how to defeat him? You playtest this game every day for your job. Don't tell me you weren't tempted to—"

She shook her head. "I was doing Whitebox testing for this last expansion, so I wasn't in the trenches actually fighting the bosses."

Heath's forehead wrinkled. "And you weren't tempted to go in and find out a loophole or gimmick or even a solid legit strategy on how to defeat this guy? He was frustrating as hell."

"Well," I said, turning to Adam with raised brows of expectation. "You gonna share?"

He shrugged back at me. "How should I know? You think I'm in there designing the new bosses on an expansion while trying to run the entire company?"

"It didn't occur to either one of you to investigate?" I pressed further.

Adam and Kat met each other's gaze and then both shrugged. "That's cheating," Kat said.

"Yeah," Adam pointed at Kat. "What she said. I mean it would be boring for me to play with you guys if I knew all the answers."

"That's the only reason we keep you around," I snapped back good-naturedly.

Meanwhile, Heath was hunched in front of his screen, scrutinizing something. "I'm on GameJunkie's Youtube channel. They have an entire walkthrough on the mob."

"Cheater," Adam sneered. He hated those spoiler websites. Not like he could do much about them, because they cropped up like mushrooms on a pile of poop in a cave within hours of a new expansion going live.

Heath ignored him and then passed along some tips on how to approach the mob without giving the exact play-by-play the gaming streamer had revealed.

We were on our third try and getting really close to kicking this guy's ass when the baby started crying.

In fact, we were so deep in the thick of it that it took a minute, and Heath was the one who said. "Isn't that the baby?"

"The Slayer's at thirty percent, guys. We got this." Kat said excitedly.

Adam turned to me. "Her Imperial Highness is summoning you."

But I was leaning forward, ready for my moment. "When the boss gets to twenty percent, he spawns all those orc adds," I replied. "I need to be here for crowd control. Go get her and bring her here. You can one-hand it."

Adam sighed heavily. "I don't have any of my macros set up on this machine. I can't one-hand this part."

Heath was in the middle of tanking—and trying to keep The Slayer mad enough at him that it wouldn't attack any of the squishier characters. Especially Kat. As the group's healer, she was the most important to keep alive.

"One of you grab her and bring her back. We can do this," Kat said breathlessly.

"Don't take him down to twenty percent until I get back," I shouted, half out of my chair as I pressed a couple buttons, then sprinted to the nursery to grab the baby and bring her back.

"Okay, Palps is back," I said, returning through the doorway with her crooked in my arm. She wasn't due to eat for another hour so I could only imagine it was a diaper change or just general crankiness driving this. After one quick check, I saw her diaper was still clean.

Sometimes, she was just done sleeping and wanted to be held or put under her mobile.

Adam had angled my laptop so that he could reach it, pressing a few buttons on my keyboard. I blew out a breath. "You took him down to twenty already?"

Adam frowned at my screen. "Put Palps in the baby swing. That should keep her happy 'til this is done. I got this for a few more seconds, at least."

"Two-boxing the DPS *and* crowd control." Kat shook her head. "Mad respect to you, Adam."

"If Eloisa doesn't get back here in the next minute, it's not going to be so impressive," Adam replied, tension in his voice.

I carefully laid Palps in her baby swing and fastened the buckle to keep her secure. With a quick flip of the switch, the light-up mobile started to play tinny music, stars and moons rotated just above her head, and the swing swayed slowly, back and forth.

Then I raced back to my chair and plopped down, snatching my laptop back from Adam. "Wait, what? You did *not* fire off my group daze spell. I needed to save that for five percent."

"I was desperate," Adam replied, pounding his own keyboard to keep FallenOne up front and center, delivering damage with the quick swipes and fancy maneuvers of his quarterstaff, brown monk robe flying about as he kicked and whirled around The Slayer.

Me? I had to concentrate on keeping all the orc minions that The Slayer had summoned under control so they wouldn't swarm and overwhelm us.

And apparently, the baby was having none of her swing because she started grousing.

"Your turn, I gotta keep these orc adds under control," I said to Adam.

He didn't reply and the baby groused again.

"One of you take care of it. I do not want to hear my niece in distress," Heath said, staring intently at his own screen.

"She's not in distress, she just wants to be held and Adam can do his job one-armed," I shot back.

Again, my husband didn't move from his computer. "She can feel your anger. Strike down these orcs with all of your hatred, and your journey towards the dark side will be complete."

I snickered. "Everything that transpires is according to her design, don't you know." I hit a refresh on the daze spell the minute it became available. Adam had done a decent job of playing Eloisa, my spiritual enchantress, while I'd been gone, but he didn't understand the subtleties of the class. Which made sense, since I'd been playing this character off and on for over five years.

Adam returned from fetching Palps from her swing and bobbed her on his arm as his free hand flew over his keyboard to fire off maneuvers. "Anger her and she'll execute Order 66 and then we'll all be done for."

Heath glanced up at both of us through narrowed eyes. "My beautiful niece is not a Sith Lord dictator of the galaxy."

"Give her about twenty years. She will be," Adam fired back. The baby, for her part, seemed perfectly content where she was, propped against her daddy's chest as he balanced her on a muscular arm.

Daddy Adam was the hottest version of Adam. Not gonna lie.

But I didn't let that thought distract me long, and ultimately, we were victorious in the fight against The Slayer and his hordes of orc minions.

In the aftermath, as we sifted through the loot, I took the baby from Adam. She immediately started to cry.

I frowned at her. "Well, I won't take that personally. Or maybe I will."

Adam snickered but didn't ask for her back.

Heath appeared at my side. "Here, she wants her Funcle Heath, clearly."

And damned if that kid didn't stop crying the minute Heath picked her up and bobbed around the room with her. Apparently, I was just the milk truck these days.

Our old house sold, and the boats were removed to a slip at a nearby yachting club so we could still make use of them when we wanted. Meanwhile, we grew into the darling small town that was Canyon Hollow and the kind, and sometimes weird—sometimes really weird—inhabitants that occupied it.

And I still had worlds to conquer so April and Lindsay met with me the following week to go over the progress on the legal stuff and the establishment of our non-profit organization. It would be years, yet, before the clinic was up and running and ready to go, but we were getting there.

Lindsay fawned over the baby and seemed stunned by how much she looked like Adam. "I mean, I don't see you in here at all. Do his genes not play well with others? Because that would track."

We laughed over that. I suspected that as Sabrina grew up, there would be more of me peeking out here and there. Or at least I hoped for it.

After Lindsay left, April was gathering up her notebooks and laptop and packing them away as I finished feeding Sabrina her second lunch. Maybe we should have nicknamed her Bilbo or just the Hobbit?

But Palps had stuck, at least for a little while.

April bent toward me and asked quietly. "So hey, you can tell me if this is none of my business but...I was wondering. How did that whole situation with your senior resident resolve?"

I blinked. "Well, my maternity leave is up in two weeks, and he has three months to go before he's done with his residency. The hospital has opted not to extend an offer to hire him as a fellow."

Her brows twitched up. "Oh wow, and how are you feeling about that?"

I blinked. "Mixed, actually. He'll have a good career and he's had offers elsewhere, from what I understand. I just hope he's learned from this experience and that he'll look at his mistakes and correct them."

April nodded. "Are you comfortable enough to have a conversation with him about that?"

I shrugged. "It's not my place, and I really don't think I need to do more than I've already done. It's on him to be better."

She smiled wide. "You are brave, girl. Braver than I would have been."

I shook my head. "It sucks that women have been so long in the workplace and we're still dealing with BS like this. It gets better, or at least I'd like to hope that it does."

"It gets better when we learn to speak up and support each other to subvert the patriarchy when we can. That's why I love our project so much. You, me, Lindsay. All powerful women. Girl bosses in our own right."

I smiled. "You got it. It's up to us to make this world a better place for the women who follow in our path."

April glanced down at the nursing baby and smiled. "Oh, she's definitely going to be a girl boss just like her mom."

"Or hopefully, even better." I grinned.

"So how did you keep Adam from going into attack mode when you told him about it?"

I blinked, hesitated. "Ahh."

She immediately flushed. "Oh, I'm sorry. I just assumed you'd told him. Probably a good call that you didn't."

And that got me thinking...did I not trust my husband to handle the information without acting on it? What did that say about me and our relationship?

Adam came home that night from his last official day at the office. In the future he'd be going in on an "as-needed" basis and for board of directors' business only.

When he walked through the door and gave me a kiss, I pulled him into my arms and hugged him tight. "Dinner's almost ready but I wanted to talk to you really quick about something." I directed him to sit down next to me on the couch in our front room.

His brows twitched together. "Okay."

"Well, before I say anything, I want you to know that this is just to inform you about something that's happened and that I've already handled. But in the interest of being open and honest, I think you should know about it."

Adam kept his features remarkably schooled, but I could see a flicker of concern pass through his dark eyes. He said nothing, nodding at me to continue.

"Do you remember that guy who you noticed at the holiday party and when you came to the hospital for my birthday last year? The senior resident, Dr. Iverson."

"I do."

"Good, okay. Well, things weren't great with him. I have no idea what motivated it and I really don't care but he took every opportunity to be an asshole to me at work."

"I remember you complaining about scheduling a lot and I did the math months ago that it had something to do with him, since that's his job."

I nodded. "It goes a little bit beyond that." I then recounted, briefly, some of the encounters. Adam showed no emotion beside the sudden irritated twitch of his eyes, a slight flush of color at his collar.

"Remember, I said I've handled it." I added the part about him hitting on the nurse, prompting me to go to HR about it.

"He's still working at the hospital?" Adam asked tightly.

"Yes, for a few more months, with his scheduling and senior resident status revoked."

"And you're going back to work in a week. You'll have to work with him."

I nodded. "He'll have no authority over me, and we'll be on different rotations. He's been instructed to stay away. Actually, he pretty much ignored me for months before I left for leave."

When Adam looked at me with the unspoken question I responded. "I think, um, well I think the change in his behavior happened when I told people at work I was pregnant."

"Seems like you should have spilled the news sooner, if that's what finally gave the dickwad a clue that you were taken. But your wedding ring should have done that. Regardless of your status, what gave him that sense of entitlement in the first place?"

I nodded. "In a perfect world, I shouldn't have had to worry about it at all. but some guys are clueless—"

"Assholes."

I smiled, then met his gaze quietly. "So are you mad?"

He blinked. "Mad that some shithead doctor thought he could score with my wife? Hell yeah, I'm mad."

I let out a little laugh. "No, not about that. Are you mad I didn't tell you?"

He took a deep breath, let it out, then turned his head to look away, as if accessing some thought or memory. He ran a reassuring hand down my arm, rubbing it from shoulder to elbow. When he looked back, he was deadly serious. "I understand why you didn't tell me, given the past and my need to...take charge. I'm proud of you that you had the courage to take care of it. However, I'm upset that I couldn't be there as a support for you because you felt you couldn't trust my reaction."

I bit my lip. "I know you've been doing a lot of work on yourself. Neither one of us is perfect and we're always still learning. But thank you. And I'm sorry I didn't let you in so you could support me."

Adam reached up and ran the pad of his thumb along my cheek. "Promise me you'll tell me if he pulls any bullshit before he's gone."

I smiled, turning my head so I could kiss his thumb. "I promise. I'll not only tell you, but HR will also get an earful."

He pulled me in to press his lips to my temple. "Good."

I smiled, leaning in close. "Thank you for being you."

His arms tightened around me. "Emilia, you made me the man that I am. So...thank yourself too."

And with that, we kissed and kissed some more...and I almost burned dinner because of it.

Chapter

Thirty-Seven

Adam

"W HAT'S THIS?" EMILIA ASKED WHEN I BROUGHT a cup of coffee to her in her office.

She was sitting at her desk, laptop open. In front of her was the gift box I'd set there last night before going to bed. I handed her a latte in a mug that read, *Cute enough to stop your heart, skilled enough to restart it,* with an EKG graphic on it. A gift from her coworker, Louisa, during her cardiology rotation.

I nodded to the box. "Well, it's wrapped, so if you really want to know, you should, you know, open it."

She arched a brow at me over her coffee cup. "To be fair, I wasn't asking you what was inside the box. I was asking you what the occasion was. My birthday was months ago. You already got me something for Mother's Day. What is the occasion for spoiling me today?"

I grinned. "Does there have to be an occasion?" And before she could reply, I continued. "It's a push present."

Her brows scrunched together as she swallowed her first sip of coffee and set down the mug. "A *what* present?"

"The moms at the Parent and Me class were talking about what their husbands got them for push presents and I didn't know that was a thing."

She blinked. "Explain what a push present is."

"A present the husband gives the wife for pushing out a baby, apparently."

She looked increasingly puzzled. "That's a thing?"

I shrugged. "According to the Parent and Me moms, it is. And I was being neglectful by not getting you one."

"Wasn't that class called Mommy and Me?"

I gave her a sheepish grin over my mug of black coffee. "Well, it *was* Mommy and Me class, but they decided when I started taking Sabrina that they should be inclusive. So, they changed it to Parent and Me."

She laughed. "I never asked how you like being the only dad in that class."

I shrugged. "It's fine. Sabrina loves it. I'm not going to let any hangups keep me from something that's good for her."

Her eyes smiled into mine as her beautiful features lit up. "You are the best dad."

I took another sip, gave her a self-deprecating half shrug. "I try." Then I pointed at the gift with my mug. "Open it."

She set down her mug and whipped up the present with gusto. "I thought you'd never ask." She laughed.

Once the wrapping paper was removed, she slipped off the top of the box and inside was a red jewelry box. "Hmm," she said, eyes narrowing as she popped open the box. Inside, matching the one I'd given her for our first anniversary, was another rose gold

Cartier love bracelet, studded with diamonds. Her eyes lit up, but she glanced at me. "I have a matching set now."

"Well, I noticed you like to wear your other one. But read the inscription on this one. It's different."

Our anniversary bracelet read, *EKS + AD = Nat 20* along with our wedding date. This matching bracelet read, *Sabrina Kimberly Drake* with her birthdate, time, and the latitude and longitude, right down to the nearest second, of her birth location.

Emilia popped out of her chair and wrapped her arms around my neck. "This is amazing and so sweet. Thank you."

And for good measure, she planted a coffee-flavored kiss on my lips. But I loved the taste of coffee—and Emilia—so I was digging it.

She pulled back, still holding me. "Are you ready for our big day? Canyon Hollow apparently rolls out the stops for every holiday."

My hands slipped to her hips and I laughed. "Even an innocuous one like Memorial Day. I read the flyer. Looks to be an all-day thing."

Memorial Day was a hot dry holiday Monday at the end of May where we walked the mile and a half from our end of the canyon toward the town square, pushing Sabrina in her stroller, which we brought along to carry the baby's stuff more than the baby herself.

I eyed the diaper bag and the extra things packed and tucked under her seat in the stroller wondering yet again how someone so little required so much stuff. Wherever we went, we were transporting at least five times her weight in stuff. No wonder parents gravitated toward minivans. It had nothing to do with the kids and everything to do with all the stuff that came with them.

We made our way to the line of booths and trucks set up under the shady oak trees along the main drag—a roughly trapezoidal-shaped town square. It was a relatively flat clearing complete with a bandstand covered by a quaint, large gazebo, an adjacent flat field for pickup sports games and some shops and eateries along the edges. These all had open booths and free sample plates set up outside under their awnings.

Crowds had spilled in from the *flatlands*—so the rest of the county was referred to, here. I tried not to take that personally as a recently imported flatlander myself. Cars were parked everywhere with the overflow relegated to just outside the mouth of the canyon, contributing to a steady stream of people walking in and lining the square in preparation for the parade.

But before that, people wanted snacks, and Emilia declared herself dying of thirst—a common complaint of hers since she started nursing a baby. So here we were, waiting in the long line at the lemonade booth. Sabrina started crying, but before I could respond, Emilia had her unstrapped and in her arms, bouncing her.

"She doesn't need to eat, does she?" I asked.

"Oh my goodness. She's getting so big!" The owner of the local bakery, Marianne, had stepped out on the porch with a fresh tray of tiny muffins to give away and had zeroed in on us.

She approached and began to fawn over the baby and ply us with free baked goods while chatting nonstop about her grandkids. On the way over, we'd run across Miguel, the mail-carrier-slash-astronomer on his day off. He had, as usual, recounted some brand-new James Webb telescope facts. He hadn't repeated himself yet, which I found impressive.

After five months of living here, I could safely say that Canyon Hollow was a trip and unlike any place I'd ever lived before, populated by an eccentric but interesting cast of characters.

Marianne had no sooner left us to set up her tray of muffin samples in front of the bakery when Stacia, one of the moms from the Parent and Me group stepped up.

"Hey Adam! So great to see you here with baby 'Brina."

She bent and chucked the baby's cheek while giving a quick hi to Emilia, then turned back to me. "Did you read that article I texted you? What did you think?"

I nodded. "It was very interesting." And full of a lot of woo woo stuff I didn't ascribe to, but I kept that opinion to myself.

"Yeah, so it's a really great philosophy. I absolutely love it." She hesitated when I failed to elaborate on my opinion. I was one-hundred percent certain she wouldn't like what I had to say about the article and the philosophy behind it. To say nothing of the fact that I hadn't even bothered to pass the link on to Emilia because I was also certain of what she'd say.

Stacia chatted a little bit more before stating she had to run off to meet her husband and kids.

"What was *that?*" Emilia asked me several minutes later when we had our drinks in hand and wandered over to sit at one of the temporary tables that had been set up for refreshments.

I waved it away. "Oh, another article about woo woo parenting."

She raised her brows and sipped, and I could just tell by her body language that she had a lot to say that she wasn't saying.

I frowned. "What?"

She fought a smile. "I don't think she really wanted to talk to you about woo woo parenting. Not the way she was batting her eyes and shoving her chest out at you."

I shook my head. "No really, she's just really passionate."

"Or really attracted," Emilia snorted.

"She's always preaching about this stuff to me—"

"But not to the other moms?"

I blinked, thinking. Did Stacia preach to the other moms?

"She certainly was too busy flirting to be aware of *my* existence," Emilia added. I eyed her, definitely feeling an amused vibe from her rather than a jealous one.

I shook my head. "We talk about tummy time and sleep training. There's no flirting."

She laughed. "Adam, I know what flirting is. You're the one who's apparently blind to it."

I quirked a smile at her. "I'm not blind to it when you're flirting with me."

She grinned wide. "That's true. That's definitely true. But I can't help but wonder if you're the most popular participant at Parent and Me class."

I shrugged. "If I am, it's only because I'm the oddity, as the only dad."

"Yeah, the *hot* dad. The DILF, you mean."

"I'm *your* DILF and no one else's."

She leaned over to plant a peck on my lips. "Yup, just how I like it."

As we finished up our drinks, Emilia handed me the baby so she could start digging through the stroller stuff for some random essential baby paraphernalia. Across the way, I spotted Dom exiting the general grocery store carrying a paper bag.

When his gaze met mine, I smiled and waved him over. Though we'd been living in the canyon—practically his neighbor—for months now, I'd only seen him a handful of times and he hadn't accepted our standing invitation to come for dinner yet. I wasn't above noticing the many curious glances cast his way by the locals. I'd heard some whispers and hints of gossip here and there about this mysterious and enigmatic figure in their midst. But as soon as people realized we were friends, little more had been said to me. Which, frankly, was the way I liked it.

"Hey Adam," he said the moment he was close enough. "I had to duck in and grab something at the store. I can't stay long." And as if to punctuate his point, he glanced at his watch. He flashed a smile at my wife. "Mia, you're looking well. And my how the little lady has grown."

Emilia's grin widened. "Dom, thank you so much. And yes, any day now she'll be big enough to play with that amazing playhouse you sent her. It's just stunning...hell, sometimes I want to crawl in there myself."

Dom's baby shower present had indeed been amazing and unique, a handcrafted wooden playhouse with exquisite details. "Straight out of the old country," he'd told me, which only gave a small hint of the background he rarely talked about. I did know that he and his parents had emigrated from Romania when he was still quite young, which explained why he had no accent when he spoke English.

Perhaps the playhouse had been built in Romania? It was a very thoughtful, unique and lavish gift, to be sure.

"Have you put her name on the list for the academy yet? There's a long waitlist, I've heard," Dominic asked.

"Oh you mean the Helena Modjeska Academy?" We both turned and glanced across the town center toward a complex of older buildings situated partially up the canyon wall on a bluff overlooking the valley.

It was highly exclusive, apparently.

I laughed. "She's not even going to be ready for school for—"

"Get her name on the list now. I mean it. It's worth it. I graduated from there." Dom followed our gazes up toward the academy grounds and a weird expression, like a ghost, flickered through his eyes.

"Come have dinner with us next weekend," Emilia said suddenly.

Dominic smiled. "Thanks, Mia, but I'll have to take a raincheck. I'll be out of town, back up north."

"Well reach out to us with some dates on your calendar that you're available. We'd love to have you over."

He nodded, grinning widely. "Will do. I'm gonna move along before this parade starts or everything's going to be backed up for miles. Take care, you three."

I watched him go and soon after, as he'd said, the parade started, with the marching band from the academy, locals in costume on horseback, the Canyon Hollow city council driving a simple float that was basically a glorified golf cart.

Emilia held up the baby so she could see. She waved her hands excitedly as the dogs from the local animal shelter walked past on leashes. Maybe we'd have to adopt a dog at some point. I'd always wanted to, anyway. And if Sabrina got this excited from just seeing them...then I'd have to consider it.

I smiled, watching her and was suddenly remembering my most recent session with the therapist. I'd been questing to find my role, my next thing to do in life. "Has it occurred to you that you might already be doing it?" Kendra asked, a brow arched above her glasses.

I shrugged. "I'm not doing much beyond speaking and consulting here and there, though."

"No, I don't mean career wise. I have no doubt you'll be getting up to something soon. You're far too much of an achiever to sit back and retire. No, I'm just putting forward that maybe your next role in life is one you're already fulfilling."

I tilted my head and stared back at her between narrowed eyes. "You mean my role as a father?"

Her grin blossomed across her face, lighting her eyes. She reminded me of a teacher finally witnessing progress from her clumsy apprentice.

I blinked, settling back against the comfortable, wide back of my chair and let out a long breath. "I just know I want to be the best I can possibly be. And I want it for her. For *them*. I'm that little girl's protector and you know what? I am damn happy with that."

Back in the present, it was getting hot, and we were tired. And it was almost time for Sabrina to eat. When Emilia tried to put her back in the stroller for our walk to the house, however, little Miss Drake was having none of it.

"Let me take her," I said, reaching out for her.

Emilia turned to me and cocked a brow. "It's a long walk back. You want the sling?"

"Sure, lay it on me." Since Emilia had worn it last, I had to make some adjustments so it would fit me. Then Emilia handed the baby to me and helped me settle her into the sling. Emilia packed up the rest of the baby stuff into the stroller and she pushed it along as we walked.

Sabrina calmed down as soon as we started moving. Emilia and I waved to some neighbors milling about—not that we knew all their names yet, but they were so friendly.

Almost to the base of our driveway, a memory of something Jordan once said to me floated through my mind. Something about promising him I'd never wear my baby on my chest like a clothing accessory.

"What's wrong?" Emilia asked when I stopped in my tracks to whip out my phone and switch the camera to a selfie setting.

"I just gotta send Jordan a quick text." And with that, I stretched out my arms to get the baby and sling in the frame and snapped a quick pic. Then I hit the button to send the selfie and for the caption, I just chose one emoji. The middle finger, of course.

Take that, Jordan. I was wearing my baby, and I would take no shit from anyone about it.

Then, I took my wife by the hand, and we went back to the house. All three of us together.

Chapter Thirty-Eight

Mia

I'D BEEN BACK TO WORK ABOUT THREE MONTHS AND WAS starting to wrap up my second year as a resident when Dr. Iverson ended his residency.

I avoided the hell out of the small gathering assembled to see him off. Someone had brought a cake and some refreshments to the residents' lounge. I also didn't sign his card. No shocker. I wasn't his biggest fan.

After finishing my evening rounds, I was headed back to the lounge to secretly swipe a piece of cake when Louisa, on a long call, peeled off from the nurses' station to ask me if we could chat really quick.

We found an empty examination room.

"Heya, I know you're aware it's Iverson's last day today. He's still lurking somewhere around. Just giving you a heads up in case he decides to deliver a parting shot."

I nodded. "Thanks."

"You remember the nurse in psych? She wanted me to thank you for reporting. She's so thrilled he's not going to be around for a fellowship."

I smiled. "It sucks that she had to go through that. Especially because she felt her voice wouldn't be heard. I just wish I could have done more to help."

Louisa's eyes lit up and she leaned in, lowering her voice conspiratorially. "Well, keep this on the downlow, but she's decided to hire a lawyer, because there were others who had complaints about him too. They want to go after him for damages, so he'll suffer some real consequences rather than a slap on the wrist. They're looking for a little payback, you know?"

I blinked, hoping this payback plan didn't involve violence and dumping a body in the ocean or something. *Tempting, but*...no.

"How can I help?"

"They were wondering if you would testify. They are getting the case together."

I blinked. "But the things he did to me are nothing compared to—"

"They were still wrong. He's entitled and bound to keep failing upward. You know he's going to end up as chief of medicine somewhere and still treating the women he works with this way." I inwardly groaned, having suspected the same and yet felt helpless to do anything about it. Maybe this would be my chance.

Louisa reached into her pocket and pulled out a card. "She asked me to give you this card for her lawyer. If you want to help, just call him. Think about it, anyway."

My eyes widened and I bit my lip. "I'll do whatever I can."

Louisa leaned in and pulled me into a hug. "I know it takes courage to go up against a colleague, especially when you're in the vulnerable position like being a resident. You're a badass, Mia."

"Not feeling that so much these days but I do want to help where I can." And write a check to help their legal fund once I figured out a way to anonymously contribute.

Minutes later, I slipped into the residents' lounge to finish up some paperwork and wrap up my day. Ignoring the half-hearted décor—a sign and a balloon bouquet—I gravitated to the remains of the sheet cake, cutting a piece for myself. It was my favorite, after all, yellow cake with custard filling and buttercream frosting.

That's where I was, after having inhaled the cake but still finishing up my charts when Dr. Iverson entered the room. My eyes flicked up, met his, then flicked back down to the screen. This was about the extent of our interactions since my complaint was filed with HR.

Which suited me just fine. And it would have continued it like that had he not, after cleaning out his locker, ended up standing at my shoulder with his stuff in a giant gym bag slung over his shoulder.

"Uh, hi," he began awkwardly when I looked up from my work.

I raised my brow. "Hi," I replied, carefully lacing my fingers together atop the desk.

"I'd like to have a word."

I glanced around the empty lounge. We were the only ones in here. Suddenly feeling that this might go somewhere weird, I decided to be on even ground, without him standing over me. "Go ahead." I said, popping up to move to the coffee station.

I was simultaneously curious and dreading what he'd have to say. Maybe he'd find it in his miniscule hard heart to apologize. Somehow, I doubted it.

He followed me over as I plucked up the coffee pot and poured some into my mug. "So I get that you did what you felt you had to do." He paused a beat. "But you know, it might have been nice if you'd talked to me first before reporting."

My eyes flicked up at him, then back down to where I was fixing my coffee. "I *did* talk to you. *Multiple* times. Whenever I did, your reaction made me feel unreasonable for pushing back." He frowned but I continued before he'd almost inevitably interrupt me. "You have two choices, Dr. Iverson, you can become belligerent and resentful toward me, or you can take it as a learning moment. You will continue to work with people. Professionals who've spent grueling years studying and practicing in order to be here. The lesson is simple. Treat them right. Respect them. You're not the main character. Don't impose your wants and needs on them."

He flushed and I could tell that a thousand thoughts ran through his head as he processed my words. I stirred my coffee and avoided his gaze. But I stayed right where I was.

Instead, he seemed to dismiss his options and gave a half shrug, a slight roll of his eyes. "Well, agree to disagree. I just was trying to push you to be better. I figured most professionals would want that. But I guess...the biggest problem is that you may not have recognized the definite chemistry between us. We wouldn't have been striking sparks off each other whenever we worked together, otherwise. In other circumstances, we could have clicked as a couple."

I curled my lip at him. "What some people call *chemistry*, others call *dislike*."

Well, there it was. He was still an asshole and hadn't learned a goddamn thing.

He shot me a patronizing smile. "You know what they say about the fine line between love and hate." I calmly sipped my coffee showing him no response. I also glanced at my watch to carefully note the time.

In the face of my nonresponse, he seemed to flush a deeper shade of red. There was a nasty glint in his eyes. "Well, good luck with your career, Mia. You are a good doctor even without the pushing. Who knows? Maybe we'll work together again. Or you can, you know, look me up if you ever decide to dump the code monkey and find a real man."

I didn't even look at him. Just sipped my mug. "None of those things will be happening."

After another beat, he pivoted, and he and his giant gym bag were gone. I literally let out the breath I'd been holding in relief. My gaze flicked up at the security camera situated right above me. Hopefully it had caught the whole encounter. But if not, I recreated the entire conversation for my notes.

More ammo for the lawsuit. And he'd never come back to this hospital. So much the better.

When I got home from the hospital, I expected to walk straight into the arms of my waiting husband. It had been a long-ass day and he'd taken his first international trip since the baby had been born. But the house was quiet, and Adam was in bed, sleeping instead of waiting up for me.

With a sigh, I made my way into the dark bedroom and sank down on the end of our bed and watched him. He'd been gone for nearly a week to speak at a massive gaming conference, Gamescom, in Cologne, Germany. I'd watched his keynote speech on the internet and had been so proud of him.

And he'd only arrived home a few hours ago, so I surmised he must not have been able to sleep much on the long flight from Europe. He never went to sleep this early normally.

And though I was tempted to wake him up and kiss him all over, just to give him a proper welcome home, I let him sleep. He looked so peaceful and so damn gorgeous. Now well into his early thirties, he was even better looking than his younger self. I almost let loose a girlish sigh. God, I'd missed him. Rubbing the stiff muscles at the back of my neck, I couldn't help but think about the million things I had to do—the most important of which was to get out of my scrubs and get to bed. But I didn't want to...not yet.

"Are you just going to sit there and stare at me like a creeper or are you going to come over here and kiss me?" he muttered, cracking an eyelid open in the dim light.

I let out a laugh. "Did I wake you up?" I stood up, coming around to his side of the bed to land a big one on his sexy lips.

"No. I've been lying here waiting for you to get home. You took your sweet time about it, too."

I shrugged. "Sorry. Had a bunch of paperwork to wrap up." And a jerk former senior resident to rid myself of...

Adam rolled onto his back and hooked an arm around my waist. "Hmm. You have a serious emergency to handle right here, doctor." His hand slid up my back and he pulled me down to kiss him. It didn't take much effort on his part because I was more than willing to suck on that delicious mouth. His hands came up to twine through my hair, his wedding ring glinting in the low light. Soon he was pulling my long hair out of my ponytail to let it spill down over my shoulders.

My mouth moved hungrily on his, tasting every inch, every corner. I got out bits of the normal chitchat in between frenzied kisses, which also involved him pulling my scrubs off of me. "How was Germany?"

"I missed you," he said by way of answer. His hands came up to unhook my bra.

"I missed you too," I replied. He yanked my top over my head, my bra following it in seconds. I ran my hands over his bare chest and down under the sheets, noticing that he'd saved me the trouble of undressing him by going to bed naked.

"Awfully presumptuous of you, isn't it?" I snarked as I ran my mouth over the ridges of his yummy chest, tasting every valley. He let out a long, slow groan.

"Foreknowledge," he muttered, pulling my head up to his again so he could claim me with his mouth. Then his lips traveled down my jaw, against my neck, evoking delicious, dizzying sensations there. "I knew you'd be overtaken with lust and jumping my bones the minute you got home."

"So sure of yourself," I said, sucking my breath as his mouth blazed a trail from my neck, across my collarbone and chest to fasten on my nipple while he caressed its twin with his free hand. I arched my back, gasping with pleasure.

"No, it was actually *you* that I'm sure of."

When I thought he'd roll us over, I pulled away, laughing and climbing on top of him, ready to prove him right. "This cowgirl is ready to ride. Better saddle up!"

I bent over, grabbed a condom out of the nightstand drawer and deftly tore the package open with my teeth, slipping it on him in one easy motion. He laughed that breathy laugh he always did when he was turned on. "You don't waste any time, do you?"

"Not when I have a hot piece of manmeat between my legs."

"I feel so objectified." Grinning, he gripped my hips and slid inside me. We both groaned in unison. It had been a long day, a long shift. I should have been ready to collapse, but instead I was exhilarated, my blood singing through my veins in a rush of frenzy and thrill, just by being in this man's arms again.

"You love it," I breathed.

"Damn right I do."

I rode him slowly, relishing the feel of him inside me, his hands cupping my breasts, his fingers tracing over the tattoo across my old surgery scar, the constellation Draco.

Then with growing urgency, I moved quickly, sliding my hips over his, pushing us both closer to climax. He hooked a hand around the back of my neck, pulling my mouth down to his and we moved against each other, like the cloudy sky skimming over jagged mountains—he solid, hard, and me fluid and shifting over him. Our mouths locked in a long, passionate kiss. I came like that, with his thumbs gliding over my nipples, our bodies fastened together. I pushed against him and felt my world shattering around me, releasing in ecstatic waves.

In moments, Adam had rolled us over, now moving on top of me to finish, driving into me with hard, fast strokes before stilling while I caressed his back, his shoulders. He let out a long, slow breath and then bent to gently pepper my face with kisses.

After he rolled off, I lay back against my pillow, feeling as refreshed as if I'd awoken from a full night's sleep. With a dreamy sigh, I watched as he got up from the bed, went into the bathroom and then came back, settling beside me.

"Okay, now we can talk..." he said with a grin.

I rolled onto my side and hooked my arm around him. "For now..."

He laughed and kissed me. "So, tell me everything I missed."

"I got my results for my five-year scan today," I said. "Everything's good."

His arms tightened around me, and he breathed into my hair. "Of course it is." His voice was light, relaxed, but I knew how tense he got every year when I went in for my scans. And now that we'd hit the five-year mark, the chance of cancer recurrence had dropped dramatically.

Thank god for that.

We talked some more—about his trip and the latest goings on with the gaming industry, me recounting things that had happened at work, the latest from our friends and family members. I left out the weird conversation I'd had with Iverson not two hours before.

Adam held me for a long time, his hands moving over my body as if he'd never touched me before. His hands slid slowly across my breasts, my belly, past my c-section scar that ran just above the pubic bone, before slipping lower. I smiled, opening my legs. I was ready for round two.

But a shrill cry pierced the air, and we froze. Adam stiffened against me and I reached over to turn down the monitor on the nightstand. He moved to sit up, but I stopped him. "Don't go. Most of the time she rolls right over and goes back to sleep."

He pulled away and gave me a look as if to ask, *are you kidding me?* And promptly slid out of bed and into his closet to pull on his pajama bottoms. Sighing, I sat up as he left the room. I reached over and turned off the monitor, got up and grabbed my own nightshirt and pulled it on. So much for round two. That was a rare gift, these days, anyway.

A minute later, he was back in the room with the other love of his life in his arms, planting kisses on her teary cheeks. She had a chubby fist in her mouth. Her dark hair, the same color as his, frizzed in a curly aura around her angelic face.

"Hey baby girl," I said, holding out my hands for her but she turned her head away, tucking in under Adam's chin. "Ah, so now that Daddy's home, my name is mud again."

Adam sat down on the bed, lying back and settling our daughter on his hard chest. I grabbed a pacifier from the nightstand and held it up to her. She took it and in less than two seconds flat, her long, dark lashes lay against her soft cheeks.

"You spoil her," I whispered.

"Daddy's prerogative," he answered, giving me a smile, and taking my hand in his while he kissed the top of her head. My heart skipped a beat like it always did when I watched them together. Even now, as little as she was, I knew a special relationship when I saw it. "I haven't seen *her* in a week, either. And she got bigger."

I smiled lazily, squeezing his hand. "Babies do that. And fast."

I was so entirely grateful for all that I had. Him, her, our wonderful life together.

I reached out and traced the tattoo on his chest, spelling out his sister's—and now our daughter's—name in beautiful jade script. And the other tattoo, still freshly inked. Weeks ago, he'd surprised me with it, "closest to my heart," he'd explained. when he'd come home, surprising me with it spelling out my name, *Emilia.*

Because I was Dr. Strong, MD to some, Mia to everyone else, Mommy to Sabrina. But I was—and would always be—*his* Emilia.

Chapter
Thirty-Nine
Dominic

What the hell is she doing here?

My hands ball into tight fists at my sides and I can all but feel the blood pressure soar in my veins, filling my ears with the sound of rushing blood. Is it really her or am I just imagining it? There's no possible way. But as I angle my head to get a better look, I recognize the familiar curve of those dark eyebrows, that tiny mole just above her lip. My gut clenches with realization.

She's lying naked in a bed of banana fronds and carefully crafted sushi. Her thick, shiny dark hair is arranged in a fan around her head, carefully out of the way of the food.

And she's a fucking vision. A sensual goddess without imperfection.

And yet all I can think about right now are the heated, red thoughts accelerating in my mind like particles in a supercollider. Those memories, the humiliation. I don't think I could ever forget what she did. Ayla Polat—the woman I wish I never laid eyes on, even though she was once a seemingly innocent girl. Once so brilliant. So full of promise.

And here she is now, nothing more than eye candy for the leering gazes of random businessmen whose eyes roam that expanse of smooth, glowing skin, the bare breasts tipped with strategically placed tiny bright pink flowers. How far she's fallen.

At my shoulder, one suit whispers not so quietly to his friend how he wants to take those flowers off her tits with his chopsticks. The other wonders why the hell he'd want to use chopsticks when he could use his teeth and, with a slip of his tongue, "get a taste of that" himself. Their banter descends into even more base commentary as they progress towards her head. They both snicker, and I'm certain she can hear them, though she doesn't react or even move.

It's enough to turn my stomach.

And suddenly, despite having looked forward to eating top quality sushi, the best that the Bay Area can offer, I have no appetite.

Still, my eyes are glued to her. She lies so quietly, unmoving. Apparently well-practiced at what she does. And she's flawless. Her golden-brown eyes stare blankly upward from an expressionless face. Will she see me if I come closer?

Will she recognize me if she does? And why do I care?

"Dom? You okay?"

I dart a glance toward the head of the serving table. Adam is standing very close to her head. And he's just about the only one here not ogling her body. Her perfect body.

She's so fucking beautiful. *Still.* After all these years. And even with those dark memories, those angry thoughts bouncing around inside my head, I can't help but notice. Can't help but fantasize touching my mouth to her beautiful, full lips.

I blink when Adam calls my name again, then peel my gaze away from that confusing vision before me.

"Huh?" I blurt.

Those amber eyes that could stare right through you with the cutting accuracy of a laser beam. Instead, they stare at the ceiling into nothingness, fringed by thick dark lashes, barely blinking. What must she be thinking as she overhears what is said around her? Is she humiliated? So much the better. I hope every second she has to lie there, she feels every bit of it.

That mind of hers, more stunning than her body, really...was it still?

And yet my eyes betray me, sliding down the expanse of those perfect breasts, the shapely hips, those long, curvy legs. I swallow. Hard.

Fuck this. And fuck her.

I turn and make a wide berth around the table to meet up with Adam on the other end.

He frowns with concern. "Is everything okay? You seemed kind of spooked back there."

I shrug, shaking my head. Maybe that will help me shake off this feeling...like I've seen a fucking ghost. But that's ridiculous. She's a figure of the distant past. That of a trusting boy who no longer exists. The memory, the vision of Ayla haunts that boy. Not me.

"The model looks like someone I used to know," I explain lamely, then move hastily to the table we'd chosen with a half-full plate.

We sit and somehow the next hour or so passes while I pick at my food and give Adam monosyllabic replies whenever he asks me something. He can tell something's up. I can tell by the way he eyes my untouched plate without saying a word about it.

A few others try to approach and after a few attempts to exchange contacts with me, they give up. Thankfully.

I'm in no mood for this. I want the fuck out of here now. And yet the entire time I'm sitting here, I feel an almost uncontrollable desire to turn my head back toward the serving table and look at her again.

I succeed in resisting that urge, however. And half an eternity later, we wrap things up. By now, the model has been wheeled into the back. Of course, I know this because the first thing I do while standing up to button my coat is to turn and check.

"Are you still up for that shoot-'em-up?" Adam asks.

In reality, I'm not. I'd rather go home and brood in the dark and try my hardest to forget what I saw here.

"Sure." I say, regardless. "Hold up a minute, will you? I'm just gonna give my compliments to the chef."

I turn away from Adam's frown and walk over to the cashier. I want to make sure this goes directly to *her* so I explain my predicament. I want to leave a tip but specify it goes to the sushi model. The cashier offers me an envelope.

I open my wallet, pull out all available cash on hand, around five hundred dollars, and stuff it into the envelope. I'm not above noticing how the cashier's eyes bulge.

After sealing the envelope, I label the front to the "Sushi model" and then on the back, add a nice little note. It gives me a stab of heated satisfaction to write out the message.

I scan the room to see if the chef is still about, preferring to leave the thing in his hands, given the way the cashier was eyeing the hundred-dollar bills I'd stuffed in there. After asking a few questions, I'm directed to the kitchen door where I find him, just on the other side. There's no sign of *her* anywhere and that's a relief.

With a quick, jerky gesture, I hold the envelope out to the chef and spin, walking away without explanation. He'll probably read the note meant for Ayla. I don't really care.

The more eyeballs on it, the better, to increase her humiliation all the more.

To Ayla, the sushi model,

Here's some pocket change. Go out and buy yourself a dress. If you're going to bother selling your naked body for filthy lucre, you'd probably earn a lot more out on the street.

Just one tiny fraction of the payback she truly deserved, after everything she'd taken from me. Which got me thinking...maybe real payback was just what I needed to deliver.

And since she'd proven quite handily that she could be sold, so much the better.

My own thoughts began racing...and forming a plan. Payback, indeed.

Brenna Aubrey is a USA TODAY Bestselling Author of contemporary romance stories that center on geek culture. Her debut novel, At Any Price, is currently free on all platforms.

She has always sought comfort in good books and the long, involved stories she weaves in her head. Brenna is a city girl with a nature-lover's heart. She therefore finds herself out in green open spaces any chance she can get. She's also a mom, teacher, geek girl, Francophile, unabashed video-game addict & eBook hoarder.

She currently resides on the west coast with her husband, two children, two adorable golden retriever pups, a bird and some fish.

More information available at www.BrennaAubrey.net

To sign up for Brenna's email list for release updates, please copy & paste this link into your browser:
http://BrennaAubrey.net/newsletter-signup/

Want to discuss the Gaming The System series with other avid readers? Brenna's reader discussion and social group is located on Facebook
https://www.facebook.com/groups/BrennaAubreyBookGroup